She **intent on showing him**
what she needed.
What she craved.

His moan of pleasure vibrated through her veins, assaulted her lips, and sent a rush of longing straight to her core.

"Zoë?"

"Hmm?"

When he didn't respond, she raised her lids and read the wonder in his eyes. In that moment, she knew she wanted Theo Maragos to be her lover for however long she remained on earth. "Are you coming in?"

"Believe me, there's nothing I want more, but it's late and we have to get an early start tomorrow."

Confused, she nodded.

Was he rejecting her, a daughter of the mighty Zeus? If anyone on Mount Olympus found out about his rebuff, the citizens would ridicule her until the end of her days. He was lucky his renovation project was important to her success, or she'd clock him where he stood and transport him to Hades in a hand basket!

By Judi McCoy

MAKING OVER MR. RIGHT
ONE NIGHT WITH A GODDESS
ALMOST A GODDESS
WANTED: ONE SEXY NIGHT
WANTED: ONE SPECIAL KISS
WANTED: ONE PERFECT MAN

JUDI McCOY

Making Over MR. RIGHT

AVON

An Imprint of HarperCollinsPublishers

AVON BOOKS
An Imprint of HarperCollins*Publishers*
10 East 53rd Street
New York, New York 10022-5299

Copyright © 2008 by Judi McCoy
ISBN: 978-0-06-134143-4
www.avonromance.com

First Avon Books paperback printing: March 2008

Avon Trademark Reg. U.S. Pat. Off. and in Other Countries, Marca Registrada, Hecho en U.S.A.

HarperCollins® is a registered trademark of HarperCollins Publishers

Printed in the U.S.A.

10 9 8 7 6 5 4 3 2 1

*This book is dedicated to all my loyal fans
and the goddess that dwells in each of you.
Thank you for enjoying my words,
identifying with my characters,
and spending your hard-earned money
buying my books. Your devotion
is greatly appreciated.*

Prologue

Mount Olympus

Zoë jumped at the ear-shattering crack of thunder and raced into the marble-tiled hall. Though the racket was Zeus's dictatorial way of reminding her, Kyra, and Chloe they were due in his office on the double, it didn't mean he would see them on time. One never knew where one stood with the quixotic father god, and that was exactly the way he liked it.

She knew that arriving late for her one-hundred-year performance review wasn't a bright move, but Zoë had been forced to stop on the way. Aphrodite's handmaidens were a disheveled group of lazy and self-absorbed women. As the Muse of Beauty, it was her duty to make certain their scarves and accessories matched their chitons and sandals, whether or not they agreed, which they usually didn't.

It was tough inspiring something that most gods thought was a joke. No one recognized the depth of her vision or the brilliance of her creativity. Throughout the centuries, Zoë had conjured hundreds of clever ideas: the bustle, bell bottoms, the kilt, snowshoes, chaps, she claimed them all, yet she was never given credit for her innovative designs.

And now, after centuries of hard work, Zeus planned to criticize her work and probably demote or reassign her to some nonsensical chore that required little brains and even less flair.

Thunder echoed ominously. She was still running when a jagged bolt of lightning split the sky. The soles of her sandals slapped in time with her jittery pulse as she careened around a column and practically bowled over Kyra and Chloe, her sister muses.

"Oops, sorry." She whooshed out a breath. "Had to take those slovenly graces in hand—again. You know how bent Aphrodite gets when her girls are in disarray." Still gasping, she asked, "Has he called for us yet?"

"He's just about finished with Polyhymnia," said Kyra, twisting a strand of her glorious red hair. "Her wailing's slowed to a subdued whimper."

While they waited, Chloe prattled about the

depths to which the muses had been forced to sink, thanks to their father's scheme to run Mount Olympus like a Fortune 500 company.

"I hear he's reassigned most of our sisters, charging them with inspiring things that fit better in the modern world," Zoë added, wishing one of them would tell her she was wrong. Still, if given a choice, there were other areas she might find interesting. "I, for one, wouldn't mind being the Muse of High Adventure. Maybe rock climbing or spelunking or—"

"You're afraid of heights, sister dear," Chloe interjected, tossing her head of satiny blond curls.

Chloe was right as usual, which only annoyed Zoë further. "Maybe so, but I blame these ridiculous performance reviews on progress and all it implies. Technological advancements are nothing but a pain in the neck. First the telephone, then the radio, then that miserable box with sound and moving pictures—"

"It's called a television," said Chloe. "And it's nothing compared to his latest gadget. The skinny is we're all expected to use a computer."

Their shared horror segued to dismay when Polyhymnia stumbled out of Zeus's office. Mumbling something about "blogs," the Muse of Sacred Poetry wobbled down the stairs as if ready to faint.

When Kyra peered in the doorway, their father's

voice boomed, "Don't stand there gawking, daughter, enter. And bring those two good-for-nothings with you."

As one, the sisters glided into his private chambers.

Zeus gazed at them with his bushy brows raised. "I assume you know why you're here?"

"Yes, sire," they chorused.

Chloe began an immediate recitation of her achievements over the last century, making one excuse after another for her failures. Much as Zoë loved her beautiful sister, Chloe was the true diva of the group. In fact, she'd taught Mata Hari, Maria Callas, and Beyoncé everything there was to know about getting their way in life. And the moment she came up for air, Kyra, the most sensible of the muses, began her own lament.

By the time Zeus got to her, Zoë was ready for his put-downs, so she began her own litany of successes. "Thanks to Martha, at least the mortals' home decor is exciting," she began in self-defense.

"*Martha-smartha.* What about those ridiculous plastic shoes, lava lamps, toe rings? You haven't inspired a single sensible thing since washable paint, and I have my doubts about that," he pronounced.

"But everyone loves Martha," Zoë insisted. "And they especially like my most important contribution. 'It's a good thing' has become a worldwide catch phrase."

Zeus threw up his hands in disgust. "Perhaps you should have given the woman a tip on how to better handle her stocks instead of decorating advice." He pointed a bony finger. "The three of you are not going to talk your way out of your failures this time. I'm still top god around here, and it's going to stay that way."

He rifled through a file on his desk, then stared at them long and hard. "You three are the least successful of my daughters. None of you has inspired much of anything, therefore mortals have never taken you seriously. I created a dozen muses, but the history books speak of just nine. Not only have you lost your edge—you never had one to begin with. If there were another way to discipline you, perhaps a bit of time as handmaiden to Hera . . ." He appeared to consider the thought. "No, no, not after that last fiasco."

Kyra began to plead, but Zoë knew better and kept quiet. Yes, the three of them had darted through the pasture with water pistols, but it wasn't their fault the stupid pigs had taken off at a run and charged into the dovecote. And they'd certainly had no control over the terrified birds that flew over Hera while she was drinking ambrosia on her patio.

"Hear me out and be grateful for my benevolence," Zeus commanded. "You have two choices. First, you may stay on Mount Olympus and accept a loss of status. Instead of gossiping or flirting the day away, you can muck out the stables, toil in the kitchen, or work in the dairy. There are any number of chores that will allow you to earn your keep."

Zoë moved closer to her sisters, hoping to fend off the distasteful tasks.

"The second offer is more challenging, of greater risk, and therefore eventually of more value. Each of you may go to earth and take a final stab at fulfilling your destiny, which means doing that which you were created to inspire in mankind. If you succeed, you may return here and live forever in splendor—no more performance reviews, just frolic and fun. But if you fail . . ." He leaned forward. ". . . you will remain on earth and live as a mortal until your dying day."

"Impossible," murmured Kyra.

"Unbelievable," Chloe added.

"While handmaiden to Hera the Harridan is both," moaned Zoë, "the other choices threaten our very existence."

"I have no intention of pulling udders or shoveling horse droppings until the end of forever," said Chloe. "We are demigoddesses, created to inspire. What else can we do?"

Kyra turned to Zeus and asked, "Is that all?"

"Not quite." He gave a demonic grin. "Since I'm sending you to earth on an important task, falling in love with a mortal will not be allowed. Dally if you must, but stick to business. Dire consequences await if you return here more impassioned by a mortal than your job."

"It'll never happen," vowed Chloe.

"Not bloody likely," said Zoë. She'd met men who had appealed to her in a sexual way, but not one, be they mortal or god, with whom she would have entrusted her heart.

The sisters locked gazes and mentally agreed. After joining hands, they stepped closer to the desk and said in unison, "We accept the challenge."

"And are grateful for it?"

They nodded.

Zeus gave a grimace in lieu of a smile. "Good, good. Now here are the conditions. You shall live independently of each other, hundreds of miles apart, for a single earthly year. During that time, Kyra must inspire mortals to believe in good fortune. Chloe, you must help however many mortals you meet to believe they will have a future filled with happiness." He raised a brow in Zoë's direction. "You, daughter, must find a way to enhance their lives through appearance or design, but no more idiotic ideas or tainted mavens." He raised a finger skyward. "And above all, remember the love thing. If you fail in these tasks, beware my wrath. Are there any questions?"

"How many mortals must we inspire?" asked Zoë.

"I'll decide how many when I'm good and ready, and not before. Do I make myself clear?"

"Yes, sire," they singsonged.

He jerked a thumb over his shoulder, indicating his computer. "Oh, and you'll need to use one of those, so we can keep in touch."

"Why can't we use Hermes, as we have always done?" Chloe asked, her tone defiant.

"Hah! Shows what you know. That boy hasn't taken to wing since the day I installed the telephone. He's in charge of networking the system and providing technical support. I'll allow you a day or so to become proficient, then—"

Chloe stomped her foot. "That's not fair. The others don't have to—"

Zeus rose, looming over them. Thunder shook the clouds as lightning speared the sky. "Silence!"

Without warning, Zoë was swallowed up into a vortex of howling wind. For a scarce second her sisters dangled like marionettes beside her, then disappeared. Alone in a great blackness, she plummeted toward the unknown.

Chapter 1

New York City

"Anybody who looks at these so-called publicity photos is going to have nightmares. The least you could have done was trimmed your beard and had your hair styled." Chad Thomas slapped the pile of proofs on top of the two-drawer filing cabinet next to a work station. "The pictures have to be retaken, and you still need to do something about this barn you call a home."

Distracted by the outburst, Theodore Maragos combed his fingers through the facial fuzz in question. Sure, it was a little on the bushy side, but it saved him time getting ready in the morning, and what was wrong with shoulder length hair? He had no reason to waste precious minutes shaving or making trips to the barber while he had a company to lead.

Scowling, he glanced up at his partner, the Chief of Operations at Marasoft Enterprises. "I'll be out from under in a couple of weeks. Can't it wait until then?"

Chad stopped pacing and stuffed a hand in the pocket of his charcoal gray Armani suit. Thanks to his pale pink shirt and striped silk tie, he resembled a model straight out of a men's fashion magazine. Combine his fashion style with his knowledge of art, gadgetry, and restaurants, and he was the poster boy for the original metrosexual.

"Three weeks is the extension I was able to coerce *New York Entrepreneur* into giving us for these disasters you call photographs. You wore that suit for our college graduation, ten years ago, for shit's sake, and it was out of style then. What were you thinking?"

"I guess I wasn't," Theo said, refocusing on the monitor. "What's the big deal?"

"The big deal? Let's see . . ." Chad began ticking off fingers. "One, if the pictures don't meet *NYE*'s standards, they'll replace you on their list of the ten most promising young businessmen in Manhattan. Two, if you're not on the list, we lose a ton of free publicity. Three, there goes our best chance at opening high and going higher the day the company hits the NASDAQ, which means that, four, Marasoft could bomb its first week as an IPO." His sigh echoed his impatience. "Come on, Theo. We've worked eighty-hour weeks, practically sweat blood for the company. We owe it to our investors—hell, we owe it to ourselves—to do everything in our power to get Marasoft recognized as a competitive power in the IT market."

Frustrated, Theo pushed away from his desk. His best friend was right. They'd spent years building his baby into a real player in the world of computer technology, not only to thank his father for taking him on, but to show a certain old goat, whom he despised, that he wasn't a useless idiot. If getting prettied up for a stint as one of New York's up-and-coming entrepreneurs would add to his prestige and put the cherry on top of his professional sundae, he'd be a fool not to take advantage of the opportunity.

Even if he hated every minute of it.

"Okay," he said, giving Chad a smile. "What do I have to do?"

"We've been over this about a hundred times—"

"I know. And I've ignored you just as many. Now I'm ready to listen."

"You'd better, because it's my last try at getting

you to pay attention. My stylist can see to your grooming problem. In the meantime, I'll take you to my personal shopper at Barney's for a couple of suits—"

"A couple? Won't that be expensive?"

"You need at least two, and you can afford it. It's this . . . this shell of an apartment I'm worried about. You vetoed my pal Andre's decorating firm, so we'll just have to pick a designer from the Internet, maybe someone on Craig's List, and pray they can work us in."

"I'll see a stylist, I'll even go so far as to work with a personal shopper, but I draw the line at letting a complete stranger turn my home into something they *think* it should look like. Isn't there anything else I can do?"

"This isn't a home, it's a barn with packing cartons for seating, a mattress and box spring for a bedroom, and a computer station for a conversation center. Maybe we could use my apartment, or borrow a fully furnished one—"

"No."

"No?"

"You heard me. This is where I live. If the magazine doesn't like it—tough. Whatever happened to judging a man on his work ethic and his morals? Since when do appearances count more than character?"

Chad rolled his eyes. "You above all people should know the answer to that one. Or have you forgotten the lousy time you had in college? If not for the fact that impressing your father was so important, you probably would have dropped out before graduation, even though he went to bat for you with the admissions board."

Theo twisted the gold ring he wore on the fourth finger of his right hand, a constant reminder of his place of birth. He'd been a geek, the nerdiest of nerds, and he still was, only now he sometimes wore a T-shirt that read, I'M A GEEK AND PROUD OF IT. His college experience would have been nonexistent if not for Chad, his party boy roommate. Together, they'd muddled through, with Theo tutoring Chad in the math courses he needed to get his degree, and Chad dragging him to parties and sporting events so he could have some semblance of a social life.

His dad had put great stock in a college education. So much stock that he'd pulled strings at his alma mater and gotten his son admitted on a scholarship, even though Theo only had a GED. When he'd graduated with perfect grades, he and Chad made a pact to earn their fortune together. After ten years they were very close to meeting their goal, but close wasn't good enough.

"How could I forget, when you won't let me,"

Theo goaded. Then he sighed. "Okay, I'll try to work with a designer, but I'm not promising it'll be pretty."

Chad furrowed his brow.

"Genius at work. I smell the rubber burning."

The COO snapped his fingers. "I have an idea. Why not go window shopping? Literally. Check out a couple of stores, say Bloomingdale's or Macy's, or one of the home decor windows, and see what they're doing. Find one you like and ask the manager if you can speak to their decorator. They have people on the payroll, sometimes they use freelancers trying to drum up business and get a client list going. You like to walk, so take a stroll and see what's out there."

"I have to finish this program," Theo insisted.

"You also have to eat, breathe, think. Where else better than in the smoggy, exhaust-filled air of Manhattan?"

"I don't know . . ."

"It's close to one. I have an appointment with our marketing firm or I'd tag along. Take a cab to ABC Home, buy a hot dog, and look around. If you don't find something that appeals to you, I'll call Andre and see if he can recommend someone, but get it done because you're running out of time."

* * *

Zoë adjusted the crystal and brass lamp on the side table next to a green leather club chair and took a step back to survey her handiwork. Though she didn't have much room to maneuver in the cramped space, she didn't think it necessary to go outside and check the window display from the sidewalk. As an expert in her field, she knew this cozy yet dramatic room was the perfect display for ABC's Valentine's Day theme.

It was her last chance to impress her designs upon a half-million people all at once, since it was the final department store with which she'd contracted before her return to Mount Olympus. She had a few more weeks to work her personal touch with the women at Suited for Change, but that venture was small potatoes compared to the number of mortals she could inspire with a single window in one of the biggest stores in Manhattan.

Checking her watch, she decided to spend a few more minutes on her final job. She'd managed to work efficiently, even with the handful of passersby who stopped to scrutinize her product, tap on the glass, and offer advice. The small crowd had broken up about fifteen minutes ago . . . except for the man still peering at her with a curious grin crinkling the corners of his eyes.

When she'd arranged the paintings on the wall, she gave him a sidelong glance, noting his tall frame, dark, shoulder length hair, and scruffy beard. She wasn't bothered at first; people stopped all day to peruse her designs. In turn, she usually enjoyed waving hello and pantomiming her thanks at their smiles of approval.

Something told her this guy was different. Though he wore a somewhat dated jacket with elbow patches, a button-down shirt, and patterned tie, he appeared too young to be a college professor. His clothing was definitely not that of a homeless person, but it wasn't fine enough for a lawyer, stockbroker, or other corporate type Manhattan was famous for.

Student crossed her mind.

She peeked over her shoulder and his grin broadened, showcasing his even white teeth.

Nope, too old. At least thirty. And he was wearing sneakers. Definitely not a businessman.

She put the finishing touches on the vase of white silk roses, intermixed with foiled red hearts, sitting on the coffee table. Then she gave a final adjustment to the brass statue of Eros, also known as Cupid to many mortals, that overlooked the entire scene from the majestic walnut sideboard. She'd give anything to see the haughty god's face when he again saw himself portrayed as a diaper-wearing tot sporting a bow and quiver of arrows.

Ducking her head, she stole another glance out

the window. Uh-oh, the guy was studying her backside. She sighed. Great. Just what she needed. A pervert!

She recalled Stacy, a decorator she'd met when she started this career, who had acquired a stalker. He began his reign of "rudidity" by showing up at every window Stacy designed, ogling and drooling and making himself a general nuisance. One day he dropped his drawers and exposed himself, but by the time the police arrived, the creep had fled—and Stacy decided she'd decorated her final display.

Now she knew how the young woman had felt, and it wasn't amusing or complimentary.

Hoping to nip things in the bud, Zoë spun on her heel, but the man was gone. She exhaled the breath she hadn't realized she'd been holding and told herself she was losing it. Not every man who stared at her backside or her legs was a pervert. Some of them were normal guys, checking out the scenery and hoping to score.

Besides, she was used to it. She and her sister muses were Zeus's finest creations. Chloe was, of course, the most beautiful, and Terpsichore a close second, but Zoë thought she held her own. Her winged black brows set off her thickly lashed hazel eyes, and her gold-streaked dark hair held a nice curl. Having a curvy figure didn't hurt, even if it was what mortals called full-figured. Her father bestowed life on shapely women; never would a goddess have the childlike body so many of today's fashionistas considered attractive.

And truly, she didn't care one iota if someone approved or disapproved of her lush figure or her take-charge personality. The few men she'd bedded over the past year had been nothing more than a pleasant diversion, and she planned to keep it that way. There were only a couple of weeks left of her stay, and she was determined to focus on each and every one with her main objective firmly implanted in her brain. Returning to Mount Olympus and living the rest of her days in splendor had to be her first consideration.

A tingle of pride skittered up her spine when she gave the display a final perusal. This design, with its cozy yet trendy edge of elegance, was worthy of a spread in any number of home decor magazines. All the rooms she designed spoke to the customers who viewed them and, in turn, inspired those customers to recreate what she portrayed.

Aware that she was due at Suited for Change in an hour, Zoë stepped through the curtain leading into the main showroom—and slammed straight into a wall of muscle. Bouncing back, she stared at the gawker-cum-stalker from the sidewalk.

"Oh, jeez. Did I hurt you?" he asked in a deep baritone.

Okay, so he was a caring pervert. "Um . . . no." She smoothed the lapels of her jacket. "If you'll excuse me—"

"Are you Zoë Degodessa?"

A clairvoyant pervert? "Who wants to know?" she asked with her best New York bravado.

"Oh, sorry. I'm Theo Maragos." He held out his hand. "I've walked half of Manhattan hoping to find you."

She accepted the gesture, noting his palm was warm and dry. "Half of Manhattan? That's a lot of territory."

"Well, maybe not half," he said, giving a polite smile. "I spotted one of your windows in Macy's. When I asked the manager about it, she gave me your name and told me she thought you'd be working at Barney's today. I stopped there, and a floor manager sent me to a decorating store, and they sent me to a women's boutique on Forty-third. A sales clerk there said you'd finished up yesterday, and directed me here." He stopped for breath. "I took a good look at every display you did for each establishment, and I want my place to look the same."

His blue eyes sparkled behind his wire-rimmed lenses, while his honest smile showed the hint of a dimple hiding beneath his scruffy beard. Without his ratty retro hairdo and unkempt appearance, she thought, he might even be attractive.

Not my concern, Zoë reminded herself as she brushed past him toward the employee locker room where she'd stored her coat and handbag. "What type of store do you own?" she asked over her shoulder, then spun on her heels and held up a hand. "Never mind, forget I asked. I don't have any time for a new client right now. I'm booked until . . . well, I'm just booked."

"I guess I didn't make myself clear. I don't own a store."

"I'm still booked," she said as she plowed through the lounge door. After shrugging into her tan, full-length cashmere coat, she picked up her Chanel bag. Ready to make a beeline for the exit, she turned and met his still smiling face. "Did I say something amusing?"

"Not exactly, but I should be more clear about what I need."

What he needed was a life, she thought. "I don't have time to chitchat. I'm late for an appointment."

"Then I won't keep you any longer." He handed her a business card. "I need a designer for my apartment, and I think you're the perfect person for the job. Your work will be showcased in the spring edition of *New York Entrepreneur.* I'll see to it you get full credit, which should add to your portfolio and impress everyone who has anything to say in the field of design."

"Did you say *New York Entrepreneur*?"

"The 'Fling into Spring' edition, due on newsstands in about nine weeks."

Zoë knew of the magazine. She'd admired their full-color layouts featuring the homes, lofts, and apartments of Manhattan's most wealthy businessmen and -women. Having her work showcased in such an important publication would top the window she'd just constructed and was sure to convince her father she could inspire the world of fashion and design and bring it to new heights of elegance and glamour.

"There's just one problem. The entire job has to be finished and ready for a photo shoot in a little more than two weeks."

Amazed that the date coincided perfectly with her return to Olympus, she tucked the card inside her bag. "I'm not promising anything," she said, giving herself some wiggle room. "How about if I show up at about six and take a look at the place?"

"I guess that's fair."

"Great. Now I have to run or I'll be late for a meeting."

Chapter 2

"Thanks so much, Zoë. I don't know how I'll ever repay you or the rest of the consultants here." Regina Hopewell squeezed Zoë's fingers. "Wish me luck."

Zoë stepped back and gave the middle-aged woman a final once-over, then added a leather belt and held out the color-coordinated pumps she'd secretly conjured to go with the woman's recycled suit.

"Why wouldn't they hire you? You're smart, savvy, and dressed like a professional." She adjusted a suit sleeve. "And more than good luck, I wish you a world of fashion success."

A befuddled expression graced Regina's face. "Thanks—I think." Waving farewell, she left the fitting room.

Zoë knew many of her clients thought her wish for "fashion success" a bit odd, but she didn't care. The perfect accessories brought an outfit to life, which in turn gave the wearer an attitude of confidence that carried through to their goal. Most women felt on top of the world when they knew they looked their best. They needed to wear what complimented their personal style, not a cookie cutter copy of whatever was in a monthly fashion magazine.

"Another happy customer," someone behind her said.

Zoë turned to find Elise Sutton, smiling in approval. Elise was director of the local branch of Suited for Change, a charitable organization that helped women get back on their feet after a divorce, widowhood, or other personal setback. She had also become her friend.

"We're going to miss you," Elise said, following her into the break room. "I don't know where we'll find another designer with your flair for fashion or your kindness." She poured a cup of coffee, opened the fridge, and brought out milk for her java and a can of pomegranate juice from the stash Zoë kept for emergencies. "The day's almost over. Sit and chat with me awhile."

Zoë checked the time on the wall clock above the sink, noting she had a few minutes before she left for Theo Maragos's apartment. "And I'm going to miss being here." She popped the top on her can and poured the liquid into a paper cup. "I've dropped a hint with a couple of fellow designers. I'm sure someone will volunteer to take my place."

"But they won't be you," Elise said after sipping her coffee. She ran manicured fingers through her tousled blond curls. "None of us has a clue how you're able to come up with some of the things you say you found hanging on the racks. Tell me the secret, please, so we can do the same when you're gone."

"It's nothing really," Zoë answered. "I just have a good eye for knowing what goes with what. The clothes are there. It simply takes a little imagination to put the right scarf or handbag with the proper suit or dress."

Zoë had come upon Suited for Change while walking the city shortly after waking in her hotel room a year ago. She knew on her first visit that it was a place where she could influence women, one outfit at a time, and she volunteered that same day. Out of professional courtesy, she'd informed Elise before the holidays of her departure at the end of January.

"So, how'd the ABC window go today?" Elise asked. "Did you draw a crowd, as usual?"

"It's amazing how curious people can be when they see someone assembling a window display. I even got a potential job from the session."

"Another job?" Elise set down her cup. "I thought the home store was your last assignment before you left for Greece?"

"I did too. Let's just say the guy made me an offer I couldn't refuse. I'm due at his apartment in half an hour."

"His apartment?" Elise's grin showcased her wide mouth and softly rounded chin. "That's a funny place for a store window."

"It's not a window, exactly. I'll explain it to you after I talk with him."

"Still, going to the apartment of a man you just met? What's he look like? How old is he?" She raised a finely arched brow. "Is he straight?"

Zoë grinned at the comment. She guessed that Elise was just past thirty, though the director sometimes acted older than she herself did. "Get your mind out of the dating pool and onto dry land, my friend. I'm not sure about his looks, his age, or his sexual preference, and truthfully, I don't care. The discussion was completely professional, and besides, he was too hairy to tell."

"Ugh. I hate it when a guy wears long hair."

"Not to mention a rather bushy beard."

"Double ugh." Elise shrugged. "I'm the first to

admit that decent straight men are scarce as hen's teeth in this city, but it wouldn't hurt if you had some fun before you left for your family reunion. You're an attractive woman; men hit on you, but you always turn them down."

"Not true. I went out with Sharon Feifer's brother, that corporate attorney fellow, a few days after she brought him to our Fourth of July party, remember?"

"Went out. Once. No relationship, just a one night stand. And I'm not judging you," Elise added, holding up her hand when Zoë sniffed. "But I do wish you'd find someone who'd appreciate you for more than a single date."

"You should talk. Have you had any kind of interaction with a man since your divorce?"

"No, but my situation is different."

Elise had told her that she'd gotten married right out of college, stayed home and was the model wife, until her jerk of a husband cheated on her. With another man. Devastated, she'd cut herself off from her friends and family for six months before going to counseling. After a few sessions with Suited for Change in Washington, D.C., where she was living at the time, she moved to New York and opened a branch office.

"What do you mean, my situation is different?" Zoë asked.

"I might not be good at picking the right man, but I'm an expert at finding the duds. All you have to do is pass one by me for a quick hello, and I'll give you a rundown; my gaydar's been resynchronized, my slobometer is working at full steam, and my cheater-reader is on high alert."

"Marrying someone unsure of his sexual orientation was not your fault. And you cannot blame yourself because he cheated on you. That was his problem."

"But I should have at least suspected something. Instead, I went merrily on my way thinking I had the perfect marriage, until I found out the embarrassing truth." Elise sighed. "I'm still not convinced the entire debacle wasn't my fault."

"That's ridiculous," said Zoë. "Your ex-husband is who he is, and it has nothing to do with you. I thought your psychologist made that clear."

"She tried, but it's hard not thinking there might have been something I could have done—been more feminine, read the clues, I don't know. But I will say this—I won't be fooled by a man again."

"You won't be if you never go on another date."

"I might. Someday."

"Right."

"Hey, it could happen. It's only been two years. Maybe I'll change my mind in another twenty."

Elise stood and brought her coffee cup to the sink. "Isn't it time for you to leave? I'd hate for you to be late for your date."

"It's a business meeting, not a date." Zoë slipped on her coat and grabbed her bag. "I'll be in on Wednesday to work with Marjorie Barris, ten o'clock sharp. See you then."

Theo stood in the doorway of his TriBeCa loft, studying the large open space before him. He vaguely remembered that Chad had mentioned *NYE* would need pictures of his private digs when the subject first came up. Unfortunately, he'd been in the final stages of writing the code needed to bring him a step closer to his end goal: launching Marasoft's final installment in their suite of software on the day the company's IPO took center stage on the floor of NASDAQ. He was now paying the price for his inattention.

Unlike Chad, he didn't give a lot of thought to his surroundings or his appearance. Not that his COO was vain, but Chad had style. His apartment could double for a movie set, and he dressed for success, as if making a good impression was paramount to having a booming career. Maybe it was, Theo admitted, but he'd rather give the world a simpler way to manage data, which in turn would make things easier for everyone on the planet.

Earning his father's approval also fit into the equation. His dad had sacrificed to make sure his only son received the best he could afford. Now, with his father retired and close to shutting down with Alzheimer's, he had only a short time to make the man proud.

Intent on being brutally honest, he inspected the apartment as if seeing it anew. When he signed the lease a few years back, he'd just wanted a place big enough to double as a home and office, because finding the perfect spot for his computer and its accompanying paraphernalia was his primary concern. From where he stood, the apartment appeared huge, mostly because the single room had no interior walls.

A kitchen setup, complete with the basics, took up space to the right of the entryway, and a large full bath ran the length of the wall to his left. His bed—a mattress and box spring resting on the hardwood floor—sat in the far corner next to an antique armoire he'd brought from his dad's place when they moved his father to a nursing home.

Ensconced in the center of the open space sat his baby, his fortune, his future: a computer setup with a main server, several desktop systems, printers, monitors, and enough professional equipment to catalogue, run, and support an entire business. He'd spaced a ring of cardboard boxes around the hub, interspersed with filing cabinets holding paperwork that couldn't be stored on CDs. But the bulk of his work was here, in the system he'd lovingly assembled over several years.

Never before had he worried about another person's opinion of his personal space. Chad was right. This "home" did resemble a high-tech barn. And a woman he desperately wanted to impress was due to arrive in the next few minutes.

After dogging her innovative window designs like Hansel following a trail of bread crumbs, he couldn't help but admire Zoë Degodessa. Her elegant yet comfortable-looking designs spoke to his soul and made him imagine himself living in a setting she'd created. But when he'd seen her in person, constructing one of the spectacular showcase windows at ABC, the ring on his finger started to warm and his heart stopped beating for a good three seconds.

Seen from behind, she had long legs, a dynamite ass, and a waterfall of dark wavy hair streaked with gold. Viewed from the front, she was every man's fantasy, especially his. Black winged brows brought attention to her golden eyes, her heart-shaped face took his breath away, and her full-lipped rosy mouth . . . well, he'd imagined immediately what it might taste like and what it could do. Meeting her in person had been even better, because she smelled great, had a warm smile, and sounded intelligent enough to carry on a conversation with just about anyone . . . including a computer nerd.

Theo shook his head, again twisting the ring he wore on his right hand. *Get a grip, pal. Remember your mother's warning.*

He'd been enamored with the fairer sex growing up, but as his mother had pointed out, those women didn't count because they could never be his. He didn't recall the last time he'd been head over heels about a girl—college, probably—but the ring hadn't reacted to any of them. He'd been so immersed in his software project since graduating, he couldn't remember his last date. It had been years since he'd thought of romance, and he was positive this was the first time the ring did what he'd been told it was capable of doing.

Was Zoë Degodessa the woman he could trust with his life, the only female he'd be able to love, the one who'd understand his past and share his future?

He answered his phone on the second ring.

"So, do I call Andre and beg, or did you find someone to tend to your personal space?" Chad asked tersely.

"Where are you?" Theo replied, though he had a

pretty good idea that his COO was at Marasoft, Inc.'s headquarters. The main floor had a spacious waiting room, several conference areas, an office for Chad, plus one for the president, which Theo rarely used. The second floor was home to the salesmen when they were in town, and the men and women who installed and did troubleshooting on the system, plus the programmers and support staff.

"At the office," Chad said, just as Theo expected. "Now answer my question."

"I found the perfect someone, and she's due here any minute, so—"

"I'm only a cab ride away. Don't do anything until I get there."

Theo yelled, "No, wait!" then said, "Well, damn," to the droning dial tone. Slamming the receiver in place, he sighed in frustration. There went his chance at getting Ms. Delectable alone. Once she got a look at his suave and handsome COO, he wouldn't stand a chance.

He walked to the bathroom and stared in the mirror. The unkempt man gazing back at him sported stringy hair and a beard the birds could have used to build a nest. No wonder the adorable designer had gazed at him as if he were a serial killer. Thinking back on the encounter, he was amazed that she'd agreed to meet him at his apartment.

Then again, business was business, and the design field in this city was competitive. His offer gave her the opportunity to showcase her work in one of the trendiest and most upscale magazines in New York. Anyone with a head for success would kill for a mention in *New York Entrepreneur.* To have an article touting your talent would be a dream come true, which was why he and Chad had said yes to the periodical's offer.

He ran a brush through his hair and secured the ponytail, then tamed his runaway beard with a comb and vowed to get his grooming under control tomorrow morning, or afternoon at the latest. He had a feeling his new designer wasn't into men who resembled the great American bison.

When the downstairs buzzer sounded, he rushed to answer it.

"It's Zoë Degodessa. I'm here for our appointment."

"Come on up," he said, pressing the button. Ignoring the heat building on his finger, he ran into the bathroom and brushed his teeth.

Zoë shook her potential client's hand for the second time that day. Still warm and dry, she noted, pleased he didn't seem nervous or self-conscious, as did so many of the men she met. It was a drag, dodging guys with prying eyes that centered on her chest and fast hands that seemed fascinated by her bottom. Theodore Maragos might look like the apeman, but he could also be a really nice guy who was simply not interested in a woman for anything but her brains and personality.

She stepped around him, and he darted in front of her. "Before you have a look, I want to explain."

"This is where you live?" she asked, peering over his shoulder. Her voice echoed in the humongous space.

"Yes."

She sidestepped to her left, and he followed.

"Mr. Maragos—"

"It's Theo, please, short for Theodore."

"I know."

"Know what?"

She moved to the right, and he blocked her view again. "That your name is Theodore. It's on your business card."

"Oh, yeah. Of course." He ran a hand through his beard. "I just don't want you to get the wrong idea."

"I can't get any idea at all if you won't let me see what I have to work with," she countered. This time she went right, then quickly danced left, skirting around him. Blinking, she took in a large and mostly barren space the size of Madison Square Garden. "Oh, my."

"I know. It's a mausoleum, a warehouse, a decorator's nightmare of mammoth proportion," he said, turning to stand beside her. "I don't blame you for not wanting the job."

"Not so fast." She brushed by him and took another couple of paces farther into the room. Her eyes focused on a spacious U-shaped counter with an ergonomic desk chair in the center, surrounded by cartons and filing cabinets. "This is where you work?"

"This is it."

"And live?"

"Afraid so." He stuck his hands in his pockets. "I know it's pretty bad, but—"

"Bad would be ratty carpeting and faded chairs, walls that were painted black, and a smell that reminded one of a trash dump in the middle of August. This is something else entirely."

He frowned, and Zoë thought she'd hurt his feelings, but who could tell when it was impossible to see his expression through all that hair?

"Then you're not going to take the job?"

Her mind worked at warp speed, envisioning the space as an experienced artist might assess a blank canvas. The apartment could be molded to her liking, without any preconceived ideas or already implied themes. It was a creative spirit's dream, and if nothing else, she considered herself creative.

"Don't be ridiculous," she answered, shifting her gaze back to his face. "Of course I'll take the job."

His blue eyes crinkled at the corners as his teeth flashed white through the jungle around his mouth. She thought she spotted a dimple but, again, it was hard to tell.

"Great. Really great. When can you get started?"

"I already have."

She was about to toss out a few ideas when the apartment door opened and she turned. A man walked in, quickly crossed the entry, then stood at her side and took her hand. Gazing into her eyes, he said, "Hello. I'm Chad Thomas, COO of Marasoft and Theo's best friend," in a smooth voice laced with a hint of humor.

"Zoë Degodessa," she said in reply.

"And I want it understood from the get-go that this isn't my fault."

Zoë tugged from his grasp and glanced at a scowling Theo. "This?"

Chad waved a hand, meaning, she imagined, to include the entire apartment in his appraisal. "All of this . . . empty space. I've been on his case for years to put up walls, buy furniture, hang a picture, for cripe's sake, but did he listen?" The COO raised a brow. "Of course not."

Hoping to defuse the tension she sensed radiating from her new client, Zoë took a step back in retreat. "May I have a closer look, take a few measurements and view things from the other side of the room?"

"By all means," Chad answered, as if he were the proprietor. "Help yourself."

When Theo nodded, Zoë walked to the center of the huge room, keeping both men in her line of sight while she pretended to scope out the area. In truth, she found it a lot more interesting taking stock of the men than the room. The new arrival was a tad taller than Theo, maybe six-one, but instead of the caveman look, his face sported the beginnings of a sexy five o'clock shadow, his hair was neatly styled and gelled, and he wore a pale pink shirt and pink and gray striped tie under his up-to-the-minute three-piece Armani suit. Though Chad had a good build, Theo appeared more muscular, but it might have been the lumpy shoulder pads in his ancient tweed jacket, rather than a bulging bod, that gave that impression.

The men huddled, their voices an inaudible low rumble, and Zoë reminded herself she'd be gone soon and she planned to leave in a blaze of decorating glory. Taking a battery-powered gizmo from her tote bag, she began to measure the space.

"I told you I didn't need any help," Theo muttered, stepping in front of Chad.

"And I can see why," his pal answered in an equally subdued tone. "That's one attractive interior decorator, and I haven't even seen what she's hiding under that coat."

"Never mind what she looks like under her coat."

Chad grinned. "That good, huh?"

"I hired her because I admired what I saw in the windows she designed, not her figure."

"Let me guess." Chad gazed over Theo's shoulder, his eyes appraising. "She's what, five-eight? I bet she's got legs up to her armpits and the body of a Reuben's model. If I remember correctly, you always were drawn to women with meat on their bones."

"Shut up," Theo ordered, again stepping in front of the COO.

"Uh-oh. This sounds serious. Look, I'm not about to poach on your territory, so give it a rest. That lady seems very sure of herself. You know I want my women a little more . . . needy."

"You enjoy women—period," Theo reminded him.

"So, have you asked her to dinner yet?"

Theo grabbed Chad by the elbow and dragged him into the kitchen section of the apartment. "No."

"Why not?"

"Because I'm not like you, you moron. I don't just ask a woman on a date the first moment I meet her."

"Too bad. Think of all the time you waste doing the will-she-won't-she dance."

"I don't dance."

Chad waggled his eyebrows. "And that's a damn shame too, because women love a guy who has moves, on the dance floor and elsewhere."

"You're an idiot," Theo said, hissing the comment.

"I'm a genius. If not, you wouldn't let me run things at Marasoft while you slave away here, over a hot computer."

"What happened with your stylist?"

"Roberto? I'm happy you decided to use him, because he's going to have a field day when you walk in the door."

"I don't want a field day, I want an appointment. Tomorrow morning, first thing."

"You're kidding."

Theo gave him a quelling glare, and Chad leaned against the refrigerator. "You're not kidding."

"Can you call him now?"

"It's past six. He's been off duty for hours."

"Give it a try, okay?"

Chad sighed, removed his cell phone from a clip on his belt and pressed a button.

Leave it to Chad to have his stylist on speed dial, Theo thought, and then Chad was holding the phone toward him. The taped message came across loud and clear.

When it finished, Chad left his name, number, and a request for Roberto's first available appointment, then looked at Theo. "Sorry, stud, it's the best I can do."

Theo glanced over his shoulder, then back to Chad. "Just let me know as soon as you hear."

"Of course, but I won't be able to go with you. I'm booked tomorrow."

"Doing what?"

"Interviewing the programmers and support staff."

"Can't Sally do that?"

"Sally, our intrepid administrative assistant, has her hands full dealing with head hunters and handling questions from our broker for the IPO. The woman is a genius at multitasking."

"Most women are," Theo replied. "Something about their right brain and their left being able to work in harmony."

"Unlike ours," Chad added. "I know, because you've told me so about a hundred times."

Theo spotted Zoë heading in their direction. "Not a word about Roberto," he ordered. "And isn't it time for you to go home?"

"Can't," Chad answered. "I've got a date."

"Who's the lucky girl?"

"Anne Marie."

"Anne Marie who? Do I know her?"

"I don't know her last name, and yes you know her. She's one of the baristas at the coffee shop across the street."

"About five-two, dark hair, big brown eyes?"

"The very same."

"That child can't be more than twenty."

"She's twenty-two, graduates from college in May. And believe me, she's no child."

"First date?"

"Second, but who's counting? I haven't scored yet, but I might tonight. Depends on the lady."

"I'm finished here," said Zoë as she neared them.

"Great. Then you're ready to start?" Chad prodded.

"First thing tomorrow morning." She smiled at Theo. "You said we have a couple of weeks, correct?"

"Yes. I know it's not a lot of time, but—"

"Not a problem. I'm leaving the city at the end of the month, so I'll have to be done before I go."

"Leaving?" Theo asked, not quite comprehending her words.

"I'm going home for a family reunion of sorts." She gazed at the room. "So, tell me, what look are you going for? Contemporary, casual, period? Do you have any color no-nos? Are you allergic to any fabrics—wool, for example?"

"Um, I like open space and light, and I'm not crazy about purple, but I'm willing to consider anything else. And no allergies that I'm aware of."

"Great. I have to make a few calls in the morning and contact a couple of warehouses that specialize in getting things to the customer within forty-eight hours." She hoisted her bag over her shoulder. "One more thing. What's my budget?"

Theo glanced at Chad.

"Sweetheart," Chad said with a grin. "The sky's the limit."

Chapter 3

Zoë smiled a hello to the evening doorman as she entered the Trump Tower. In return, he tipped his hat and sketched a bow. Life at the posh hotel always amazed her. The mortals residing there dressed in everything from evening gowns, furs, and diamonds to leather, jeans, and studs. She'd even seen guests toting pint-sized dogs wearing jewel-encrusted collars in equally ornate carryalls.

"Ms. Degodessa," said the concierge by way of greeting. "I passed ABC on my way in and recognized your excellent work. Love the little cupids."

"Thanks, Fran," said Zoë. "I'm in for the night."

Riding the elevator to her suite, she prepared for another quiet evening. During her stay, the staff had come to treat her more like family than a guest. There weren't many mortals who could afford a year in one of the Trump Tower's penthouses, though she hadn't realized that until she'd lived there awhile.

When she first arrived on earth, she awoke in a sumptuous bed to brilliant sunlight flowing from between crushed velvet draperies. Unsure of what might be waiting for her, she checked out the spacious walk-in closet and found it overflowing with everything she'd need in the way of personal embellishment. Shoes, boots, and handbags lined one side of the area, while designer clothes in every style and color hung from a rack on the opposite side.

The well-stocked bathroom showcased perfumes, bath salts, scented soaps, and makeup. Besides a laptop computer with Internet access that sat on a cherry-wood desk, the opulent living room was equipped with a bar, refrigerator, and period furniture that she suspected were real antiques. When she'd opened the Chanel clutch on the low table in front of the massive sofa, she found a picture ID, a cell phone, a room key, a roll of bills that amounted to several thousand dollars, and the receipt for a year's rent.

Assuming Zeus had sent her to this particular place for a reason, she'd gazed out onto the busy street and did her best to understand his logic. She was in Manhattan, New York City, the capital of the fashion world. Her residence had a bird's-eye view of some of the most important stores on the planet. Every couture house and design showroom was within walking distance, waiting for her inspiration.

In seconds a lightbulb clicked in her head, and Zeus rose several steps on the ladder of her respect. Her father had given her every opportunity to fulfill her destiny in the time frame she'd been given. If she didn't succeed in the Big Apple after all he'd done, the failure would be hers alone.

On a whim, she'd picked up the cell phone and fiddled with the buttons until she found an address book holding both her sisters' numbers. She called Kyra first, then Chloe, and after hearing the details of their arrivals, acknowledged that their father, the old softie, had done everything in his power to make certain the Muse of Good Fortune, the Muse of Happiness, and the Muse of Beauty attained their goals.

Of course, Kyra and Chloe hadn't see it in quite the same manner. Kyra complained about having to use a computer, and Chloe groused about the lack of single men. As the year passed, both changed their tune. Kyra, it seemed, had been promoted and learned to use a computer in her new job; and Chloe, well, she'd had more men in her bed than she could count.

Zoë didn't have a complaint about Zeus's dictums.

Yes, their father was a bossy old coot who demanded respect whether he earned it or not, but he was top god. He'd given them life and a purpose. Granted, she, Chloe, and Kyra hadn't filled that purpose to his liking, but it wasn't Zeus's fault.

He might have warned them of their impending doom sooner, of course, but he'd been wrapped up in his loss of status with the mortal world. No one believed in gods anymore. Instead they worshipped things: money, elaborate homes, expensive cars . . . power. Mortals had injured his pride and, in turn, he'd reigned terror and threats on the residents of Mount Olympus.

Over the past several hundred years, most of the gods had taken Zeus's challenges seriously, while she and a few of her sister muses hadn't listened at all. And even those who'd tried to make the father god happy had faced a raft of problems. No one wrote sacred poetry these days, so Polyhymnia had nothing to inspire; therefore, Zeus renamed her the Muse of Blogs, because the bloggers' daily ramblings were now an up and coming Internet reality. If Poly could inspire the mortals who wrote them, it followed that the quality of the blogs would improve.

The same could be said about epic poetry, lyric poetry, even astronomy, now a well-accepted science. Mortals were so fascinated with the ability to search the universe that astronomers fulfilled their destiny without Urania's heavenly inspiration.

She sighed as she sat at the desk and scanned the room service menu. She'd eaten so many meals at the Tower that she almost knew the listings by heart. It wasn't that she hid in the hotel, but she'd rather be alone than make friends she would eventually leave. Aside from a few lunches and dinners with Elise, conversations with the clients of Suited for Change, and random dates with a couple of men, she'd kept to herself. She refused to let an intimate relationship interfere with her chance at eternal glory in the home she loved.

After dialing the kitchen and placing an order for hot tea and a burger, she opened her day planner and started phoning suppliers and services that had helped her in the past. By the time dinner arrived, she'd already secured appointments with two furniture companies for the next morning, and two more in the afternoon.

She was sure that Theo Maragos was going to love what she had in mind for his apartment—as soon as she decided what that might be. To know for certain, she'd have to assess his likes and dislikes and come up with choices. She never foisted her personal opinion on anyone, but she always did her best to inspire her clients. Unfortunately, time was of the utmost importance. To do the job right, she'd have to eat with him, shop with him, and practically set herself in the middle of his life.

She couldn't help but wonder what kind of man lurked behind all that hair. She suspected he had a dimple, maybe two, and his blue eyes appeared kind behind his wire-rimmed glasses. She also guessed he had a nice body, but it was impossible to judge, thanks to the style of clothing he wore. Though he wasn't as suave as his handsome business partner, she thought him more appealing, more likable, even more fun.

Striving for honesty, Zoë admitted she found her new client intriguing. And with nothing else on her schedule except a few consultations at Suited for Change, she was willing to spend her remaining weeks on earth finding out what made Theo tick.

"Roberto's willing to see you at five o'clock as a special favor to me. In return, I had to promise we'd give his salon a mention in the *NYE* article, so we'll have to work it in somehow." Chad leaned against the counter in the area Theo called his kitchen. "And please don't embarrass me when you get there by playing the nerd, okay?"

"I don't act like a nerd when I'm out in public," Theo groused. Damn, but his partner was irritating.

"Right. Just remember, talk in normal sentences,

not technogeek; don't tell Roberto you could transfer his customer list to a database or inventory his hair products in return for services rendered either. Think of the cost of a stylist as part of the cost of doing business."

"The guy's a fortune."

"That's it," Chad pronounced. "I forbid you to talk at all. Let him do whatever he wants to you, pay him whatever he charges, and include a big tip. You got that?"

The sarcastic bite Chad gave to his jocular warning held a grain of truth. Theo knew that his expertise in everything technical often made people's eyes glaze over, but hey, his computer skills were as much a part of him as his arm or his leg. He'd been picked on in one way or another his entire life. Long ago, Chad had accepted his geek quotient. But there wasn't a soul on earth with whom he could discuss the life he'd led before he met Chad, prior to his eighteenth birthday.

"People can't choose their inborn talents," he said now, "just like they can't pick their parents. You know I'm a geek as much as I know you're an egotistical snob, but I don't ridicule you or—"

"Yeah, yeah, yeah." Chad ran a hand through his perfectly cut hair. "Sorry." But he didn't sound sorry. In fact, he sounded pissed.

Theo gave the situation some thought. "Do you

think I should go to a barber *before* I see this Roberto character?"

"Don't be ridiculous. I'm just in a foul mood."

"Because last night didn't go as planned?"

"That's one way to put it."

"What happened? Did Anne Marie bring her teddy bear on your date?"

"No, smartass. She wanted to go to a club, and I obliged. We weren't there ten minutes when some kid asked her to dance—"

It took a bit of doing, but Theo managed to hold back a grin. "You mean a man closer to her own age."

"He was dressed in separates that screamed The Gap, and he couldn't have been more than twenty-five," Chad said, his tone incredulous. "And when he asked her, she said yes. The next thing I knew, they disappeared."

"I keep telling you to date women instead of little girls."

"Today's women are too suspicious. They wonder what's wrong with a man who hasn't been married by thirty, and as soon as they do decide the guy is worth their attention, they expect something I'm not—*he's* not ready to give." He shrugged, as if resigned to the situation. "But this isn't about me and the women I date. I'd rather continue discussing your grooming habits or lack thereof.

What's the point in going to a chop shop so some old geezer with bad breath and worse eyesight can hack at your hair and your face, when you'll be taken care of by a pro at the end of the day?"

"Because I wanted to look my best this morning," Theo argued. "By the time I see Roberto, my chance at making a stellar first impression on my interior designer will be lost."

"I hate to tell you this, buddy, but it's too late. The adorable Ms. Degodessa met you twice yesterday, so you've already blown your initial quest to impress." Chad rinsed his coffee mug and set it in the sink. "I know you want her to see you in a more personal light, but how do you know what type of man interests her? Maybe she appreciates the Yeti look."

"Somehow, I doubt it. Besides, I've been thinking about everything you've hammered into me for the past couple of years, and you're right. I don't want to stand on the floor of NASDAQ and have those tight-assed stockbrokers think the company is run by a slob. And if my picture's going to appear in *New York Entrepreneur*, I guess it should present me in a positive manner." Theo glanced at his watch. "Zoë will be here in thirty minutes. We're supposed to shop for furniture this morning and again this afternoon. I was hoping to get the grooming thing done in between."

"What? Not chaining yourself to your computer today?"

"I'm caught up, nearly finished, really. I sent the final module over to the guys you hired last week for testing. I just have a few more details to take care of and I'm through. How are the newbies settling in?"

"The cubicles turned out better than expected. They're roomy, with comfortable chairs and a good amount of work space. Add that to our top-of-the-line equipment and sign-on bonus, and the new associates don't have a thing to complain about."

"I suppose I should meet them," Theo said, but he had no idea when he'd find a free hour to do so.

"That might be a good idea, seeing as you're president of the company. But I told them you were a recluse, the Howard Hughes of the computer world, so they aren't too worried."

"Thanks—I think." He paced to the bathroom door. "I have to shower and do something about this hair," he muttered, though he never thought those words would pass his lips.

"Don't let me stop you, my Yeti friend. And good luck with the bodacious Ms. Degodessa."

When Chad left, Theo recalled how often he and his friend had eaten breakfast in this loft while they held planning sessions and discussed the future of their company. His COO had always been the doer of the team, while he was the thinker. As of today, he was stepping into Chad's world—a frightening thought, but one he was ready to accept.

The ring on his finger warmed as a vision of the lovely designer flashed in his brain. He was certain the misery of being scrutinized by a "stylist" would be worth the trouble if the end result got Zoë Degodessa to see him as more than a client. Although his grooming appointment was later in the day, he'd at least be clean and dressed decently. That had to count for something, didn't it?

After showering, Theo pulled his hair into a ponytail and ran a comb through his beard. What had possessed him to let things get so far beyond his control? When had he decided the Grizzly Adams look was back in vogue?

Because I have this crazy idea that it's safer to bond with a laptop than a woman.

Oh yeah, he'd forgotten about that.

He pulled a pair of fresh jeans out of the armoire, as well as a long-sleeve dress shirt and a fairly new sweater. The jeans were a little faded, but Chad wore his like that, so Theo assumed it was the style. To his credit, the shirt had all its buttons, the collar was intact, and the gray sweater was free of those annoying balls of fuzz that collected like crumbs in his beard whenever he ate.

The buzzer sounded, and he jumped, then rushed to make certain it was his morning appointment. "Yes?"

"It's Zoë Degodessa, Theo. Are you ready for me?"

Ready, willing, and able. He almost blurted it. "Come on up," he said instead, and pressed the front door entry. *Get a grip,* he commanded himself while waiting. Ms. Degodessa was just a woman.

Yeah, but what a woman, his brain shot back. When the warmth of the ring echoed the thought, he smiled. Every once in a while even a geek got lucky and was able to talk a good-looking woman into a date. If he played his cards right, this week he'd be the lottery winner.

A soft knock brought him back to reality. After straightening his sweater, he plastered a friendly smile on his face and opened the door. "You're prompt. I like that."

"If there's one thing I find annoying in myself and others, it's being tardy." She set her coat and a huge black leather tote bag on the counter. "Before we leave for our meetings, I need to ask you a few questions."

More than willing to do whatever she requested, Theo admired her glorious waterfall of hair and her perfect face. Dressed in high-heeled boots, fitted black slacks, and a body-hugging red sweater,

Zoë Degodessa managed to appear incredibly sexy yet totally competent at the same time.

"Fine, great, seeing as I have a few of my own."

As if she'd just made an error, she bit her lower lip. "Do you need to see my references? I didn't bring my portfolio, but I could give you some names and numbers to call—"

"No, no. I've inspected your work, remember?"

"But they were only store windows. I won't be upset if you tell me you've had a chance to think it over, and you're not sure I'm qualified to design an entire loft of, what, two thousand square feet?"

"About twenty-one hundred, and I haven't changed my mind. I know you're the right person for the job."

She propped her hip against the counter. "Okay, what do you need to know?"

If you'll have dinner with me, tonight, and every night for the rest of my life. The ring burned his finger, giving him hope, but it was too soon to ask such a question. "I want to know if you, ah, have a—a—website. If so, I could look at a few more samples of your work—to see if there's anything you've done that would translate well here."

"A website? Sorry, but no."

"No?" he said, taken by surprise. In today's Internet world of e-mails and instant messaging, everybody had a website, even kids. "Why not?"

"I don't need one. From the day I arrived in this town, I was able to find clients. It started with a window for Bloomingdale's. I walked in looking for a job the same day their window decorator quit. They asked me to show them what I could do, and that was it." She shrugged. "I guess you could say I was lucky, but I also know I have talent."

"And your confident attitude kept you in customers?"

"It helped. I took pictures of my first successful project. Carried them to the next store on the block, got another job, and took more pictures. Word spread, and both ABC and Macy's offered me a permanent position, but I turned them down. I like variety."

"And you make more money, I'd imagine."

"Yes, that's true. But I don't do it for the money."

"Really? What are you, independently wealthy?" He regretted the question the moment it left his mouth. Her financial situation was none of his business. "Sorry, that was too personal."

She shook her head. "I don't mind. Most people would say that I'm set financially, but I enjoy my career. Being happy in what you do is more important than earning a hefty income."

Theo couldn't fault her line of thinking, especially since he agreed with her. Which was one more reason he wanted to explore the crazy sensation that had his ring acting like a Bunsen burner whenever he was in her presence. "I think so too."

"Great. Now what else do you need to know?"

"Uh . . . I forget. What did you want to ask me?"

"I need to find out about walls."

"Walls?"

"You know, room dividers, partitions, whatever you want to call them. I can have a company in here by tomorrow morning to do an inspection and put something up in a couple of days, but first we have to do the layout."

"Forty-eight-hour delivery on the furniture, and now a construction company that's willing to do a job in a couple of days? Are you a magician?"

She gave a mischievous smile. "Not exactly, but I have connections. Of course, they'll charge double what they normally would to meet the deadline, but your COO did say money was no object."

"Yeah, well Chad sometimes goes overboard, as you'll soon find out."

"Then there is a budget?"

"Not if he said there wasn't."

"Good. Let's sit down and draft the floor plan."

"I think that about does it," Zoë said as she and Theo stood in the middle of a trendy gallery in the Village. She eyed the last piece of artwork he'd chosen. The three pen and ink sketches of nudes in repose had delighted her and embarrassed him, but he'd been incredibly agreeable to her suggestion that they were perfect for his apartment. "We'll hang these in a staggered line on the far side of the armoire in the bedroom."

"That's good, because I certainly wouldn't want them in my office."

"Art Deco is very in at the moment. And they'll go great with the theme of the room."

"The room has a theme?"

"It will after you give final approval on the furniture. In case you haven't noticed, everything you've been drawn to is bold and masculine. These pictures will hint at your softer side."

"I'm not sure I like the sound of that."

"The rooms need balance, a little something that catches the eye yet flows to the next room. For you, it will be the unexpected graceful edge of the art work." She flipped through her day planner then smiled. "Buying a bed is next on the list."

"I already have a bed. You must have seen it."

"It's hard to miss a mattress and box spring sitting on a floor. How old is it?"

"I don't know, seven, maybe eight years."

"You need new. And don't forget the linens."

"You mean sheets and stuff?"

Was she imagining it, or was he blushing? Darn,

but that hairy face made it difficult to assess his reaction to things. "Sheets, comforter, pillow shams, area rugs, the works. I use a cash-and-carry place on Designer's Row for most things. We'll go in a few days, after the construction people are through with the job. I'll make sure the hangings are up and the carpets are down before the furniture is delivered."

"You weren't kidding when you said you had connections, were you?"

"I never kid where design and fashion are concerned." She checked her watch. They were narrowing down their choices in furniture groupings, but she had a sneaking suspicion choosing paint colors, draperies, and rugs would be a more difficult task. To complete the experience, she had to learn more about him. "It's almost five. Do you want to share an early dinner?"

He snapped to attention. "Five? I've got to run."

So much for spending some personal time with her client, she thought, though now that she'd worked with him for an entire day, she had a pretty good idea of his likes and dislikes. "Okay then, I'll see you—"

"How about later, say eight?" He walked backward toward the subway entrance as he spoke. "At the Villa Italiano on Seventy-fifth?"

"If you're sure you want to, then yes."

"I want to," he shouted. "See you at eight." With that, he disappeared down the stairs.

Hefting her tote bag over her shoulder, she shrugged. Now she had time to drop in at Suited for Change and go over the outfit she'd planned for Marjorie Barris. But thanks to the immediacy of Theo's remodeling project, she'd have to slip the woman into her new schedule for her final fitting. She guessed that dressing Marjorie would prove difficult. Sometimes it was hard for a woman who stood five-foot-ten and wore a size twenty-four to find decent business attire.

Still, she was up for the challenge, especially since Theo had agreed to dinner. The more they were together, the more she could get into his head and learn what he preferred in style and design. She planned on leaving earth in a blaze of glory, with *New York Entrepreneur* singing her praises and Theo Maragos one of her most satisfied and inspired customers.

With those impressive credentials, she was sure to be welcomed back to Mount Olympus with open arms and her bossy father's longed-for approval.

Chapter 4

Zoë paid the cab driver and included a handsome tip. He'd done his best to maneuver the taxi through traffic in order to get to the restaurant on time, and it wasn't his fault she'd asked the impossible. But at eight-fifteen, nothing could save her. She was late.

As she pushed through the restaurant's double doors, the enticing aromas of rosemary, basil, thyme, and lemon, mingled with the basic Italian scents of olive oil, garlic, and tomato, made her mouth water. She loved every type of food mortals prepared, especially fare with a hearty Mediterranean flavor.

Some people might believe that living in paradise high above a mountaintop in Greece would allow the gods to feast on flavor-filled dishes with an exotic bent, but they were wrong. Due to Zeus's recent unsuccessful fling with modern food and a bout of acid reflux, his stomach had proved delicate, so the citizens of Mount Olympus were forced to eat what he preferred. Ambrosia, fruit, stuffed grape leaves, and a few basic meats and vegetables were the norm, not the tangy spices, tempting herbs, and tart-sweet tastes she craved.

Luckily, it never mattered what or how much she ate. Thanks to a father who demanded perfect physical form in all his creations, her body would forever remain the same. Instead of wrinkles, sags, and cellulite, every inch of her skin was toned, taut, and smooth, and showcased in a generous package designed specifically to please a man's eye. If Zeus ever decided to set up a body-sculpting shop on earth, mortal women would flock to his door for a single moment of his magic touch.

"May I help you?" asked the maître d' standing behind a podium in the foyer.

"I'm supposed to meet someone, but I'm late. Is Theo Maragos here?"

"Yes, madam, he is. May I take your wrap?"

She passed him her coat. From nowhere a woman appeared and whisked the garment away.

"Please follow me," he continued.

She trotted behind the maître d', weaving past customers and around waiters and busboys until they stopped at a secluded alcove. Pulling out the chair, he said, "Your table, madam."

Zoë smiled sheepishly as she gazed at the handsome man who rose from his chair across from her. "Sorry, there's been a mistake." She glanced at the maître d'. "I think you misunderstood. I'm here to meet Theodore Maragos."

The maître d' grinned at the tall, good-looking customer, then at her. "This is his table, madam. Please have a seat."

"Yes, but—"

"It's all right, Tonio," said the stranger in a deep voice she recognized immediately. "I'll take care of the lady."

Still on her feet, Zoë opened and closed her mouth. Then she noticed her tablemate's gray sweater and snug faded jeans.

"It's me, honest." Theo ran a hand over his clean-shaven jaw. "I had no idea it would be such a surprise."

Incapable of uttering a word, she sat with a plop and stared. Theo's pale skin, the result of not having seen the sun in a while, she guessed, glowed, while his dark wavy hair shone in the soft candlelight of the wall sconce. His blue eyes twinkled behind wire-rimmed glasses, and his chiseled lips held a sexy grin, revealing the dimples she suspected lurked beneath his beard when they first met.

"Is it too much?" he asked, his expression concerned.

She inhaled a breath, as blown away by his square jaw and princely appearance as she was by his voice, so much deeper than she remembered. "I—I'm—I don't know what to say," she blathered.

He ran a hand over his expertly styled hair. "It was supposed to be a surprise, but I had no idea you'd come close to fainting. I hope that means you're not disappointed."

Fat chance, she thought, still studying his face. "I'm sorry." Heat rushed from her chest to her neck. "It's just such a . . . shock? No, that's not the right word. How about I call it what you suggested? A surprise."

"Fine by me, as long as you don't run screaming from the restaurant. I was caught off guard too. It's been a while since I've seen the real me." He passed her a menu. "Let's order, then we can talk."

Zoë opened the bill of fare, but instead of reading the offerings, continued to sneak a peek at him in case she'd only imagined the transformation. When a curl fell gently onto Theo's forehead, it took real effort not to reach out and brush it into place.

His sharp-bladed nose wrinkled and straightened, his full lips turned down at something he read, then lifted in approval. He raised his gaze and grinned, showing one of the first things she'd noticed about him—his perfect teeth. "See anything you can't resist?"

Yes, you, she almost blurted. Positive he knew she'd been staring, she turned her attention to the menu. "Everything. Why don't you order for both of us?" That way, she could enjoy looking at him a little longer.

"Do you like lemon, chicken, and capers, because this place does a mean chicken piccata."

"That sounds wonderful."

"How about an appetizer?"

The heat continued to rise from her neck to her cheeks as a sudden urge to nibble on his lips invaded her brain. "Um, no thanks."

The waiter arrived, and Theo took charge. After giving their order, he said to her, "Do you drink wine?"

She suppressed her usually negative response. The one time she and Elise met for drinks, it had taken only a few sips of a peach margarita to get her light-headed and giggly. The cocktail's delicious taste didn't make up for the out-of-control feeling that invaded her senses. But now that giddy tingle might be just what she needed to counter the shock of her client's new and improved image.

"I'm not big on alcohol, but a glass of something light would be nice."

He gave his selection to the waiter by name and vintage. After handing over both menus, he leaned back in his chair. "Did you take care of whatever you had to do to clear the rest of your calendar?"

"Sort of. I'm fairly certain I can work what's left of my responsibilities in between our appointments. Then I'm off to Greece."

He turned the ring on his finger as his sensuous lips flattened, almost to a grimace. "I thought your last name had an ethnic ring. What part of Greece are you from?"

"The mountains," she answered, purposely vague. When he didn't comment, she said, "I suspected we shared a bit of the same heritage when I saw your last name too. Is your family from there?"

"On my mother's side."

"Does she still live in Greece, or are your parents here in the States?"

He frowned before he answered. "Mother's there, as are, I assume, the rest of her relatives, but I haven't seen them in over fourteen years."

"And your father?"

"My dad is from Wisconsin, but right now he lives in a nursing home in New Jersey. I try to visit him every weekend." He took a sip of water. "Why are you going back?"

"A family reunion of sorts. My father is expecting me."

"Will you stay long?"

"Um . . . I'm not sure. Probably."

His eyes narrowed. "But you are returning to New York?"

"I don't—"

The waiter arrived with their wine and held out the bottle for Theo's inspection. He checked the label, then waited while the bottle was opened and a splash of golden liquid poured into his glass. After taking a taste, he nodded.

"That's perfect."

The server filled their glasses, then set the bottle in a stand supporting a chilled bucket. Zoë guessed by the flex of Theo's clenched jaw that her impending departure upset him, so she changed the subject as deftly as possible.

"I'm curious. What made you decide to alter your appearance?"

"Truth?"

She grinned. "Always."

"Chad's been after me to update my personal

style ever since we knew the company would be featured in *New York Entrepreneur*. I had pictures taken about a week ago, and they turned out lousy, mostly because, as Chad put it, I could have doubled for a member of ZZ Top. He insisted that both the loft and I undergo major renovations or the magazine would kick me out of their lineup."

"You did the right thing finding an interior designer. But why me?"

"Because he told me if I didn't get someone on my own, he'd have one of his friends do it, and I've met enough of his friends to know that's not what I wanted. Since I didn't feel comfortable choosing a stranger from the Internet, he suggested I check out store windows, and there you were."

"Sounds as if this photo shoot is important to the success of your company."

"Vital, might be a better word. There'll be pictures of the main office and my loft in the magazine, but it's extra important that I make a good personal impression. According to my COO, image is everything. It can make or break the company on the NASDAQ."

"That's why this project has no budget."

"Right. Chad's the front man. He believes in the old adage: you have to spend money to make money. He handles the finances, our investors, and the day-to-day operations, while I focus on product development."

"So that explains it."

"Explains what?"

"Why your friend reminds me of an ad for Armani," she said with a smile. "Or a model in *GQ*."

"But I'm not Chad."

She opened her eyes wide in an expression of innocence. "Really? And I thought you were twins."

"Very funny." He ran his fingers through his jet black curls. "I guess I'll get used to the new me in a couple of days." He tugged at his collar. "According to Chad, I need a wardrobe update. He's been threatening to take everything I own to the local homeless shelter so I'll be forced to buy new."

"And he's going to help with that?"

"Not if I have anything to say about it. I'm worried I really will end up looking just like him, and that is definitely not me."

Suddenly, Zoë had an idea. One that would allow them to spend more time together . . . for the job, of course. "May I make a suggestion? Actually, more of an offer?"

"Sure. At this point, I'm up for anything."

"How about if I take over for Chad? I promise

that, in the end, you'll be your own man, dressed comfortably but in a style you like and he'll approve of."

Clearly surprised by her offer, Theo's shocked expression quickly changed to one of approval. His eyes crinkled and dimples creased his cheeks. Then he raised his glass of wine and held it out to her. "You've got yourself a deal."

Theo gazed at the Trump Tower Hotel, one of the most expensive and impressive places to stay in the city. His eyes darted to the valets and bellmen rushing to assist guests with their automobiles and luggage, then to Zoë. "You live here?"

"Yes." She walked into the lobby and nodded to the impeccably dressed doorman. "Hello, Charles. Has it been busy tonight?"

"About usual, Ms. Degodessa. Thanks for asking."

Not quite able to believe what he was seeing, Theo caught Zoë's elbow and turned her to face him. "Let me get this straight. You *live* at the Trump Tower, full-time?"

She smiled at his obvious amazement. "It's my home."

"Wow. Business must be booming."

"You could say that. Do you want to come up to my apartment?"

More than anything, he thought. Instead, in an attempt to display a man-of-the-world attitude, he said, "If you're sure it won't be an imposition."

"Of course it won't," she answered, still grinning.

He followed her to an elevator marked private. Once inside, she pushed the button for a top floor. Flummoxed, he bit his tongue. Zoë was a class act, but she certainly didn't behave like the people he'd met who had money. He figured she had designer taste, but assumed she was able to get the stuff at a discount because of her profession. He now realized he was wrong, because Zoë Degodessa had to have a trust fund, family wealth, or a business that could put his to shame in the accounts receivable department, maybe all three, to live at the Trump Tower, twenty-four/seven.

As the elevator glided upward, she said, "I can hear the wheels turning. What are you thinking?"

He leaned against the car's rear wall, growing used to the ring's heat against his skin. "Promise you won't take this the wrong way?"

The elevator stopped, the doors slid open, and he followed her into the hall before she responded. "I promise."

"I've had to work for every dime I have—"

"I work too." She led him to a door, inserted her card in the lock, and stepped inside. "But I do have family connections that make things easier. Remember what I said about having a profession you love?"

"Yes."

"Well, if this lifestyle were gone tomorrow, I'd still be decorating windows, dressing women who need fashion help, and looking for ways to improve life through better design. I assume you feel the same about the use of the computer programs you write?"

"I guess so," he responded, not fully concentrating. Instead, he blinked at his surroundings, taking in the elegant appeal of a suite filled with ornate furnishings and luxurious carpets. It wasn't a place he'd care to live, but he imagined many of the upper crust would.

"Make yourself at home," she encouraged. "There are beverages in the fridge, though I'm not sure of the brands. If you don't see what you want, we can call room service." She hung her coat in the closet, then reached for his.

He interrupted his inspection to keep her in sight. This was her residence, he thought, which meant he was so far out of her league he might as well return to his boyhood home. Even if his company ate up miles on the Internet highway, he would never catch Zoë Degodessa and her millions.

She went to the bar area and dug through a basket laden with goodies. "Do you want a drink, or . . . pretzels, macadamia nuts, chocolate?"

He remembered staying at a hotel with his father once, and his dad hadn't allowed him to touch a single thing in the honor bar. "We can't afford it, son," his father had said. If that were true a decade ago, it had to be doubly true now.

"No, thanks. I'm still full from dinner."

"Me too."

She turned on a light next to the desk, and he spotted a laptop computer, which told him that even if she didn't have a website, she knew enough about technology to make use of it from time to time.

He waited while she switched on and dimmed several of the lamps. When she sat at the opposite end of the sofa and slipped off her black half boots, he caught sight of her toes through sheer stockings. Each toenail, painted a shimmering pink, beckoned like a beacon guiding him through the dark.

"Hmm. That feels good." She wriggled the dainty digits, then leaned back into the cushions. "Unlike my sister, I'm really not much of a shoe freak."

"You have a sister?"

"I have several sisters. The one with the shoe fetish is Chloe. Kyra likes shoes too, but she loves clothes, the more expensive the better."

Zoë, Kyra, and Chloe. The names rang a bell, but he couldn't figure out why.

"What about you?" he asked. "What are you into?"

"Me?" She raised her arms over head and stretched, drawing attention to her generous breasts. "Clothes aren't that important to me, personally. I'd rather make sure others look good. That's what I was made, er, born, er, what I enjoy doing most. Besides interior design, I love helping people feel positive about themselves. It's the reason I volunteer at Suited for Change."

Theo shifted on the sofa. "What's Suited for Change?"

"It's an organization that helps women find their way back into the job market by dressing them for success," she stated in a serious tone. "They think the same as your COO—that a good self-image is important, especially to a woman who's been dragged down by her situation in life. They operate exclusively on donations and assistance from people in my profession."

"What do you do for them?"

"I take the donated clothes and match them to the right client, update the outfit with the proper accessories, and make sure the woman appears her very best before she goes on a job interview."

"Like Cinderella's fairy godmother did for her before Cindy left for the ball?"

"Exactly." She turned toward him and tucked her legs underneath her. "Will your company offer corporate sponsorship or a charitable donation to a needy organization once it goes public? Maybe take Suited for Change under its wing?"

"Maybe. I'd have to discuss it with Chad."

She rose to her knees, inching closer. "That would be great. When can Elise and I talk to him?"

Thanks to his COO's misguided comment about money, Theo realized, Zoë thought he and Chad were in her financial league. In fact, start-up costs had dropped them in a hole they were only now beginning to dig out of. Since hiring a full-time staff and giving them healthy sign-on bonuses, they barely stayed in the black. They also had a half-dozen college buddies who'd invested in their firm and were eager to see a profit. That's why the success of their IPO was so important, as was the *NYE* article.

"You can talk to him whenever you catch him free," he told Zoë. "I don't involve myself in what he does on a day-to-day basis, but I know he's been spending most of his time in our new headquarters."

"So you won't mind if I make an appointment with him to discuss a donation?"

"Fine by me." Theo leaned forward and rested his elbows on his knees. "What's our schedule for tomorrow?"

"I have a client fitting at ten o'clock at Suited for Change, then I'm free. We should go to my supplier and check paint colors, then make a final decision on the furniture. The wall men will be at your place first thing in the morning. You'll have to be there to go over our floor plan and answer any questions they might have."

"Questions?"

"They'll probably ask about the placement of electrical outlets and light fixtures, things like that. Especially in your office and the kitchen."

He sighed. "The kitchen really isn't my area of expertise. Maybe you could explain it to me again, and I'll tell them to do whatever you've written down."

Just like a man, Zoë thought. Why were kitchens always so out of their realm of understanding? Most of the top chefs on the Cooking Channel were men, so why couldn't an ordinary guy handle a simple detail regarding the most important room in a home? She scooted closer to him, opened her tote bag, and brought out her day planner. Then she flipped to the pages with the schematic of his new living space.

"Okay, let's run through it one more time. Here's

the entry, with the guest bath to the right, only we've cut it down to a more manageable size and used the freed-up space for a coat closet." She pointed to the drawing. "Got it?"

"Yep."

She shifted her attention to the kitchen layout. "This wall will hold all the appliances and swing around to the refrigerator. I've added a pantry here," she indicated a corner, "and the countertop will double as a work area and a room divider, as well as provide extra storage underneath." When he didn't answer, she raised her head.

Instead of studying the plan, Theo was studying her.

"Um . . . you're supposed to be inspecting the layout."

His lips quirked up at the corners. "Looking at you is far more interesting. Has anyone ever told you you're beautiful?"

Thousands of men, over and over again, she thought, though none of them had caused her nerves to tingle the way they were doing right now. "I've heard it before, but it's nice of you to say so."

"I'm still trying to figure out the color of your eyes," he continued, his expression softening. "Sometimes they're green, then they fade to a lighter shade and turn almost amber, then they darken to the color of a fine, aged whiskey, sort of a golden brown." As he spoke, he slid closer. "It's very disconcerting, not being able to put a name to the color. And your hair . . ."

The same blast of heat that had overtaken her in the restaurant rose in her chest and crept up her neck. "What about my hair?"

"First it's a chestnut brown, then it catches the light and turns a deep red, but the streaks of gold make me think of a butterfly's wings changing color as it flits in the sun."

Theo's mouth was only inches from hers. When he took a deep breath and exhaled, she caught scent of the wine they'd shared at dinner mingling with the fresh citrus aroma of whatever aftershave his stylist had used.

"That's very poetic," she murmured, her eyes drifting closed for his kiss.

Seconds passed and nothing happened. Zoë snapped up her lids and found him standing, the plans she'd drawn clutched in his white-knuckled fist.

"I'm sure we'll be okay with the . . . the schematic," he muttered. Racing to the closet, he pulled out his leather jacket and opened the suite door. "I'm going home. Alone." His handsome face crumpled. "I mean, to be by myself, 'cause that's how I live . . . alone . . . so . . ." He rolled his eyes to the ceiling. "See you tomorrow."

The door shut with a bang. Zoë heaved a breath. Well, golly, that had never happened to her before. Now she was embarrassed. And annoyed. Ticked off, really. Theo had made her feel foolish, and she hated when she did something stupid. Sighing, she rested against the sofa cushions and muttered a curse.

Of all the mortal men she'd met on earth, Theo Maragos had to be the most confusing. If she wasn't so certain that his renovation project would earn her kudos from Zeus, she'd tell him to find another decorator to torment or—

Her cell phone rang, and she dug it out of her bag, suddenly recalling that tonight was her scheduled weekly chat with Kyra and Chloe. Vowing to keep her dealings with Theo private, she flipped open the phone. "Hey."

"There you are," said Chloe. "I thought you might have forgotten us."

"Sorry, but I sort of did. I was with a client, and it skipped my mind."

A few seconds later all three muses were on the line. "So, how is everyone? Anything new?" Chloe inquired.

The ensuing silence told Zoë she'd better speak

before one of her sisters asked a question she wasn't prepared to answer. "Why don't you go first," she suggested to Chloe. "Your life is a lot more exciting than mine."

"If you insist." The Muse of Happiness began a litany of her latest adventures, ending with, "Bryce is positively the last guy I'll have to deal with, since we'll be leaving soon. And don't even ask me about Belle's grandson."

"I'm sure Miss Belle is thrilled with your revolving door policy where men are concerned," Zoë offered with a snort. "You are shameless. How many has it been?"

"Twelve, but who's counting? Miss Belle thinks a woman should sample a bushel of fruit before she picks a favorite orchard. It's not my fault mortal men are so easy."

"For a senior citizen, your employer sounds like a very progressive woman," added Kyra.

"She is. And I really do care about the mortals I've dallied with. There isn't a single god I'd bother taking to my bed after seeing so many good-looking men down here."

Zoë knew Chloe was joking. The stunning demigoddess loved voicing shallow statements just to get a rise out of everyone within hearing distance.

"May I remind you," said Kyra, "that it might

blow your chance at eternal glory if our father finds out you've been playing around instead of doing your job. Have you been keeping track of the happiness you've inspired?"

"Of course I have, just as I know you're keeping tabs on the good fortune, and Zoë is hitting it big in the world of fashion and interior design. But Zeus did give us permission to mess around with mortals, as long as we don't fall in love."

After another long pause, Kyra said, "Zoë, what's going on in New York? Any new problems . . . or new men?"

"Not a one," she lied, because as of about five minutes ago she'd decided Theo would not be a problem. "The women at Suited for Change are inspired by my suggestions, the window dressing job is a success, and I just took on a challenging project."

"Is the guy cute?" Chloe asked, her usual one-track mind steering her thoughts.

"Who said it involved a guy?"

"I could tell by the sound of your voice, silly, and it might do you good to have a final fling before you leave. We all should."

"Don't preach to me about a final fling," Zoë answered, hoping to switch the subject. "Kyra hasn't had any affairs at all. She's the one we need to worry about."

Kyra didn't say a word, which had Zoë concerned.

"Hey, sis, you still on the line?"

"I'm here."

"Is there something you don't want to tell us?"

"It's just been a couple of interesting days."

"Define interesting."

Kyra proceeded to explain her current working relationship with a man, including the fact that he was a twelve on the kiss-o-meter.

"You can't be serious," chimed Chloe.

"I am, but I can handle it."

"Just don't let Zeus hear you," advised Zoë, continuing to divert the discussion. "Our father might be listening to this conversation as we speak."

"Hah! I doubt it. It's going to be so rewarding when he admits our triumph and gives us our due," said Kyra.

"That's the spirit," Chloe encouraged. "It will be very satisfying to see the great father god humbled."

"And don't forget Hera," Kyra added. "The witch."

"I think you've got the first letter wrong," said Zoë with a chuckle. "I believe the word to describe her should start with a capital B."

After a few more minutes of chitchat, they

wished each other well and said good-bye. Zoë turned off her phone, strode to the desk and set the earthly device in its charger. Had Kyra and Chloe confessed everything that had taken place in their relationships with mortal men? she wondered.

Or were they holding back, the same as she was?

Earthly males could be a drag, and rarely were they worth the trouble they put women through. Theo was a prime example. First, he'd acted as if he couldn't get enough of her; then, when she made it clear she would welcome his kiss, he backed away as if she had the plague.

Talk about mixed signals.

But it was no big deal, because with little more than two weeks left of her stay, and a big project to bring to fruition, there was no point in starting an affair with a man who didn't know what he wanted.

Her goal was clear, and nothing would stop her from reaching it. A triumphant return to Mount Olympus was her heart's desire, and she refused to accept less.

Chapter 5

Marjorie Barris's eyes sparkled with tears as she ran shaking fingers through her newly cut russet hair. Then she dabbed at her damp cheeks, careful not to ruin her freshly applied makeup. Turning in the three-way mirror, she continued to study her reflection, as if doubting her own image.

"Good lord, Ms. Degodessa, I can't believe it. It's a miracle. Plain and simple."

Zoë folded her arms, studying the knot she'd tied in the red silk scarf adorning her client's black and gray tweed suit. "Please call me Zoë, Marjorie. And it's not a miracle, it's simple fashion sense."

The woman glanced down at her size eleven feet and scowled. "Fashion sense to you, but a darned impossibility for me. I never thought anyone would find stylish shoes for these big old boats, but you did. The question is—how?"

"It was easy, once I gave the shoe area a thorough search," Zoë answered, crossing her fingers to offset the fib. The "shoe area" she'd perused had been the window of a high end boutique, where she spotted the pricy Ferragamos and took a mental picture in order to recreate them when she was alone in the storage closet. "Law of averages says there are a few wealthy women who wear a size eleven, just like there are a small percentage who wear a size five. And those ladies tire of styles as quickly as the rest of us."

"Hah! I haven't worn a five since I was eight years old." Marjorie picked up a handbag that matched the shoes, showing off a perfect manicure. "And I've never owned a real leather purse before." She held the bag to her nose and inhaled. "Don't you just love the smell?"

Locating the right handbag could be attributed to smart hunting as well, because Zoë had found it buried in a box of donated accessories that had yet to be catalogued. "I imagine it's like the scent of a new car," she said, even though she'd never been in any motorized vehicle other than a taxi, and those conveyances smelled more like the inside of a musty cave than a new automobile. "I'm glad you approve of everything."

"I just hope I ace the interview. I really need this job, for my sanity and the sake of my three kids."

"I have no doubt you'll impress your prospective employer." Zoë glanced at her watch. "It's getting close to ten."

Marjorie gathered her things, threw back her broad shoulders, and drew to her full height. "Wish me luck?"

"More than luck, I wish you a world of fashion success," said Zoë, smiling.

As if she'd just been hit with an idea of true genius, Marjorie's face brightened. "I like that. I think I'll turn it into a motto for my daughters to live by: fashion success is business success, or something like that."

"Sounds good to me," Zoë agreed. "And be sure to let Elise know how you make out today."

Marjorie left the room, and Zoë heard a hum of voices in the hall. Seconds later the director of Suited for Change pulled back the curtain and peeked into the dressing room. "Got time for a little refreshment?"

"Sure." Zoë followed Elise to the break room. "I need to talk to you too."

Elise went to the fridge, retrieved a can of pomegranate juice, and set it and a glass in front of Zoë. "Marjorie teared up like a mother of the bride on her daughter's wedding day just now." After adding milk to her coffee, she took a seat at the table. "I still don't believe you found those Ferragamos in our shoe closet. Who in their right mind would toss out a perfectly good pair of five-hundred-dollar shoes? And in a size eleven no less."

Unwilling to tell another lie, Zoë poured her drink into the cup. "Was there something else you wanted to talk about, because if not, I have a question for you."

"Good or bad?"

"Good, with the possibility of being *very* good."

"Then you have my undivided attention," said Elise, setting down her coffee. "Fire away."

"It's about corporate sponsorship."

"Do you have a particular company in mind, or have you been on a fishing expedition?"

"A specific company, and yes, I have been fishing. Remember that guy who invited me to his apartment for a decorating job?"

Elise raised a brow, then took a swallow of coffee as she gazed at the ceiling. "You're talking about the hairy buffalo who's scheduled to have a spread in *New York Entrepreneur.*"

"Yes, only he's not hairy anymore, and he owns a company called Marasoft, Inc."

"And he said they're willing to sponsor the clients of Suited for Change?"

"If you set up a meeting with the COO and make

a good impression, I think so. I told Theo every-thing was up to you, since I'm just a volunteer."

The director caged the coffee cup between her palms. "Get me an appointment and I'll be there, but I'd feel more comfortable if you came along to smooth the way."

"I'd be happy to. I've been meaning to ask, how's the Personal and Professional Development pro-gram going?"

"Marjorie is one of our first graduates, so I'd say it's doing great. I just wish a few more companies would get on the bandwagon and agree to train on the job. Most of the women we help don't have enough skills to compete in today's technology-laden workforce without some instruction."

"All the better that you meet with Marasoft, because you may get more assistance than you expect." Theo's computer software company was exactly what Elise's clients needed, not only for the charitable donation, but also for training and jobs . . . if Chad could be convinced. "I'll talk to Theo's COO, set up the appointment, and let you know where and when."

"Sounds like a plan." Elise stood, brushed imaginary lint from her hot pink skirt, and walked to the counter to top off her coffee. "Where are you going after this?"

"I'll grab a sandwich and bring it to Theo's.

Once I'm sure the construction people have a handle on the job, we'll head for the paint store, then Designer's Row for furniture. Area rugs too, if there's time."

"All that in one afternoon?"

"Well, maybe not," Zoë agreed. "But with only a short while left before I'm gone, I have to make things happen fast."

"Don't remind me," Elise said, pouting her full lips. "I don't know how we'll get along without you,"

"You'll manage." Though Zoë knew she would never forget Suited for Change and all the women she'd helped. "I have to run, but I'll call you as soon as I get that appointment."

Theo sat at his desk attempting to concentrate on a bug the testing staff had found in one of his latest modules. He'd been at work since 8:00 A.M., when his buzzer had rung and he'd allowed a cadre of wall men into his loft. After going over the plans, the construction supervisor sketched a more detailed schematic, had Theo approve it, and decided to immediately start the job. Now, at close to noon, a half-dozen men were measuring lumber, raising wallboard, pounding nails, and installing wiring and pipes in order to make his living space fit for human habitation.

And the racket, clutter, and general chaos the project created was driving him crazy.

In truth, waiting for Zoë Degodessa was the real reason he'd spent most of the morning drumming his fingers and finding it difficult to pay attention to his program module. After last night's idiotic performance, he couldn't imagine her ever again speaking to him in anything more than a professional manner . . . if she spoke to him at all.

He could still see the expression in her eyes, the shape of her lips, and recall the way his body had responded to her presence. The urge to kiss her had been so strong it almost strangled him . . . until he'd had the good sense to walk away. But in doing so, he'd sent Zoë a message that no doubt left her confused and frustrated, exactly as it had left him.

In fact, he'd become so used to the feeling, he barely noticed the ring heating his finger whenever he thought about her or spent time in her presence.

He owed her an explanation, but there was no way he could tell her the truth, because she'd never believe him if he did. Positive there was no form of damage control he could initiate that would redeem him, he vowed to worship her from afar until he was absolutely certain she was *the one.*

Once that happened, he'd take a chance and believe the words his mother had told him in secret.

The faraway sound of the downstairs buzzer inched into his brain, and he jumped to his feet. Tripping over slabs of discarded lumber, he bumped into a whistling workman, stumbled to the kitchen area, and stabbed at the button in hopes it was his delectable designer. "Hello?"

"Theo? It's Zoë. Can I come up?"

He pressed the door lock without answering, then ran to the bathroom for a fast personal inspection. Perusing his image, he made certain his hair was properly tussled and his cheeks and jaw smooth, as he'd been instructed by Roberto. Then he grabbed a toothbrush, intent on getting rid of his coffee breath, and finished in time to answer Zoë's knock. Racing once more into the chaos, he shoved a construction worker aside in his quest to reach the door.

"I thought you'd never get here," he said, letting her in.

She trotted past him, leaving the scent of a summer meadow in her wake. Placing her tote bag on the only bit of free counter space, she picked up an envelope the foreman had left for her and tucked it in her bag. Then she waggled her fingers at the construction workers standing in a stupor and staring in her direction. After several of them shouted a rousing hello in return, she withdrew a brown paper bag from her tote.

"I brought lunch for both of us, but if you've already eaten I'll stick yours in the fridge."

Overwhelmed by her thoughtfulness, Theo shook his head. "No, no, that's great. I haven't had time to eat since this gang showed up—"

"Bright and early, I imagine?"

"Too early." He frowned at the wreckage that was once his apartment. "And there's no free space to eat in here."

"I guess not," said Zoë, following his gaze. "How about we find a quiet spot, maybe at your headquarters?"

"We have a lunch room, if you don't mind sitting with the employees."

"Not at all. Besides, I want to ask your COO about that appointment for the director of Suited for Change."

The name of her pet charity brought to mind the promise he'd made. "Give me a minute to find out if he's free." He picked up the phone and hit speed dial. "Hi, Sally, it's me. Is Chad around? . . . Great, thanks."

Settling his backside against the counter, he tried to relax, but Zoë's mere presence caused the ring to warm and his stomach to knot like the laces of a five-year-old's sneaker. What did she think about his totally ridiculous exit from her hotel suite? And what was she thinking now, with that too serious expression on her lovely face?

"Theo?"

Chad's voice pulled him to the present. "Do you have a few minutes to spare this afternoon?"

"For you, of course," his COO answered in an amused tone.

"Not for me, for Zoë. She wants to discuss something near and dear to her heart."

"Near and dear to her heart? Does that mean you've struck out with the woman and she's decided to let me have a try?"

Ignoring the comment, Theo told himself he'd build a snow fort in Hades before Chad heard about last night's embarrassing moment. "Just answer me, you pea brain."

"No need to get testy. It was a simple question."

He sighed. "We'll be there in thirty minutes, maybe sooner if we catch a cab right away."

"I'll be here," Chad said with a laugh.

Theo hung up the phone. "He'll see us whenever we get there. Let me grab my coat." After running the obstacle course to his sleeping area, he shrugged into a leather jacket and was back at her side in seconds.

They made small talk in the elevator until they

reached the ground floor, where he guided her to the curb in time to catch a taxi dropping off a customer. "We can eat as soon as we arrive, then you can go to Chad's office to set up the meeting while I introduce myself to a few of the new employees," he said as they settled into the cab.

"Are there really people working at your company that you've never met?"

The taxi took off with a squeal of tires, and Theo latched onto the front seat to stay balanced. "Yes, but I have an excuse. Besides working on product development, we've only been in our new space for a few months, and since Chad does all the hiring and firing . . ."

"What about your sales staff? Surely you've talked with them about the product they're selling?"

"Most of the salesmen are guys we met in college. After graduation, they knew enough about the IT business to get jobs in the field. Chad kept in touch with them, and once we were ready for public use, made them offers they couldn't refuse. They're usually on the road pushing the product, as are a couple of guys who install and troubleshoot. Stats show we're growing, and since we only have one real competitor, we're doing well. Once our latest suite of modules is announced, our offerings will be complete and orders should start rolling in."

As the cabbie made a sweeping turn, Zoë slid across the seat and smacked into his side, and Theo immediately wrapped her in a protective embrace. When he glanced down, she was gazing at him as if he'd come to her rescue like a knight of old.

"Sorry," she muttered, but stayed glued to his thigh.

"You okay?"

She nodded. "I don't mind taxis, but sometimes . . ."

"Yeah, I know what you mean." Mesmerized by her amber eyes, he was unable to look away. "Zoë, about last night—" he began, thinking this was his chance to make amends. "I'm sorry if I acted like a—"

"Don't give it a second thought," she answered, inching backward. "It's for the best that we keep things strictly business. Anything more . . . intimate would only make this job difficult."

The taxi swerved again, and she banged into him a second time. When he caught her in his arms, she blushed. "Sorry, I'm squashing you."

"Not at all."

She drew away from him. "Still, I'm no lightweight."

"I don't mind." He lowered his voice to a whisper. "In fact, I think you're perfect."

"I'm afraid today's fashion designers would

argue that point," Zoë replied, though she didn't seem embarrassed. "According to the Hollywood hotline, thin is in, and that certainly doesn't describe my figure."

"Those so-called experts are small-minded boors. Every woman should be lucky enough to look like you."

The compliment brought a deeper blush of pink to her cheeks. "How sweet of you to say so."

"That'll be eight dollars."

At the sound of the driver's nasal voice, she pulled away. "I think we're here."

"Here?" Theo repeated.

"Eight dollars, folks." The cabbie leered through his rearview mirror. "Unless you want me to take another spin around the block for the hell of it."

Great. One more reason for Zoë to think he was a moron. Theo mumbled a curse, fumbled for his wallet, and handed the man a ten dollar bill, then held the door and waited while she slid out after him.

Standing on the sidewalk, Zoë studied the multi-storied building that housed Marasoft, Inc. "Nice place. How many floors do you occupy?"

"Only the first two, but we have an option for more if a tenant leaves."

They entered the plush waiting area, and a young woman with short spiky hair the color of a tangerine glanced up from her computer. "Hi, may I—" Stopping short, she did a double take worthy of a cartoon character. "Theo? Is that you?"

"Yeah, it's me. Is Chad in his office?" he asked, hoping to head off the administrative assistant's remarks about his appearance before they began.

"He is." She eyed him from head to toe, blew a huge bubble, and let it pop. "He said I'd be surprised when I saw you, but I had no idea . . . I mean . . . wow."

How in the hell did Chad know what sort of transformation had occurred?

"Is that any way to talk to the president of your company?" he asked in a stern voice.

"The president? No. But to the regular guy who signs my weekly paycheck . . ." She gave him another once-over. "Just let me say it a second time, then I promise I won't mention it again, okay?"

They'd hired Sally because she was efficient and had a mind of her own, so Theo doubted he could stop her. "Go ahead, because you're bound to say what you want anyway."

The admin's cherry red lips broadened. "Wow."

"Finished?"

"For now. The guys in the back will be happy to finally meet you."

"Is that right?"

"Chad's been telling them all sorts of stories.

Talked you up so big, they think you're the god of computer software."

Theo smiled, though he found the comparison distasteful. "This is Zoë Degodessa. She's going to be working with us for a while. Zoë, Sally, Chad's right hand, and mine too . . . sometimes."

The woman grinned. "You don't look like a computer geek to me," she said in a conspiratorial tone.

"I'm not," Zoë confided. "But working with Theo has proven interesting so far."

"Really? How so?"

Theo put a hand on Zoë's back and guided her forward. "Sorry, but we haven't had lunch. If anyone's looking for us, we'll be in the break room," he called as they walked through the double doors.

Zoë heard Chad speak to someone in the hall before he sauntered into the room. Certain she would be entertained by the cocky yet amusing man, she grinned as she took his proffered hand. "I hope we haven't come at a bad time."

"Talking with you is never an inconvenience," he said smoothly. Then he gave Theo an exaggerated stare. "Who's your neatly groomed and expertly coiffed friend?"

Zoë giggled while Theo grumped a curt, "Very funny."

"Wait, I recognize that voice." The COO scanned his buddy with narrowed eyes. "Good lord, it *is* you."

"Yeah, now move on."

"Roberto said he'd created a masterpiece, but I—"

"I said 'move on,'" Theo insisted. "We're here to discuss business, not chat about the latest hairstyles for men."

"Touchy, isn't he?" commented Chad as he took a seat at the table. Pointedly ignoring Theo, he again grasped Zoë's hand and gazed into her eyes. "So, Ms. Degodessa, what did you want to see me about?"

Zoë politely pulled away and made a production out of unwrapping her sandwich. She liked Chad well enough, but suspected he was going over the top because it seemed to annoy Theo. It was fun watching the two men play off each other, but the COO was too flirtatious for her. Besides, she was here to make the perfect pitch for a worthy cause.

"Elise Sutton, the director of Suited for Change, would like an appointment to discuss the possibility of Marasoft becoming a corporate sponsor for her firm."

"Suited for Change?" Chad leaned back in his chair. "I don't believe I've ever heard of the organization."

"It's a nonprofit company that operates solely on donations. They provide professional clothing and job training for women seeking to join the job market."

"Sounds like a worthwhile endeavor. How are you involved in the company?"

Zoë glanced at Theo, read the approval in his expression, and forged ahead. "I volunteer there as a fashion consultant. I meet with the women, help them choose and accessorize the outfit they'll wear for their first interview, and assist them in picking out the rest of the clothing we supply."

"And the clothing comes from . . ."

"Sometimes from fashion shows or department stores willing to donate, but mostly from patrons who give us suits, dresses, shoes, and bags they no longer want. If they don't have any clothing, they donate to our 'Fill a Hanger' program, another way to ensure our clients get a good start in the job force."

Chad folded his arms and gazed at the ceiling, then glanced at Theo. "I take it you've heard this pitch already?"

"Not put quite the same way, but yes, I've heard it."

"And what's your opinion?"

"If you think we can afford a contribution, meet with Elise Sutton and hear what she has to say."

Chad sat up straighter in the chair. "Hey, not just me. This will be your call too, Mr. President."

Zoë held her breath when Theo entwined his fingers and set his hands on the table. He'd led her to believe this was his COO's decision alone. Did he truly like the idea, or had he merely pushed her request off on Chad hoping he'd refuse?

"I'm only asking because you're the money man," Theo answered. "It's already a done deal, as far as I'm concerned."

"Okay, then." Chad focused on Zoë. "I'm free for dinner tonight. How about if you, Ms. Sutton, and I share a meal and form a plan? Meanwhile, I'll draw up a list of questions, points I'm curious about, that sort of thing. Seven o'clock?"

"Sounds good to me," Theo responded.

Chad snorted. "Who invited you?"

"I invited myself."

"I thought you said this was my decision?"

"It is but . . ."

Zoë let the two of them argue while she thought about Elise. The director had said she was willing to meet with anyone, anytime, anywhere, which meant dinner with both men was acceptable. Besides, mingling with a couple of attractive guys was exactly what Elise needed. She'd hidden away far too long, especially from the opposite sex. If nothing else, Theo and Chad's good-natured bickering would make for an enjoyable evening.

"Excuse me," she interrupted, smiling when they sputtered to a halt. "Where do you want to have dinner?"

"The French Pavilion," said Chad.

"The Villa Italiano," Theo stated at the same time.

"I thought you and Zoë ate there last night?"

"We did, but it won't hurt to go again."

Chad rolled his eyes. "You have absolutely no imagination." He turned to Zoë. "How about you choose?"

"Me?"

"Yes, you. You do eat out, don't you?"

Technically, thanks to room service at the hotel, she ate out every night, but she knew Elise rarely went anywhere if it didn't pertain to business. "How about Cossette?" she said, giving the name of a quiet yet elegant restaurant that served a variety of food. She'd had dinner there with a group of window dressers a few months back and remembered the meal had been tasty and the atmosphere enjoyable.

"I've heard of it, but I've never been," said Chad. "It's fine with me."

"I'll call Elise and give her the news. And while I'm here . . ." She reached into her tote, brought out the envelope left by the construction crew manager, and passed it the COO. "This is for you."

Chad opened the envelope, took a look, and slid it across the table to Theo, who opened and closed his mouth without uttering a word while he read it. Then he swallowed and said, "I guess I'd better get busy and design another module for our system, because it's going to take a new suite of products to pay for this job."

"I did tell the lady money was no object," Chad reminded him.

"Okay, okay." Theo still didn't seem at ease. "It's just that I'm not used to spending this much on myself."

"It's a tax deduction, and a company can never have too many of those. Now, if you'll excuse me." Chad stood and gave Zoë a nod. "See you and your friend tonight at seven." He shifted his gaze to Theo. "You too, if you insist." Whistling a happy tune, he left the room.

Chapter 6

"We're late, and I loathe being late, so stop complaining and hurry up," Zoë muttered as she, and then Elise, slid from the taxi.

The unseasonably warm January night had allowed both woman to dress more for spring than winter. Zoë wore a gold-colored wool blazer with her black cashmere turtle neck and slacks, while the narrow black tie Elise sported over her white silk shirt perfectly complimented her hot pink jacket and matching skirt.

After contacting Elise earlier in the day and giving her the details of the meeting, Zoë had been forced to cancel her afternoon with Theo and rush to her friend's rescue. For a reason she now suspected was personal and not professional, Elise had blown like a volcano when she heard about the dinner plans Zoë had accepted in her stead. She had no intention of spending a private evening with two strange men, she'd said, especially if they were single and the meeting wouldn't be held in formal surroundings.

Getting the director to agree to the dinner had been as difficult as her attempt to stop Britney from shaving her head. Elise had refused her assistance with this meeting much as the pop diva had with the clippers, which Zoë was certain the silly woman now regretted. After more than an hour of fast talking, Elise still wasn't happy about the arrangements but finally agreed.

"The business meetings I attend are held in boardrooms with plenty of space between me and the corporate donor, or in an office where I'm on one side of the desk and the company sponsor is on the other." Elise repeated her admonishment as she stood on the sidewalk, rigid as a fence post, scanning the restaurant's cheery yet elegant exterior. "Not on a double date or at a . . . a . . . bar."

"Will you please give it a rest?" Zoë clutched her friend's elbow. "This is an informal get-together at a perfectly respectable eating establishment. Look, here's a menu." She dragged Elise to a window next to the door and pointed to the displayed bill of fare. "Nowhere does it mention loud music, all-you-can-drink beer, ladies' night, private dining salons, male strippers, or anything else tacky or illicit."

Grim-faced, Elise eyed the menu, then peered through the glass. It was clear the properly attired patrons were holding conversations and enjoying their meals in a pleasant atmosphere of refinement and good taste.

"You did say you would do just about anything to ensure Suited for Change's success, didn't you?" Zoë asked, posing the same question she'd brought up a dozen times that day.

"Yes." Elise sighed. "But that was before I realized I had issues from my past I couldn't ignore."

"So you *have* dated since your divorce." Zoë's statement sounded more like a fact than a guess.

"A couple of times, and each was a disaster of titanic proportion. I know I have to overcome my distrust of men—"

"Tonight's the perfect night to start, because it will benefit Suited for Change. If you handle the negotiations correctly, Marasoft will offer opportunities to clients who depend on you, and you'll overcome a serious hurdle on your road to a new life."

The sensible advice seemed to sink in slowly as Elise inspected her reflection in the window and squared her shoulders. "You're right, of course." She fluffed her head of blond curls. "I'm being an idiot. I'll do my best to sell our organization and try to have a good time, I promise."

Giving herself a mental high-five, Zoë turned to enter the restaurant, but stopped when she realized the director was still rooted in place. "Now what?"

"Who is this COO person again?"

"Chad Thomas, and Theo trusts him with the day-to-day running of the company. I got the impression he makes most of the decisions that pertain to Marasoft's public image. Theo's main interest is product development, but Chad consults him about most everything whenever he needs a second opinion."

"Humor me. Tell me they know tonight is strictly business and not a double date."

"I don't have any reason to think they feel otherwise," Zoë responded, though she wasn't positive about Theo. Since he'd already given his approval for the donation, she wondered about his determination to attend the dinner, especially because it sounded as if Chad viewed tonight as nothing more than a professional evening.

Satisfied Elise was willing to interact with the men as allies instead of sleazy swinging singles, Zoë caught the strap of her friend's black leather bag, intent on reeling her inside. After all, only so much business could be handled over a phone or in a corporate setting. For this venture, the mortals she intended to inspire had to make merry with each other, and this informal not-exactly-a-date dinner was ideal.

They walked through the double doors and gave their names to the hostess standing behind a podium in the waiting area. "Ah, yes, table twenty-two," said the woman as she glanced at a short rotund gentleman wearing a tuxedo and a smile. "Please follow Armand."

The Marasoft executives stood when Zoë and Elise neared their table. Dressed in an open-necked white shirt and his usual tweed jacket, Theo's out-of-style clothing faded in comparison to his dimples and clean-cut good looks. Chad, of course, was perfectly attired in trendy, three-piece Hugo Boss and a smile sure to melt the hardest woman's heart.

"Sorry we're late." Zoë sat in the chair Theo held out for her. "There was a small . . . crisis at headquarters that had to be handled before we left."

His gaze shifted to Elise and he offered his hand. "Not a problem. I'm Theo Maragos, and this is Chad Thomas, COO of Marasoft, Inc."

Elise accepted his greeting. "Elise Sutton, director of Suited for Change." Turning to Chad, her smile flattened. When he tried to shake her hand, she continued to stare without speaking.

"It's a pleasure to meet you," Chad said, as if she were smiling brightly.

Still ignoring his outstretched hand, Elise drew to her full height of five-foot-three. "Thanks for agreeing to talk with us," she said in a hesitant, almost breathy, voice.

Chad's suave expression shifted to concern. "I hope the office situation wasn't anything serious."

"Not really," said Zoë when her friend failed to reply. On the upside, Elise did take her seat, unfold her napkin, and place it in her lap, as would any normal mortal.

After listing the specials, the waiter passed out menus, and Zoë pretended to study hers while she observed Elise from the corner of her eye. What the heck was wrong with her? Had she met Chad before tonight, only he didn't remember? Or was she so in awe of the COO's *GQ* appearance and courtly manners she couldn't find the words for polite conversation? One thing was certain, if Elise started to drift into a catatonic state, she would be forced to come to her rescue.

"See anything you like?" Zoë asked, in order to bring Elise back to their surroundings.

With her gaze focused firmly on the offerings, Elise shrugged. "I'm not sure. Maybe the seafood pasta."

Chad closed his menu. "I think I'll have the same."

The waiter returned and took drink orders. Theo asked if anyone wanted wine, and Elise said she'd stick to club soda, as did Zoë. When Chad made a wry comment on his boss's expertise in choosing fine spirits, everyone chuckled.

They gave their dinner choices to the waiter, and Theo picked a wine. Then he smiled at Elise. "Zoë explained the basics of your organization, but Chad is interested in the particulars. He spent most of the afternoon compiling a list of questions."

"Then, by all means, he should ask them," Elise said, though she continued to focus on Theo.

"First off," Chad began, paying no attention to Elise's dismissive attitude, "if Marasoft decides to give Suited for Change a donation, how will it be used?"

Zoë waited for Elise to answer. It was odd to see her usually professional and businesslike friend blush pink before she met the COO's stare.

"I brought a folder containing our organization's goals and objectives." Reaching into her bag, she removed the file and set it on the table. "I'm sure it will take care of all your concerns."

Chad set the folder aside and grinned boyishly. "If you don't mind, I'll read this through at the office tomorrow. Right now, I'd like to hear your personal thoughts on what you expect Marasoft to do for your company."

Elise took a quick swallow of water, then said, "Well, that depends on the size of the donation."

Breathing a sigh of relief at her friend's sane attitude, Zoë turned to Theo and smiled. Perhaps she'd have a relaxing and fun evening after all.

Zoë crossed her arms to ward off the chill as she, Theo, and Chad stood in the restaurant entrance. When she'd left the restroom, Elise had been reapplying her lipstick and fussing with her hair, and Zoë returned to their "nondates" to make polite small talk. Since the day's warm spell had given way to a more seasonable temperature, she didn't relish going outside to brave the cold, and was hoping one of the men would walk to the curb and hail a cab for her ride home.

"I can't imagine what's taking Elise so long," she said. "I need to go over my notes on the loft renovations, especially since I had to reschedule all of today's appointments."

"How about if I wait for Elise, while Theo escorts you to your place?" Chad suggested. "That way, you can leave knowing your friend is in good hands."

"Great idea. I'll get a taxi," Theo called over his

shoulder as he bounded out the door. "Wait here until I come back to get you."

Zoë turned to Chad, unsure of how her friend would react when she realized that she and the COO would be alone. During dinner, Elise had appeared more comfortable as she sang the praises of Suited for Change. Meanwhile, Zoë had held her own conversation with Theo, talking more about the loft renovations than contributing to the other couple's conversation. Suited for Change was her friend's pride and joy, and Elise knew a world more about its inner workings than she herself could ever remember.

"I'm not sure where you live in relation to Elise's apartment," Zoë said. "Seeing her home might be an inconvenience."

"That's what cabs are for, and I don't mind." A corner of Chad's mouth curled in amusement. "Besides, I'm afraid Theo would fire me if I didn't give him a chance to spend some time alone with you."

Aware of the COO's flirtatious manner, Zoë grinned. "He's a nice guy, and I enjoy his company. I just don't want Elise to think I've deserted her."

"I promise to see her safely to her door. What more could she ask for?"

"A man who's on his best behavior?"

Chad's expression turned to surprise. "Have I

done something to make you think I'd act other-wise?"

"Hmm. It's possible you poured on the charm a little too thick," she said, remembering the suave manner and teasing comments he'd thrown in both her and Elise's direction throughout the evening.

"I can't help it if I come across as articulate and witty," Chad confessed. "Inside, I'm really shy and insecure."

Zoë rolled her eyes. "Sure you are."

Theo took that moment to poke his head into the foyer. "Taxi's waiting. You ready?"

"Tell Elise I'll call her tomorrow, okay?"

"Will do," said Chad, tossing her a salute.

After helping Zoë into the cab, Theo gave the driver their destination and turned to face her. "I'd say the evening was a success. What do you think?"

"Your COO is a very entertaining man."

"Chad's been that way ever since I met him, un-like some of us poor self-conscious guys who find it hard to concentrate in the presence of a beauti-ful woman."

"You don't have a thing to be self-conscious about. I have a good time when we're together. Especially since you—" *Lost that hideous beard and ponytail.* "—you've been so agreeable to my sug-gestions."

Theo shook his head. "You're not fooling me. I

know what I looked like at our initial meeting, and it wasn't pretty. It's just that I sometimes get so wrapped up in my work I forget about the personal things."

"Taking care of those 'personal things' from here on out has to be a priority, since you're scheduled for a new head shot in, what, a few more days?"

"Three, which means we've got to get busy finding me appropriate clothing—if you're still willing to take the job."

The idea of inspiring a man with no fashion experience thrilled Zoë to her core, but she didn't want to overplay her hand. If Theo knew what she was up to, he might think all she wanted from their relationship was recognition, which was only partially correct. At first she'd agreed to remodel his apartment to impress her father. But now that she'd spent a few afternoons with the computer expert, she had to admit his company was stimulating, in more than a professional way.

She was curious to find out why he gazed at her as if she'd hung the moon and then shied away when she offered him a chance to get close. After going over his strange behavior, she decided to tackle the challenge he presented.

"I doubt we'll have time tomorrow, but certainly the day after. Barney's might work, though there are several men's boutiques that could be interesting."

"Somehow, I can't see myself shopping at a *boutique*. I usually stop in whatever store is handy and get what I need. I guess that's not how it's done, huh?"

"Not if you truly want to impress. Would you feel more comfortable using a store Chad recommends?"

"Maybe, but he's all over the map. He goes to Barney's, but he also uses a style consultant. He shops at one place for shirts, another for suits, and another for shoes. He buys at so many specialty stores it boggles my mind."

"Choosing the proper clothing doesn't have to be overwhelming. Once you spend a day with me, you'll be . . . inspired."

The cab stopped and he paid the driver, then climbed out and held the door.

"I can go up alone if you're in a hurry," said Zoë. Though her insides churned with pleasure at the thought of being in his company awhile longer, she didn't want to experience another embarrassing episode.

The hand he placed on the small of her back to encourage her forward sent a jolt of warmth zinging along her spine. "Not a chance. It's my responsibility to see you to your door."

They crossed the lobby in silence. In the elevator, she pressed the button for her floor, then raised her gaze and caught Theo staring at her with a faraway look in his eyes. Her stomach clenched and she shuddered, surprised that she suddenly felt shy and unsure. Those dimples of his really made her crazy.

The elevator slowed to a halt, and he swept his arm toward the open door in a courtly manner. "After you."

A tingle spiraled from Zoë's chest to her cheeks. She'd met hundreds of mortal men, and none of them had rattled her insides the way Theo Maragos did. But the one time she'd given him a chance to get close, he raced away as if his backside were on fire. However, she planned to be magnanimous tonight and offer him another chance.

When they arrived at her door, he took the key card from her hand and their fingers touched, sending a flurry of goose bumps up her arm. Theo returned the card to her palm, gazing at her with the same mix of expressions he'd worn last night—concern, uncertainty, and an intensity she found appealing as well as exciting.

Moments ticked by as he focused on her lips. Her stomach coiled tight and she sighed. With no more thought, she swayed into his chest. He grasped her upper arms, and his nose brushed her cheek.

"I'm going to catch fire if I don't kiss you," he murmured.

Her eyelids fluttered open. "It would be pretty silly to burst into flames when the fire extinguisher is standing right in front of you, don't you think?"

"I'm not sure. I haven't . . . I've never . . ." He huffed out a breath. "Oh, hell."

Bending forward, Theo captured her mouth as his arms slid to her back and drew her to him. Zoë melted into his body and molded herself to his chest, his stomach, his pelvis. Hard and throbbing, his erection pressed against her while his hands skimmed her spine, then his fingers threaded through her hair. His lips grew demanding, and his leg slid between her thighs. The kiss became urgent as his tongue tasted and tormented hers.

She palmed his buttocks and pulled him closer still, intent on showing him what she needed. What she craved. His moan of pleasure vibrated through her veins, assaulted her lips, and sent a rush of longing straight to her core.

Gently cradling her jaw, he eased from the kiss and rested his forehead against hers. "Zoë?"

"Hmm?"

When he didn't respond, she raised her lids and read the wonder in his eyes. In that moment, she knew she wanted Theo Maragos to be her lover for however long she remained on earth. Certain it wouldn't take much to convince him, she asked, "Are you coming in?"

"Coming in?" His voice echoed both disappointment and amazement. "Believe me, there's nothing I want more, but it's late and we have to get an early start tomorrow."

She looked at him, confused.

He released her and took a step back. "I'll pick you up in the morning. Nine o'clock?"

She studied his expression, thinking he had more to say, but he remained stoic. Too humiliated to respond, she raised a brow. Was he truly rejecting her, a daughter of the mighty Zeus, again? If anyone on Mount Olympus found out about his continual rebuffs, the citizens would ridicule her until the end of her days.

Suddenly, she was angry. He was lucky his renovation project was important to her success, or she'd clock him where he stood, and transport him to Hades in a handbasket. The big . . . big . . . nerd!

He gazed at her with a concerned expression. "Look, Zoë, I know you don't understand . . ." He backed away. "I can't explain why, but I will, when I get it all sorted out in my mind. See you in the morning."

The elevator doors slid open, and he was gone.

* * *

"You don't have to walk me to the door." Elise tossed a bill into the front seat of the cab and got out on the street side before Chad could stop her. Hoping he would be carried off into the night, she called over her shoulder as she trotted up the steps of her brownstone, "Thanks again for getting the dinner tab."

"Hang on a second. I'll see you to your floor."

Damn! He was right behind her. "I said that won't be necessary. I'll be in touch about the donation."

"Elise."

She stilled when he caught her by the elbow, but didn't turn his way.

"What the heck is wrong with you?"

"Wrong? With me?" Wrenching from his grip, she pushed through the front door. "Nothing. I'm tired, and it's been a long day. Good night."

When she used her key to enter the building's foyer and take the stairs, he stayed on her heels. Halfway up the flight, she slowed and huffed out a breath. "Why are you following me?"

"I promised Zoë I'd see you to your apartment, damn it, and that's what I plan to do."

"Fine." She resumed her climb. "It's only one flight, so you'll be free soon."

Annoyed that he'd followed her, she stopped on

the landing and peered at him. "Here's my floor. You can go now."

"You live in the hall?" He smiled. "Must be interesting when you want to take a shower."

Glaring, she pursed her lips. "I imagine you find yourself extremely entertaining."

"Sometimes." He took the last two steps, reached her side and held out his hand. "How about giving me the key?"

"What for?"

"So I can open your door and see to it you're inside where it's safe and warm. I can even come in and make sure there's no one lying in wait."

"In case you haven't noticed, I'm an adult. I can do that for myself."

"I'm sure you can," he responded in a teasing tone. "I'd even be willing to join you for a drink, if you'd let me."

"What?"

"I said, I'd like to come in for a drink. If not now, maybe another night?"

"Why in the world would you want to do that?"

"You're joking."

Still gazing at him, she sighed. "I'll meet with you again if you have questions about Suited for Change, but it will have to be in my office." She walked to the apartment marked 2C and unlocked the door. "When exactly might that be, by the way? Because the sooner you voice your concerns and have my response, the sooner we can get this transaction over with."

Chad stuffed his hands in his pockets as if through with her and her business. "I'll call you after I've looked over the file and let you know the extent of Marasoft's interest. We can set up an appointment in your office, whenever it's convenient for you."

"Great." She opened her mouth, ready to tell him off, then snapped it shut. She had to get a grip. Suited for Change needed all the donations and corporate sponsorship it could get. For the good of her company, she'd simply have to deal with him. "Good night."

Elise slipped through the door and rested against the wood as Chad Thomas's footsteps faded on the stairs. Closing her eyes, she willed her heart to calm and her brain to take over, but it was a hard sell. Though annoyed with him, she was more furious with herself.

What in the hell was her problem? Did she have some weird physical ailment, or was it psychological? With her luck, it was a combination of both, but either way, her therapist back in D.C. would have had a field day if she told her the truth.

She had the hots for another gay man.

Damn, damn, damn. She banged her head on the door, then pushed off and headed down the hall. Men had hurt her before, not just her sexually confused husband, so why was she even thinking about opening herself up to another round of misery?

What was the jerk up to, acting as if he wanted to be in her apartment or, heaven forbid, in her bed? Did he need a cover for his next business venture or a safe date for his college reunion? If so, it wouldn't be her.

Marching to the bathroom, she stared at her reflection, stuck out her tongue and inspected her face for any visible sign of a deformity that would cause her to be enamored of another man who put himself first. The moment she'd stood in front of him in the restaurant, her breathing had increased, her heart rate accelerated, and her hormones started to purr. But when he began to wax poetic over the restaurant's "ambience," the quality of its table decor, and the choice of the background music . . . well, it all sounded too much like her ex, and she didn't want to be reminded of him ever again.

He'd even had the nerve to comment on her handbag, for Pete's sake, as well as telling her how much he liked Gucci!

She had yet to meet a straight man who would admit to admiring any designer, unless it was the guy who'd come up with the Budweiser logo. And, even then, his comment would probably be something like, "Hey man, nice keg."

Still fuming, though less so than before, Elise kicked off her heels, stripped out of her suit, blouse, and thigh-highs, and toted everything to her bedroom. After dragging a sleep shirt over her head, she plodded back to the bathroom to brush her teeth and remove her makeup.

Finally calm, she walked to her bed, sat on the edge of the mattress and brushed her hair as she replayed the evening in her mind. There was no doubt the COO was a devastating man who felt at home charming women, but there had to be an ulterior motive in his trying to wheedle his way into her apartment. Was it possible he wanted to inspect her closet, or ask for permission to go through Suited for Change's vast array of designer fashions in hopes of finding something for himself?

She grinned at the thought; somehow it was hard to imagine Chad Thomas as a cross dresser, but stranger things took place in today's world.

Sighing, she turned down the covers and snuggled into the sheets. Too bad, really, because the man was way better looking than her ex and a lot more entertaining. He had a wonderful sense of humor—dry and sarcastic, but not biting or cruel. Combine his debonair personality with his perfectly styled hair and thickly lashed brown eyes, and he was every woman's dream guy . . . if they were in the market for a best friend to lunch, shop, or dish with.

Been there, done that, she reminded herself.

The next time she took a lover, they'd form a friendship only after he brought her to orgasm a couple dozen times in every way her ex never had. And she'd be the single most important thing on the guy's brain, morning, noon, and night—all of her, from the top of her head to the tips of her toes, and everywhere in between.

Once that happened, she'd consider getting serious enough to live the fairy tale she'd dreamed of as a girl. Babies, family vacations, making love on Sunday morning, reading the paper in bed, then a walk in the rain, and another bout between the sheets with a life partner who was one-hundred-percent male. She wanted —no, she deserved—it all.

It was a damn shame, really, about Chad Thomas. Because he just wasn't that man.

Chapter 7

Theo eyed Chad over his cup of java as the two men ate breakfast in a coffee shop. They'd spent the past hour talking over details for the IPO and were now silent, though his COO appeared a bit short-tempered. Theo had no desire to bring up his latest quandary concerning Zoë, so he focused on Chad and his luck with the fairer sex. Who knew, maybe he'd learn something.

"I take it everything went okay with you and Elise Sutton last night."

Chad frowned. "Fine, if you consider being treated like Jack the Ripper a fun way to end the evening. Why?"

Uh-oh. So much for advice. "You're kidding?"

"Yeah, right, I'm kidding." He smacked his coffee mug on the table. "The woman is a nutcase."

Theo found it difficult to equate the professional and friendly woman he'd met at dinner with Chad's negative pronouncement. Ms. Sutton had seemed apprehensive at first, but once the evening got rolling, she was entertaining, and well-versed in the goals she'd set for her organization.

"A nutcase? Aren't you exaggerating a little?"

"No, and never mind," Chad groused.

"Just explain, all right? Maybe once you get it off your chest, you'll stop pouting."

"Har-har," Chad drawled, adjusting the knot of his hundred dollar tie. Then he sighed. "Tell me something. Do I look like a pervert to you?"

"Sure you do, but that's only because I know what goes on in your diabolical mind where females are concerned." When the COO drummed his fingers, Theo realized he was serious. "Wait— are you telling me Elise accused you of being a pervert? What in the hell did you say to her?"

Chad squared his shoulders. "Absolutely nothing I haven't said to a thousand other attractive females I hoped to get to know better. I simply asked if I could come in for a drink or see her again for dinner."

"Really?"

He raised a brow. "Why are you looking at me that way?"

"What way?" asked Theo, thinning his lips to hide a grin.

"Like you know something I don't. Have you heard from Zoë? Damn, I hate the way women always blab to their friends when a guy pisses them off."

"I haven't talked to Zoë today, and I doubt she'd confide in me even if Elise did call her. I just find it amusing that a man who's been able to charm every lady he's ever met didn't get to first base with a very nice, extremely attractive woman like Ms. Sutton."

"First base?" He stared dejectedly into his coffee mug. "It was torture just getting to the batter's box. I must be losing my touch . . . or maybe she's a lesbian."

Not a chance, Theo told himself. "Don't be ridiculous."

"Hey, anything goes. Maybe she's not into men."

"Now I'm really curious. How bad was it?"

Chad shrugged. "Let's just say she acted as if I had herpes or worse. Didn't even want me to walk her to the door."

"Was this before or after you tried to get personal? Are you sure you didn't say something rude?"

"I'm never rude. And I didn't lay a finger on her." He fisted a hand on the tabletop. "Not that I didn't want to. Especially since I decided to take your advice."

Theo about choked on his coffee. "*My* advice? You've got to be kidding."

"Don't look so surprised. I've been thinking about what you said when you commented on my choice of dinner companions. You suggested I might have more fun with someone my own age, and I thought I'd make Elise the first. Instead of a simple 'No, thank you,' she acted as if I was the last man on the planet she'd go out with, even for a no-strings dinner."

"Maybe she's playing hard to get?" Theo said, though he knew he wouldn't recognize that particular feminine ploy if it jumped up and bit him on the butt. "Or one of those other games women are known to engage in?"

"Is that what's happening with you and the delectable designer? Because I never would have pegged Zoë as a tease. I got the impression she'd be more of a direct and to-the-point type of female."

Considering last evening's intimate interchange, direct and to-the-point pretty much summed it up. "She is that."

It was Chad's turn to grin. "Don't tell me you haven't connected with the ball yet?"

"I tried. I mean, I did connect."

"And?"

"It was . . ." The kiss had been so unbelievable he had no way to describe it without making Chad smirk. And it didn't matter, because he had no intention of letting the conversation focus on him and Zoë. "This discussion has wandered off topic."

Chad leaned back and crossed his arms. "That good, was it?"

"It's none of your concern. Now, back to you and Elise."

Chad raised a brow. "Did she invite you into her room?"

"It's not a room, it's a suite, and I've already been there."

"You know what I mean."

Unfortunately, he did. "She asked me in the first night I brought her home. The second, I stayed in the hall."

"And that's when you tried to connect," Chad pronounced, as if he'd been there to witness the deed.

"Yeah."

"So why didn't it go anywhere?"

"It will. I just need to be sure."

"Sure of what?"

That my past won't destroy me. That I won't ruin my life and Zoë's at the same time. That she'll be safe.

"I don't want to pressure Zoë into thinking she has to sleep with me to keep this job," Theo lied, proud of his plausible excuse. "Especially if I want . . . if we decide to . . ." He heaved a breath. "Let's just drop it, okay?" He glanced at his watch. "Crap. I have to run."

"Will you be in the office later?"

"Maybe, but don't count on it. Zoë and I are finalizing rug and furniture orders. If we finish early, we're going clothes shopping." He zipped his jacket and headed for the door. "Let me know if you hear from Elise. Things might not be as out of reach as you think."

Thirty minutes later Theo stood in front of the Trump Tower, eyeing the impressive structure as he might a finely crafted automobile or top-of-the-line computer system. The building was a Manhattan landmark, one of the poshest hotels in New York. Now that he'd been inside and seen Zoë's living quarters, he realized it deserved every positive recommendation and glowing review it had been given.

Since he was a few minutes late, he rushed past the doorman, headed for a house phone, and asked the operator to ring Zoë's room. When she didn't answer, he scanned the lobby and spotted her chatting with a guy manning the bell stand. Dressed in seriously high heels, a figure-hugging, calf-length black skirt, and a pale blue sweater that outlined her every curve, she appeared tall and regal, even though it was obvious she and the bellman were sharing a joke.

Stricken with a stab of jealousy, Theo inhaled as he twisted the gold ring. He had no idea whether the object would work the way his mother said, and he had no business being annoyed because Zoë was having fun with another man. Aside from that single heart-stopping kiss, their relationship was strictly professional. All he had was a sincere desire to hold her in his arms for the rest of his life.

She took that moment to turn around. Then she saw him, waggled her fingers at the bellman, shrugged into her coat, and met him in the center of the lobby.

"Good morning," she said, her voice pure business.

"Sorry I'm late. Chad and I got wrapped up in a discussion, and I lost track of time."

"Did the construction crew arrive on schedule this morning?"

"With the sun, like yesterday. I thought about calling you but figured it was too early."

"I'm usually awake by seven, so you could have reached me. Especially if you were running behind."

"Trust me, it won't happen again," he promised, aware of her penchant for promptness. "Have you eaten?"

"Of course." She slung her bag over her shoulder. "We have a lot of ground to cover, so we'd best get started."

For Zoë, maintaining a cordial air while holding Theo at arm's length was a struggle. She'd lain awake in the dark, thinking about his reaction to her invitation, and come to the conclusion that keeping her distance was the only way to guard her heart.

Every man she'd ever let near her had tried to kiss her at the earliest possible moment in their relationship. She could have sworn Theo had that same idea in mind the first time he'd visited her suite, until he bolted like a scared rabbit. Last night had gone a bit better, but not much.

Unfortunately, since her arrival on earth, Theo Maragos was the only man who made her insides melt, her knees weak, and her heart beat like a kettle drum. And all she'd gotten for her take-charge attitude were sleepless nights as she tossed and turned while searching for a solution to her predicament.

As of this morning, her libido still wanted Theo to be her final mortal lover, but common sense told her it might be a huge mistake. Judging by his shocked expression after last night's kiss, he didn't deserve an evening in her arms or a single second of her personal attention. Now, if she could convince herself that she meant what she was thinking, things would be fine.

At her favorite furniture store, the one they'd perused the other day, Theo walked through the merchandise on display, seemingly intent on making a decision. Though he was on the other side of the room, she was drawn to his virility, his smile, his presence. And she noticed she wasn't the only woman there who found him appealing. Several of the clerks working the floor stayed close, offering suggestions as if they were the one decorating his apartment.

One of the things about Theo that attracted her was the modest way he handled his intelligence while exuding an undeniable sex appeal capable of seducing a woman of any age or profession. Was she imagining the attraction she felt sparking between them? Was she losing her goddess touch?

Worse, was she making a fool of herself whenever she encouraged him to get close?

A saleswoman placed a hand on Theo's arm, and Zoë sucked in a breath. She wasn't jealous, not really, but Theo was her client, her project, her . . . mortal. Squaring her shoulders, she dodged furniture as she hurried across the room, stopping mere inches from his side.

"I found another sofa in a pattern I thought you might like," she said, placing her palm on his shoulder. "It's back here. I can't believe I missed it."

"Excuse me," he said to the clerk, and turned in Zoë's direction. "Lead on, but please take into account my head is spinning. There's no way I can keep everything you've shown me straight in my brain."

He followed as she walked through two rooms of ottomans, chairs, and sofas and stopped in front of a large couch covered in a fabric striped in a multitude of earth tones. Sitting, she patted the cushion beside her. "Check this out. Tell me if it's comfortable."

He did as she asked, leaning back and running his fingers over the sturdy cotton fabric. "It's okay, but . . ."

"But?"

"You sure it isn't too . . . girly?"

She smiled. "Stripes are hardly girly, and it will go great with the chairs and end tables you chose. Close your eyes and try to imagine sitting on it to watch television or read a book." She stood, gauging his reaction. "Make sure it's perfect for a nap."

He swung his legs up, but kept his feet off the

cushions, stretched out his torso and closed his eyes, while Zoë settled in a chair across from him. This was the totally wrong place to lay on top of him and fit herself against his strong, hard body, yet it was the first thing that came to mind as she studied him.

Grinning, he returned to a sitting position. "How soon do you think they can have this at the loft?"

Embarrassed to be caught staring, she flipped a page in her planner. "Stay put and I'll find out."

Thirty minutes later the entire delivery was scheduled. "Time for lunch," she said as they walked out the showroom door. "Then we'll look at area rugs."

They ate at a small bistro specializing in French food and a tranquil atmosphere. But with tables aligned side by side in a tight row, there was more elbow rubbing with other diners than a feeling of intimacy.

"I don't know how to thank you for making this so easy," Theo said after they ordered. "If you hadn't agreed to help, there's no telling what I would have done. And you certainly put to rest all those horror stories men tell when they talk about shopping with a woman." He sat back in the chair. "Watching you work has been inspiring."

His words warmed her to her core. "You're

supposed to think of me as your designer, not a member of the opposite sex. I also promised I wouldn't force my personal opinion on you. I believe I stated I wouldn't be upset if you chose to ignore my professional one either."

"You definitely stuck to your end of the deal. Though I hope you like what I selected."

"I do, but I'm not the one who has to live with it."

The waitress brought their lunches, and he raised his fork. "Tell me, of all the things we looked at this past week, what was your favorite piece? Something you loved that you would have chosen for yourself, even if I didn't."

Zoë took a bite of her pasta dish as she recalled his bedroom set: scrolled wood in a dark, heavy design. "I thought the headboard you didn't choose, the one with the delicate vine carving that ran along the border, was stunning, though what you ordered suits you."

"It was a nice piece, but again, a little on the girly side. Anything else you would have wanted for yourself? Something frivolous that you really wished you owned."

She thought a few seconds. "Though you vetoed the suggestion, I loved the idea of a fireplace. The store had a green marble mantel that caught my eye. I thought it was beautiful."

"It was nice, but it also cost a fortune. I know, Chad said there was no budget, but . . . maybe I'll get it later, after I live with the new stuff."

"No matter. It's your home, not mine."

"And furniture is something you sit on that takes up space. Right now, the most important thing is how it'll photograph for a magazine layout."

"Trust me, once it's all arranged, each piece will look perfect in the *NYE* story."

"I'm sure it will." He took a sip of water. "Have you talked with Elise today?"

"No. And that's strange, because she usually calls me in the morning to give me a report on my latest client. Marjorie Barris had her first interview, and I was hoping to hear about it."

"Do you think something went wrong?"

"I hope not. Marjorie was looking forward to working for the company. She has children to support, so it's important she was hired."

"Maybe you should call Elise and see what happened?"

"You wouldn't mind?" Zoë asked, grateful for his offer.

"Of course not. I'll even visit the men's room to give you some privacy."

Once he headed for the rear of the restaurant, she pulled out her cell phone and pushed the automatic dial.

"Suited for Change," Elise said in a brusque tone.

"It's me."

"Hey, you. What's up?"

"I called because I want to know how Marjorie made out."

"Sorry, I forgot to phone you. She did great. They offered her the job and she took it. She even got the salary she needed to keep her apartment."

"That's wonderful." When Elise didn't comment further, Zoë forged ahead. "Is something wrong? You're not angry with me for leaving you last night, are you?"

"Why should I be angry? I'm a big girl. I can take care of myself."

"Did you and Chad reach a decision on the size of Marasoft's donation?"

A moment passed before Elise said, "I'm not sure there's going to be a donation."

Flustered, Zoë leaned back in the chair. "Sorry, repeat that, please. I thought you said Marasoft might not make a donation."

Elise's sigh echoed in the silence. "I'll take full responsibility if it doesn't happen, but I had a good reason for acting like I did. Honest."

"Acting like you did? What are you talking about?"

"I might have been a little curt when I told Chad good-bye."

"Curt? Why?"

"I don't want to talk about it."

"Wait, let me guess. He made a pass."

"In a manner of speaking."

"You mean you couldn't tell?" Zoë was certain a woman would know it when a guy like Chad hit on her. "Are we talking about the same man?"

"He asked to come in for a drink. When I said no, he hinted that we should have dinner together again, just the two of us. It was . . . unsettling."

Unsettling? "Okay, now I'm really confused," Zoë stated. "Unless he leered or offered more than dinner, I don't see the sleaze factor."

"How about the irony of the situation?" Elise asked in an injured tone.

"Let's see, unattached, attractive, witty man . . . single, lovely, intelligent woman . . . the two of them spending an enjoyable evening sharing a meal in a public place . . ." She waited a beat before saying, "Nope, sorry. I don't see the irony, nor do I understand your evaluation of the situation."

"How can you understand, with Theo drooling over you?"

Theo? Drooling over her? "Elise, you aren't making any sense. Just say it. What did Chad do?"

"You mean you couldn't tell?"

Ready to tear out her hair, Zoë tossed her napkin on her plate. "If you don't start making sense, I'm going to take a cab to Suited for Change and strangle you."

"I'm not antigay, just anti-lying bastard. I can't believe he'd try to pull a fast one."

"Something is seriously lacking in this conversation—like common sense. Are you telling me you think Chad is gay?"

"Are you saying he's straight?" Elise countered.

"Of course he's straight. Why would you think he's gay?"

"How could he not be?" Elise replied. "He has an opinion on fashion, food, wine, music, things even you don't comment on, and design and fashion are your business. I can imagine his apartment bathroom, magenta towels, prissy scented soaps, the latest in hair care products. He was too polished, too at ease with our waiter—and he was definitely gay . . ."

Zoë made an unsuccessful attempt at tamping down a gurgle of laughter.

"It isn't funny," grumped Elise.

"Yes it is," said Zoë between chuckles. "You couldn't be more wrong."

"I couldn't be more right," her misguided business associate insisted.

This time Zoë said nothing to contradict her.

Finally, Elise heaved a sigh. "Oh, lord, he is straight, isn't he?"

"If you like, I can confirm it with Theo."

"No! Don't you dare. I'll take care of it myself."

"Really? What do you have planned?"

"Zip, right now, but I'll think of something."

"You'd better, though I doubt Suited for Change will lose the donation. I can't imagine Chad would be so petty." She relaxed in her chair. "Any chance I can be there when you try to explain things?"

"No way. I got myself into this mess, I'll crawl out on my own. Go spend the afternoon with your fella."

"He's a client, Elise," she reminded her friend. "How about if I drop by later?"

"I'm not sure. I may be groveling."

"I don't think you'll need to go that far."

"You weren't there. I was inexcusably impolite."

"Maybe I should come in tomorrow."

"Yeah, fine. Whatever."

The line went dead just as Theo took his seat at the table. The waitress appeared a moment later, and he gave her his credit card.

When he looked up, he noticed Zoë grinning. "What's up? You look like you just heard the world's best joke."

"I did," she said.

"Well, are you going to tell me what's so funny, or is it one of those things only women understand?"

"I think it's hilarious, but I can't tell you."

"Why not?"

"I just can't."

The waitress returned with the receipt. He signed it and put the card in his wallet. "Not ever?" he asked as he stood, then pulled out her chair.

"Maybe . . . in a week or so. Let's go shopping." Zoë shrugged into her coat. "I never asked, but what do you think of magenta?"

Chapter 8

Theo studied the well-dressed and, dare he say it, classy stranger staring at him from the three-way mirror. Behind him, Zoë and the sales clerk grinned like parents viewing their firstborn in a cap and gown on graduation day. Finally, he smiled too, because he was just as pleased, though he kept his opinion of the impressive transformation to himself.

"I still can't believe I need a dozen shirts and ties," he said for the third—or was it the fourth?—time that afternoon. Zoë kept insisting he buy that many whenever he'd asked, but he enjoyed yanking her chain.

She rolled her eyes and glanced at the sales-man, a short stocky older guy with flushed cheeks and thinning gray hair who acted as if the store,

Thomas Pink, was his personal creation. "Mr. Maragos will wear the items he has on. You can ring up everything else while we take a look at your jacket selection."

"Yes, ma'am." The clerk gathered the packages, then held Theo's old shirt and tweed sport coat with two fingers, as if they were used trash bags. "And what does madam want me to do with these?"

"Do you take part in a donation service for the homeless?"

"We do."

"Add them to the pile, please. You'll find us on the other side of the store when you're through."

"Hey," said Theo, wounded. "I got that jacket for my twenty-first birthday."

"That was what? Ten years ago?" Zoë asked, marching around the display racks like a general going to war.

"Twelve. And it has sentimental value."

Stopping at a rack of sport coats, she began sorting through the sizes. "Then I suggest you have it mounted under glass or encased in plastic. That way, you can look at it whenever you feel a bout of nostalgia coming on."

"How about if I keep it in my closet and wear it around the apartment?"

"No."

"You're heartless," he said, huffing a sigh.

She held out a navy jacket, and a smile flickered across her lips. "Feel this," she ordered, thrusting it at him. "Tell me what you think."

He ran his fingers over the garment, enjoying the fabric's supple texture. "It's soft, has a lived-in sort of appeal, kind of reminds me of my old coat."

"That's cashmere for you. Try it on."

When Theo slipped his arms through the sleeves, he found the jacket a perfect fit. "I'm impressed. How did you guess my size?" he asked as Zoë straightened the collar and lapels.

"Forty long? Nothing to it. Take a look in the mirror. What do you see?"

He blinked at his reflection again. Never had he thought a geek like him would appear so put together or so in style. Turning, he faced her. "I see a guy who knows what he wants to wear."

"Exactly," she responded, back to her no nonsense attitude. Then she tugged on the cuffs, buttoned and unbuttoned the front placket, and adjusted his red and navy striped tie. "It goes with several of the tie and shirt combinations we chose. Come back to the rack and we'll find another, maybe something a little more dressy."

At the brush of her hands, Theo's heart rate accelerated and he began to sweat. Though he'd taught himself to ignore the ring heating his finger, he ached to hold Zoë in his arms. She hadn't touched him in anything more than a casual manner all day, yet he longed to pull her against his chest and steal a kiss from her ripe, expressive lips.

In a stupor, he started when he realized she'd left him standing there, mooning like a grade schooler. Whenever he got within five feet of her, he lost focus on the task at hand while his arteries pumped the blood in his body to the area behind his zipper. Just what he didn't need while being fitted for a new wardrobe.

He arrived at her side, and she held out another jacket, this one in a fabric covered in small gray checks on a black background. He slid the navy blazer from his shoulders. "What do you have against brown?"

"Brown?" She wrinkled her nose. "Nothing, if I can find something stylish in the color." She flipped through the hangers and held up another coat, this one a brown-yet-not-brown. "Will this do?"

"Does it go with the shirts and ties we picked out?" he asked, touching the fabric.

"A few. We'll need to get a couple of extras, but it'll be easy now that I know what appeals to you."

He slid the "not brown" jacket over his arms. "What do you call this color, anyway?"

Zoë bit her lower lip as she studied the fit. "Maple? Or tobacco? I'm not sure. The professional designers keep changing the names. Take the color purple, for example. It can be either eggplant, aubergine, or plum, and sometimes they're exactly the same shade. The new names just sound better with whatever the trend is for that season."

"Purple is purple as far as I'm concerned, and the only maple-colored thing I've ever seen is syrup, just like brown is brown." They returned to the trifold mirror, where he made another inspection and shook his head. "I don't know how you do it, but—"

"Madam has the eye of a true connoisseur," said the salesman as he joined them with an armful of shirts and ties that, if Theo guessed correctly, matched the "not brown" coat. "I took the liberty of selecting these." He spread the items on a table behind them. "Feel free to decide, as you wish."

Zoë grabbed two shirts, held them against the jacket, discarded one, sorted through a few of the ties, then repeated the process until she'd set aside three more shirts and ties.

"That ought to do it."

She handed the sales clerk the gray-checked

jacket, along with the one that satisfied Theo's desire for brown. "Add these to the tally, please. We'll be over to the register in a minute."

Theo heaved a sigh and donned the navy blazer. "Good thing we're finished. For a minute there I thought you were going to hold me prisoner for the rest of the day."

"Who said we're finished?" she asked, hoisting the strap on her bag farther up her shoulder. "There's still that appointment at the photography studio."

"Great. Then what?"

"You need slacks and shoes. But I have a different store in mind for each of those."

He moaned aloud as he followed her to the checkout counter and passed a credit card to the salesman. When the final total showed on the register, he swallowed hard. "I'm surprised the damned plastic didn't melt," he mumbled, signing the slip. "At this rate I can't afford pants or shoes, never mind a professional portrait."

"Of course you can." Smiling broadly, she gave the clerk a piece of paper. "Please have everything delivered to this address by nine o'clock tomorrow morning." Then she glanced at a wall clock and frowned. "Maybe you're right. It's too late for the clothes, but you can't miss your appointment with the photographer."

"How about dinner after that?" He crossed mental fingers. If things went as he hoped, tonight would be his chance to step to the plate, maybe even hit a home run. The possibility excited him so much that he took Zoë's arm and practically dragged her from the store. "You pick the spot. It doesn't matter to me."

In tune with his exuberance, she giggled. "I think tonight should be my treat, especially since I held you hostage for the entire day."

"Good. Make me feel guilty because you did exactly what I hired you to do."

"You not only complained, you whined," she stated. "And that is definitely a *girly* trait."

He gazed at the darkening sky, embarrassed she'd used his own sexist word to label his conduct. "Okay, okay, I get the picture. You were only honoring my request." He grinned. "So, where will you take me?"

"How about room service in my suite? If you don't see what you want on the menu, the kitchen will prepare whatever you like. They're very accommodating."

Theo's groin tightened. Zoë's casual invitation gave him a ray of hope. She was offering him another chance at private time, and he wasn't about to blow it.

"Room service, huh? At those prices, 'the

Donald' himself should be cooking." Hiding his enthusiasm, he hailed a cab, guided her inside, and gave the driver their destination. "I don't think I've ever spent this much money on myself. How the heck does Chad afford it all?"

"Something tells me your COO is adept at handling a lot of things you haven't had to deal with. If you want, I can help with a personal budget too."

"You're a woman of many talents."

"Only because it's forced on me. I'm always given a budget by the company I work for, and I've learned how to spend money wisely. I assume you know the amount of Chad's salary as well as what the rest of the staff makes?"

"Of course. Chad gives me a monthly spreadsheet on Marasoft's expenditures. He keeps me in the loop, or at least he tries. I'm usually so involved in the programming end of it that I don't keep tabs."

"What about a salary for yourself?"

"I take what I need, when I need it. If we have to cut corners, I'm the one that loses out."

"So you pay everyone more than you get yourself?"

"I know, Chad keeps telling me it's a dumb move. He says the company is doing well financially, but we have investors to satisfy. I intend to keep working until Marasoft is a big player in the IT field. Soon we'll have stockholders who expect a good return on their dollar, and I refuse to let them down."

"That sounds admirable, but why do you feel so responsible, if you don't mind my asking?"

How could he tell her about his unscrupulous quasi-grandfather without delving into his unbelievable past? Simple. He couldn't.

"My father always prided himself on standing firm and staying true to what he believed in. As for my salary, it pays the rent and basic living expenses. The rest goes to subsidize my dad's fees at his assisted living facility. I've made sure he gets the very best care."

"I'm sorry," said Zoë, clasping his hand. "I can only imagine how much stress is involved when you're responsible for an aging parent."

Her warmth and understanding made him sigh. "You're quite a woman. You know the exact words to bring me out of my slump. When I'm with you, I feel . . ." *Sophisticated, worldly, a giant among men.* "I suppose I should try to be more like Chad."

Zoë shifted on the seat, her eyes open wide. "Don't you dare. You're perfect just as you are."

He jerked back when a circle of heat radiated from his ring finger to his wrist.

"Are you all right?"

"Yeah, I'm okay," he answered, flexing his hand. "Probably carpel tunnel syndrome, the result of spending too many hours at a computer keyboard."

The cab took a sharp turn, and she almost slid into his lap. "Sorry." She righted herself. "No one takes their time in this city—especially the cabbies."

"You don't enjoy living in Manhattan?"

"It's fine. But I'm looking forward to going home. I miss my sisters."

"I forgot about that."

She leaned against the seat. "How about you? Do you see your father often?"

"Not often enough, which reminds me, I'm due to visit him this weekend." Only then did he realize how important it was that Zoë meet his dad before the Alzheimer's took complete control. But how would she react if he asked her to be a part of something so personal? He cleared his throat. "Do you have plans for tomorrow?"

"Tomorrow is Saturday, which means I get to sleep late and catch up on a few things. Why?"

"No reason," he said, debating on the best way to ask her along on his ride to New Jersey. If he postponed the invitation, it would have to wait until after she got back from her family reunion, and that was fine. As long as she returned to him.

"Seven dollars, folks," said the driver, interrupting their conversation.

Theo paid the cabbie, climbed out, and offered Zoë his hand. Together, they went into the photography studio, and Theo braced for the next ordeal.

Chad stopped in front of Suited for Change and peered in the store window. Other than the company name, there was little to announce the type of trade taking place inside. The items showcased in the window, an attractive grouping of feminine apparel and accessories, bespoke of a trendy women's boutique rather than the personal enhancement and job placement service he understood the company to be. At a few minutes shy of five o'clock, the business appeared deserted, even though the lights were on and the Open sign hung on the door.

After his morning meeting with Theo, he'd thought about Elise Sutton whenever he had a quiet moment. He'd even picked up the phone to call her, but changed his mind each time. After last night's abrupt dismissal, he wasn't about to give her another chance to get rid of him so easily. Instead, he decided to drop in, on the pretense of discussing Marasoft's donation. In reality, he planned to learn the true reason for her surprisingly abrupt and anger-filled attitude.

He still couldn't figure out why she'd reacted so strangely when he offered to escort her to her door. And a simple "no, thank you" would have sufficed when he asked if he could come inside for a drink or take her to dinner sometime. He'd struck out with women before, but the percentage was so low as to be insignificant, and none of them had beat feet as if escaping from an ax murderer like the testy director had.

Odder still, from the moment he'd seen Elise Sutton, he suspected they shared enough physical chemistry to create a nuclear blast, yet she'd acted as if he were the last man on earth she found appealing or even acceptable. And the harder he'd tried to make things right, the more difficult she'd become.

Before coming to Suited for Change, he'd searched the Internet to glean more information about her. Aside from the fact that Elise Sutton had lived in Washington, D.C., until assigned the task of opening the New York branch of Suited for Change, she was divorced, thirty-two, and had a business degree from a small private college in Pennsylvania.

Though the women he'd dated rarely were married before, he'd heard that a divorce, even an amicable one, could sometimes make the opposite sex swear off men for a while. But he found it impossible to believe a confident lady like Elise would continue to carry such ancient baggage. He told himself that if he had a brain in his head, he'd steer clear of her. But something compelled him to investigate whatever simmered just below the surface of her peaches-and-cream skin.

Something sensual and sinfully satisfying, he was certain, and the complete opposite of her angelic, almost prim, facade.

Taking a deep breath, he opened the door and walked into the front office, a good-sized space adorned with quality furniture that had seen better days. The end tables held a variety of business magazines, the chairs appeared comfortable, and a computer and the usual paraphernalia that accompanied a reception area sat on the utilitarian desk.

Without thinking, he sat behind the massive desk, opened the top drawer and began to snoop. The entire business with Ms. Sutton had him confused, and what he found on the Internet had left him painfully curious. If he learned more about her, maybe he could figure out where he'd gone wrong last night.

"May I help you?"

At the sound of Elise's clipped feminine tone, he grinned. Then he straightened and spun around in the chair. "I was looking for a pencil. Any chance you have one I could borrow?"

Her full lips thinned. Crossing her arms, she raised a brow without uttering a word.

"Too bad." He stood, smiling inside when she skittered backward. "I thought I might do a crossword puzzle while waiting for you to emerge from your lair."

"We don't supply that type of publication for our clients," she lectured. "This is a place of business, not a dentist's office."

"I stand corrected."

Her delicate nostrils flared. "Are you here for something in particular?"

"I came to talk. I think we left a couple of things unfinished last night."

"I didn't realize we had an appointment. Guess I forgot to write it in my day planner."

"With no pencil, I can see why." He took a step in her direction. "You seem like a modern executive. Ever think about using a PDA or BlackBerry?"

"I don't enjoy technology, and it doesn't care much for me," she said with a resounding sigh. Her shoulders relaxed slightly. "I guess that's hard to understand, since you come from a technology background and all."

"Now that you mention it, yes." He gazed directly into her eyes. "But I didn't come to discuss either of our companies. I'm here to see you."

"Me?" Her arms tightened around her body, calling attention to her slim waist and tempting breasts. "I thought we were supposed to talk about Suited for Change?"

"Not today." He stuffed his hands in his pockets, though his fingers itched to tuck a wayward curl behind her ear. "Somehow, we got off on the wrong foot last night, and I want to know why."

"Oh, that." Loosening her grip, she stared at her shoes. "I planned to get back to you."

"Funny, I got the impression I'd never hear from you again." When he continued his advance, she moved back until she reached a wall. "Now that I'm here, why don't you tell me in person what you were planning to say over the phone?"

He was close enough to read the confusion in her pewter-colored eyes. The air in the room was even more electrified than it had been the night before, which confirmed his original assessment. The tension building between them came from the inexplicable sensation that drew lovers together and made their hearts beat in tandem.

She shrugged. "I wanted to apologize."

"Apologize for what?" he asked.

Licking her lips, her gaze darted around as if she were looking for escape. "How I acted."

"Oh? Was there something wrong with your conduct?"

"Don't be difficult," she said with a sniff. "I was rude, and I'm sorry."

"I'm sorry too, because your vague apology doesn't cut it."

She blinked, her pupils expanding. "I don't know what more you want me to say."

He took another step toward her. "I want to know why you behaved as if I was the reincarnation of Ted Bundy."

She rested a trembling hand on her collarbone, just visible above the neckline of her figure-hugging burnt orange sweater. "I'm not sure I understand."

"Me neither. But I'm not leaving until I figure you out." Resisting the urge to run his tongue over the spot her fingers skimmed, he rested his arms against the wall on either side of her. "However long it takes."

"I'm not that complicated." Her face flushed pink. "Truly."

"You're not simple either. Last night I was a gentleman, in every sense of the word. What was it about me that put you off?"

Sighing, she said, "It's been a while since I've had reason to spend personal time with a man.

You seemed to be a little more than I was ready to handle."

"I'm uncomplicated and easygoing. Give me a chance to show you." He leaned forward but stopped short of kissing her. "Let's start slow. A dinner date or a concert. No strings, I promise."

When she smiled, he relaxed his stance, and she ducked under his arm. "One date is all I'm promising."

He grinned at her wheeler-dealer attitude. "One is all I'm asking for."

After dimming the living room lights, Zoë handed Theo a menu from the desk. "Here you are. Just tell the kitchen I'll have my usual. And please, choose whatever you want."

She went to her bedroom, where a fast inspection told her that all was neat and tidy, and housekeeping had already completed their turndown service. A quiver of excitement danced in her stomach. Though eating dinner was the last thing she wanted to do with Theo Maragos, she had to act as if it were foremost in her mind. She wasn't about to play the lovesick adolescent, only to be spurned by him a third time.

Striding to her closet, she inspected her wardrobe. Should she change into something more casual than she wore now? Definitely casual, she decided. Since he wasn't able to tell a designer original from a blue light special, she doubted he would care a fig what she wore while they ate.

Their busy day echoed in her mind. Theo had been red-faced for almost the entire afternoon, especially when they'd made it to a men's store right before closing. When he came out of the fitting room wearing a pair of gray flannel pants hugging his sexy butt, she had to fist her hands to keep from running them over the front placket and around to the rear. In fact, she had to order her feet to stay rooted in place with each trip Theo made to the closetlike room, just so she wouldn't follow him inside and show him what she really wanted to do.

But tonight was the end of the chase. If he didn't show any interest in her as a woman, she was finished pining over him. It had been days since she'd checked her e-mail. There were probably a half-dozen messages from Zeus, asking for a report or nagging about her possible failures. She had to concentrate on her final project, inspire Theo to take fashion seriously and earn a rave review in *New York Entrepreneur.*

She kicked off her boots and wiggled her toes. If felt wonderful to rid herself of the pointy-toed torture devices. Soon she'd be able to chuck the modern world and get back to her comfy sandals

and soft, draping chitons. An eternity of glory
awaited her when she appeared on Mount Olympus, and she wouldn't allow anything to distract
her from meeting her goal.

Moments passed while a feeling of calm washed
over her. After hanging her clothing in the closet,
she slid a diaphanous white chiton over her head
and let the silky fabric caress her body as it fell to
mid-calf. Though expert at inspiring mortals in
fashion and design, this simple garment was her
private fashion statement, what she longed to wear.
She belonged high in her mountaintop home, not
a bustling city of millions, where mortals thought
of little more than themselves and what money
could buy.

Startled by a knock at her bedroom door, she
turned. "Yes?"

"It's me," said Theo, his voice hesitant and deep.
"You've been in there awhile. Is everything
okay?"

Zoë glanced down at her flowing gown. If
viewed in the right light, it would silhouette her
lush body and show just enough of her curves to
entice her guest without screaming seduction.
The perfect number to encourage Theo to treat
her like a lover.

"Things are fine. Come on in," she answered
boldly. If she was decent enough for Mount

Olympus, she was decent enough to present herself to the man she hoped to bring to her bed.

"I don't want to intru—" Standing in the doorway, his eyes opened wide as they swept her from head to toe. "You're wearing a chiton?"

Zoë smiled, impressed that he knew the correct term for her garment. She twirled on her toes. "It's a little old-fashioned, but it's very comfortable. A lot of women in Greece still wear them."

His jaw clenched. "It's . . . I . . ."

She crossed the room and stood in front of him. "Did you call room service and place our dinner order?"

He shook his head. "No."

"Why not?"

"I decided I wasn't interested in food."

Encouraged by the confession, she reached for his tie and undid the knot. "Good, because I'm not either." Slipping the silky fabric from his neck, she dropped it to the floor. "Tell me, if you're not interested in food, what do you fancy?"

He licked his lips. "You," he whispered, shrugging out of the navy blazer. "You're all I think about, morning and night. I've been waiting . . ."

"Hmm. Me too." She unbuttoned the top button of his new shirt.

"I didn't want to rush things."

"It doesn't matter. You're here now." She undid

the second and third buttons. "I was losing hope you'd ever tell me what I wanted to hear."

"I still can't believe someone like you—"

She took care of the last three buttons, slid her hands under the fabric and skimmed her fingers around to his back. "How about finishing that thought?"

"Would care about a guy like me." He closed his eyes when she stepped into him and pressed her pelvis against his erection. "Please, Zoë," he moaned, clutching her bottom and pulling her hard to his chest. "Don't play games. Tell me you're serious about this . . . about us."

"Isn't it obvious? I'm serious about doing this." She bit the underside of his jaw, then removed his glasses and set them on the nightstand. "Very serious."

"I won't be able to see you, and it doesn't seem fair. I've envisioned you in my dreams, and I need to know if the real you is better."

"See with your fingers, your hands . . . your mouth. Know me as I want to know you." She peeled off the shirt and let it drop to the floor. One look told her he was more magnificent than she'd imagined. He had a body any god on Olympus would be proud to call his own. Standing on tiptoe, she skimmed her tongue across his lower lip. Then their mouths fused and he plunged inside her.

Opening for his assault, she wrapped her arms around his neck and purred encouragement. He cupped her bottom and raised her higher so her sensitized nipples scraped his chest. Walking them to the bed, he set her on her feet, and the chiton slipped from her shoulders and pooled around her ankles.

Zoë broke the kiss, fumbled with his belt and zipper, and tugged at his pants. In a heartbeat they stood inches apart, gloriously naked. A smattering of dark hair adorned his muscular chest, narrowed to a V that ran over his six-pack abs and covered the area surrounding his sex. The sight of his burgeoning erection sent a tingle to her core, and she clenched her thighs in anticipation.

Theo stepped into her, and they tumbled onto the mattress.

Chapter 9

Theo covered Zoë's body with his own as desire knifed through his veins. He'd waited years for this moment, never believing it would come. And now, with this woman, the right woman, he knew the next few minutes would result in a life-altering experience.

Nestling his pelvis into Zoë's softness, he caressed her back and pulled her against his chest. His mouth grazed her rounded chin, traced her lush lips, and nibbled her satiny shoulder. Moaning, he slid his straining erection down her stomach and into the cleft of her thighs.

"You smell fantastic," he muttered, nuzzling the curve of her neck. "Like a field of wildflowers after a warm spring rain."

"That's so poetic. It almost sounds as if you've

been reading one of those 'how to' books." She nipped at his ear, trembling as she spoke. "The kind that coach a guy in the art of sweet-talking a woman."

He grinned, hoping to hide his nerves as well as his naiveté. The sappy comment had shot from his lips before he had a chance to stifle the words, but now that he knew she'd enjoyed it, he was glad he said it. "I wish I'd thought of it the other night, when I made a fool of myself at your door."

"No matter. What's important is that we're here now, don't you think?" Zoë whispered. "And I have every confidence you'll do more than you'd learn from any book."

Sliding a hand down her side and around to her front, he cupped a breast and caught the nipple between his fingers. Then he lifted the swelling mound and covered the tip with his lips, drawing it deep into his mouth.

She clutched his head, arched up to give him better access, and he grazed the sensitive point with his teeth, shaping the silken globe with his palm. Following an instinct as old as time, he inhaled her essence and tasted her desire. Holding Zoë, touching her satiny skin, smelling her unique fragrance, was better than anything he'd ever imagined.

He delved lower, caressing her ribs, stroking her navel, skimming her belly, as he charted the dips, curves, and textures of new and thrilling territory. As if on autopilot, he slipped one, then two fingers into her hot slick center and found the key to her pleasure. When she moaned encouragement, he circled the swollen bud with his thumb, tormenting and teasing until she bucked beneath him.

"Now, Theo, please. Come inside of me."

Zoë's urgent, almost demanding tone so enticed him he thought he would climax against her thighs. Holding himself in check, he brought his engorged shaft to her creamy lips and rubbed along her cleft, begging entry into the place he'd so often envisioned in his dreams. The heat encircling his ring finger vibrated up his arm and straight to his heart, where it fired his blood and spurred him on.

When she reached between them and ran her nails up his cock, he grew harder, thicker, longer in her hands. She spread her thighs wide and Theo drove into her, felt her tighten around him. Pushing in to the hilt, he pumped his hips in sync with hers until they were in tune with the pounding rhythm.

As if he'd died and gone to some magical place of never ending pleasure, he lost himself in the scent of her desire, the taste of her skin, the warmth of her arms, clutching him as if she'd never let go.

Tension built to a near frenzy as he thrust into Zoë again and again, every fiber of his being attuned to her need, her enjoyment, her completion while he strived for his own. Fusing their mouths together, he hoped to make them one in body, mind, and heart. She became the meaning in his life, the reason for his existence, the woman he'd waited a lifetime to find.

Quivering, she called out his name as she joined him atop the cresting waves of passion. Positive he wanted her in his arms forever, he followed her into the abyss.

The world stopped spinning for a few incredible seconds. Minutes later, gasping for breath and grinning like a fool, he held Zoë close, rolled to his back and draped her over his chest. "That was . . ." He sighed. "Amazing."

"I'll say." Her voice sounded well-satisfied and sleepy. "You're quite the man of steel. But I'm sure you've heard that from a lot of women."

Theo swelled with pride, noting the steady heat still thrumming through his ring finger. He'd only slept with two other women, and that had been in college, when he was young and stupid, and put no stock in his mother's prediction about the ring. This rousing success only proved she'd been right. He and Zoë were destined to be together.

Unfortunately, confiding his secret was impossible. No guy wanted his bedmate to know he was practically a virgin, or that he'd been waiting for the woman his mother had told him to find. He'd had a hard enough time keeping the secret from Chad. He had no intention of spilling the beans to the girl he'd just decided would be his forever lover.

"Not any who counted," he said by way of explanation. If his luck held, Zoë would drop the subject and he wouldn't have to embellish on the lie. "And I don't think this is the proper place to discuss past affairs."

She slid to his side, but he locked her in place. "Where do you think you're going?"

"I'm crushing you."

"Not at all. Besides, you feel nice, all fragile and relaxed against me." *And warm and cuddly, and very, very sexy.* "Really, please stay."

She sighed her compliance and he gave himself a mental high-five, knowing he'd said the right thing again. Having sex with a person you loved was as compelling as he'd heard it would be. Though Zoë hadn't voiced the same sentiment, she would soon.

She nuzzled into his shoulder. "Can I ask a question?"

Theo had only one answer. "Of course."

"Have you always enjoyed sex with women who have an abundance of curves?"

In truth, he'd grown up fanaticizing about women with great tits and more than a handful of ass his entire youth, until they'd become his personal standard of beauty. He couldn't remember much about the girls he'd slept with in college, but growing up where he had, he still considered himself an expert on the subject, so his next statement wasn't a lie.

"Absolutely. But you're the most exciting. I still can't believe . . . let's just lie here and soak it in, all right? Then maybe we can—"

"Do it again?" She giggled. "Now there's a positive thought."

When his penis jerked to life at her suggestion, Zoë eased back and stared, a mysterious smile lighting her beautiful face. "I get the impression another part of you thinks it's a positive statement too. How nice to find a man who can be ready at a moment's notice."

Her pelvis fluttered against his in a seductive dance of desire. The tip of her tongue traced a line from his neck to his jaw and over to his lips. Rising on straight arms, she loomed above him, tempting him with the ruby-crowned nipples of her bountiful breasts.

He accepted the invitation, held a perfect globe in each hand and suckled, plucking a nipple as he laved its twin with his seeking tongue.

Zoë lifted her hips, guided herself over and down, and began to rock. Then she sat up and rested her thighs against his, rising and falling with abandon.

Entranced by the erotic picture, Theo raised his upper body to join hers. Thrusting in tandem, they rode to a starburst of fulfillment. Hips, hands, lips, and tongue meshing in harmony, they again climbed toward completion.

Zoë trembled from head to toe, every inch of her skin, every nerve ending, throbbing with the force of her orgasm. Theo stiffened and cried out her name, and she continued the journey. Scaling a wall of need, she jumped, and flung herself outward, gliding on the incredible sensation until she floated to earth, boneless and utterly sated.

Melting onto his chest a second time, she gasped for breath. After a satisfied sigh, she rolled to his side and spooned against him, thrilled that she'd taken this handsome, virile mortal to her bed.

For his part, Theo drew her closer and groaned his approval. Then his breathing deepened, slowed, and she sensed he'd fallen asleep. A question prodded her, and she gave it her full attention. Was it possible she could keep in contact with Theo while she enjoyed the eternal glory she'd been promised on Olympus?

There had to be a way she could have both of

the things she longed for. Zeus had made love to hundreds of women, both mortal and goddess, so if she returned home in triumph, why would he refuse her this one special man as a reward for her success?

She rolled to one side, to better look at him, and her gaze roamed Theo's expressive face, his muscular body, the slant of his wide shoulders and narrow waist, then down to his incredible male attributes. Smiling, she turned, switched off the light at the side of her bed, then rolled back, slipped a knee over his thigh, and snuggled into him.

Her final thought before drifting to sleep was of the way Theo had worshipped her body, seen to her needs above his own, and made her feel cherished with every touch. None of her past partners had taken her in that same caring manner, and she couldn't imagine anyone ever living up to Theo's prowess.

Nor did she want to.

Theo woke to the patter of sleeting rain slamming the hotel window in a raucous cascade typical of midwinter Manhattan. It figured the milder weather had been too good to last. Opening one eye, he looked over his shoulder for Zoë, but she'd left the bed. In fact, aside from the sound of pelting splatters, the suite was so quiet he thought he might be alone.

He shook his head at the ridiculous notion. He'd felt the shape of Zoë's generous breasts against his ribs throughout the night, and the curve of her thigh draping his leg, so he knew she'd slept molded tightly against him. Thanks to her, he was a man who intimately knew passion, desire, and love.

His mother had warned him to proceed with caution where women were concerned, that only one would be able to accept him for his past. He'd always thought this singular bit of advice an exaggeration, but now, with a fantastic night behind him, he realized she'd been correct.

Zoë Degodessa was the woman of his dreams, the woman he needed to fulfill his destiny.

Raking his fingers through his hair, he recalled their idyllic evening. His world would be complete if Zoë shared his feelings. Though she'd seemed pleased with his performance, he could only hope it measured up to the other guys she'd been with. If not, he had to keep trying until he convinced her they belonged together.

His goal, to erase from her memory the men who'd come before, stuck in his craw. Being jealous of her past lovers was a waste of energy, because their life together was in the future. From this moment, getting her to agree that he was the man with whom she wanted to spend eternity became his focus.

Lifting his hand, he stared at the ring on his finger, marked with the raised impression of a lightning bolt. His mother had given him the token in secret, though he had no doubt the man in charge knew what she'd done. He'd left the mountain with nothing but the ring and a set of clothes, not the best way to start life anew, but the only way his so-called grandfather would allow.

And no one dared argue with the high and mighty boss man, least of all him.

The disjointed thoughts cleared and he sat up on the edge of the bed to get his bearings. Zoë had to be somewhere in the living room, maybe having breakfast or waiting for it to arrive.

He stumbled into the bathroom and did his business, picking through the clothes on her bedroom floor until he found his own, and shrugged into them.

Then he stood in the short hallway leading to the living area and, squinting, saw Zoë, dressed in a short terry robe, poised at her computer. From where he stood, it looked as if she were answering e-mail, but without his glasses he couldn't be certain.

He cleared his throat, so as not to startle her, and sauntered toward her in his best man-of-the-world swagger. "I wondered where you were." She'd already logged off the screen when he came up behind her, placed his hands on her shoulders and kneaded her neck with his fingers. "What are you up to?"

"Just taking care of some business." She hummed encouragement as he continued the massage. "Hmm, that's perfect, wonderful."

"It can't be as great as what you made me feel last night." He worked his thumbs into her spine until she leaned forward and purred. His ring finger began to tingle but he ignored the heat, telling himself he'd simply have to get used to it, because he was going to make sure that he and Zoë spent the remainder of their lives side by side. Uplifted by the silent promise, he caressed the column of her neck and worked down to her shoulders.

"Don't stop. Please don't stop," she moaned, melting under his palms. "This is better than sitting on a cloud."

He smiled at her whimsical musing. "Sat on many clouds, have you? I think I'd like to try that sometime."

"I've sat on my fair share; you're welcome to join me on my next trip." She slumped onto the desk. "More, I want more."

"If I remember correctly, you said the same thing in bed."

She relaxed as she sighed. "This is almost as good. You have amazing hands."

"Thanks. Your hands are terrific too." He ran his fingers to the front of her robe and inched them inside, cupping her breasts and palming her nipples. Turning her in his arms, he nuzzled the tender spot under her ear, moaning his pleasure.

She stood, parted his shirt, and undid the zipper of his slacks. Freeing his erection, her nails scored his flesh as she nibbled on his chin.

"Maybe we should take this into the bedroom," he rasped. "I want you underneath me when you call out my name."

Zoë's groan of agreement pushed him over the edge. When he raised her up, she wrapped her legs around his waist and rubbed herself against his engorged shaft. Walking them into the bedroom, much as he had last night, he stopped at the edge of her bed, and she slid to her feet. Then she tugged off his disheveled clothes and ran her palms over his pecs and abs.

"Have I told you I think you have a superior body?"

Theo's penis swelled, as did his chest. "Yes, but it's nice to hear again."

"What do you do to stay in shape?"

He furrowed his fingers through her hair. "Not a thing. I'm the geek version of a couch potato."

"Then you must have excellent genes." She kissed a path from his chest to his jaw. "Lucky you."

Theo captured her mouth with his and delved into her heat, tasting honey and fruit on her tongue. When they dropped to the mattress to continue the dance, he caught the time displayed on the nightstand clock and hissed out a breath. "Oh, hell. I forgot. The clothes we bought should be at my apartment in an hour, and, unlike this fancy hotel, I don't have a doorman to accept deliveries."

"Can we call them?" Zoë asked, her tone echoing his disappointment.

He did a fast calculation. "Maybe we don't have to. I'd estimate ten minutes to shower, another ten to dress, and thirty to catch a cab to my place. That leaves a full ten minutes for . . . us."

She arched into his chest, opened her thighs, and pulled him on top of her. "A whole ten minutes? Then we'd better get started."

Zoë entered Theo's loft with bagels, coffee, and a container of fresh fruit. Their stolen moments of intimacy had finished in her shower in thirty minutes, rather than ten, but Thomas Pink's delivery was late, so everything evened out in the end. She'd given Theo the task of unwrapping and

storing his new clothes while she picked up breakfast at a coffee shop across the street.

After setting the meal on the recently installed
island, she walked through the remodeled space.
The construction crew had turned the loft into a six
room apartment with a kitchen, dining area, and
living room in front, and a master suite, guest bedroom, and Theo's office in the rear. Painting walls,
laying new flooring, and choosing area rugs would
be done, in order, at the beginning of the week, and
after that the furniture would be delivered. Once
she added a few final touches, the loft would be
ready for the *New York Entrepreneur* photo shoot.

Standing in the doorway to his bedroom, seeing Theo's broad muscular back tapering to the
waist of his tailored slacks, a jolt of desire struck
her. When he raised two shirts to the murky light
seeping through the windows and frowned in
concentration, her heart stuttered with an unwel-
come emotion.

She'd come to admire this caring mortal, maybe
a little too much, and that was wrong in so many
ways. Still, her year of toiling on earth had been
worth every second, for without this quest she
wouldn't have met such an exceptional man. And
though he'd never be a smooth talker or a smart
dresser, she would remember Theo Maragos always.

"I need a professional opinion," he said, sensing her presence. "Do both of these shirts go with the pants I'm wearing?"

Zoë pushed the forbidden feelings to the back of her mind. "By now you should be capable of figuring it out for yourself."

He groaned. "Have a little compassion, please. I'm new at this mix and match stuff."

She walked into the room, noting that the raised bed frame and dark elegant furniture they'd purchased would make the suite a showplace. "Here's a quick lesson that usually works. Cream goes with most colors, but not gray, and brown and gray aren't good together either. Avoid plaid and polka dots—"

Turning, he grinned. "That I can do."

"You did say I'd inspired you?"

He cocked a brow. "More in some ways than others."

She rolled her eyes at the teasing compliment. "Just use your instincts. If you're drawn to the combination, it's probably a match."

"If you figure a way to phrase that rule into a piece of conventional computer wisdom," he stated, "the fashion advice might stick."

"Unfortunately, that's not my area of expertise. Breakfast is in the kitchen, if you're hungry."

He unbuttoned a shirt and slipped it on, tucking

the tails in as he walked toward her. "I'm hungry, but not for food." Cupping her jaw in his palms, Theo bent and kissed her. "Mmm. I could feast on you for the rest of my life."

Tears pooled in Zoë's eyes. "I'm talking about now," she told him, blinking. "I'm starving."

They went to the kitchen hand in hand. Theo opened the bags and parceled out their food and drink. After sipping his coffee, he said, "What's on the schedule for today?"

"Not much. I have to make a few phone calls to be certain all your deliveries are in order. Then I thought I'd finish my final project at Suited for Change. Why?"

"Is Elise expecting you?"

"Not really. Officially, the place is only open another hour, but she's usually there the entire day. I imagine she's hard at work, writing proposals for grants or calling a few department stores for donations."

"I got the impression she was dedicated to her job."

"Too dedicated," Zoë corrected. "Do you think Chad called her about Marasoft's sponsorship?"

"Probably. Contrary to the image he portrays, he's a hard worker. He's simply found a way to have fun at the same time."

"Elise could use a little fun in her life. Too bad she's not ready to start dating."

Dimples creased his handsome face. "Oh, and why is that?"

"Bad past history," she said, deftly sidestepping the question. She'd promised Elise that she wouldn't mention what had happened between her and the COO, and had every intention of keeping her word. "What about you? What do you have planned for today?"

He collected their used cups and refuse and brought it to the sink. "As a matter of fact, I'm going to see my father, and I was wondering . . ."

She leaned close and rested her chin in her hands. "I'd love to join you."

"Really?" Relief radiated in his smile. "But have I told you where he is?"

She remembered, because it was evident his father had been a driving force in turning Theo into the man he was today. "He lives in New Jersey, you said. I've never been to the dreaded state across the water. Isn't that where all the mobsters live?"

He laughed. "You must be addicted to *The Sopranos*."

"Not really." She drew a pattern on the counter, realized it was the shape of a heart and flattened her fingers. "But I do recall you mentioning that your father lived there."

"You have a good memory."

"I do when it's important to me."

"That's nice to hear, but I have to warn you, he's not always lucid. If today is one of his bad days, it could get difficult. I never know until I get there."

"He's ill?"

"He has Alzheimer's, and it's progressing rapidly."

She placed her hand on his. "I'm sorry."

"Yeah, me too." He sighed. "So, are you game?"

Zoë had no idea what would happen, but she hoped to share all she could of Theo's life in the time she had left. "I'm game." She stepped back from the island to model her simple lime green sweater, black slacks, and half-boots. "I've never been to a senior housing center. Is what I'm wearing acceptable?"

His gaze slid over her skin like warm honey. "You look great. All I have to do is rent a car. It'll only take a few minutes." Theo walked to the phone, pressed a programmed number, and made arrangements for the pickup. After disconnecting, he turned back to her. "You're sure you want to do this, because I'll understand if you change your mind?"

"I have no intention of reneging on a promise. And New Jersey will be an adventure."

"Tell me that after you've seen Hackensack and

toured the Gentle Heart Care Center for senior citizens." He helped her into her coat, then shrugged into his own jacket. "My dad's not that old, but he needs constant attention, and this is the best place for him to get it."

"You must love him very much." A lot more than she cared for her own poor excuse for a parent, the autocratic and demanding Zeus.

"He was . . . he's still a great guy and I owe him a lot. He's much more than my father—"

"Why is that?" she asked, curious.

"Lots of reasons." He held open the door, and she went into the hall. "Too numerous to list right now."

"And you're driving?" she asked as they entered the elevator. She'd never ridden in a private car before, just taxis, and they sometimes terrified her.

"It's the only way to get there."

"I've heard that most New Yorkers don't have a driver's license. Where did you learn to operate an automobile?"

"In Michigan. It was one of the first things Dad taught me." Clasping her hand, Theo held it tight. "Don't worry, I'll make certain you're safe."

Zoë nodded at his promise. Somehow, she knew he would.

Chapter 10

In between talking to Theo and studying the passing scenery, Zoë pondered her time on earth. Since her arrival, she'd never been out of Manhattan, a huge city the polar opposite of Mount Olympus. Its towering buildings, smoggy air, and impatient citizens, so different from the simple dwellings, fragrant sunshine, and fun-loving gods she'd lived with since birth, had presented both a mental and physical challenge.

On Olympus there'd been little more to think about than sharing gossip, playing games, and giving her opinion on the fashions her sisters and cousins wore, as well as attempting to talk them into taking the plunge and trying something different. Back home, she was able to reach her entire family in a short stroll or a quick hike up the mountain. On earth, she'd been forced to tout her ability and exceptional vision after walking for miles or riding in one of those dreadful taxis just to get a simple assignment decorating a store window.

She'd looked upon her purpose here as routine and boring, but necessary to her survival—until she met Theo. Sleeping in his bed had been wonderful, romantic, a perfect interlude. A deep sadness crept into her heart when she thought about never seeing him again, especially since he cared enough about her to bring her to his father, a trip, she guessed, he'd never before invited anyone to make.

She'd tamped back tears at the unhappiness reflected in his eyes every time he talked about the man who had sired him. As a loving son, he wished his parent good health and a long life, instead of his father's failing mind and faltering body. If only mortals could live like the gods, in a world without pain or suffering, where no one thought about illness or old age unless the top god deemed it to be so.

And yet, even with all the uncertainty and misery in their world, mortals were proud of their accomplishments and the advances they'd made. They would never accept being held in the palm of anyone's hand, for they enjoyed something Zeus would never allow.

Control of their own destinies.

How would it feel, Zoë wondered, to live an earthly life span with someone who cared about her more than he cared about himself? Someone who would protect her, grieve with her, share her joy, and give every part of themselves to her? A mortal who would love her above all others?

A man like Theo?

She peered out the window, noting the rain had cleared and the cloudy sky had lightened to a pale gray. Staring at the imposing roadway, she observed hundreds of cars carrying thousands of people racing to and fro, so different from the lazy pace of Mount Olympus.

"I have a couple of pennies in my pocket. Maybe you'd take them in trade?"

Zoë started at the question. "In trade for what?"

"Your thoughts? You've been quiet for the past half hour. Is something wrong?"

"No, of course not," she lied. "I'm merely drinking in the wonders of New Jersey."

"It sounds as if you haven't seen much of the U.S. Why is that?"

"I guess you could say I led a sheltered childhood. My elders believed I had everything I needed in my homeland. Now that I've come here, I've experienced more. It's just that this particular area . . ."

Gazing at the industrialized complexes encompassing the Meadowlands, Theo chuckled. "I agree, this part of the state isn't so great, but the shore is nice, as is the land bordering Pennsylvania. I'll take you to Bucks County this summer. Lambertville and Flemington are a designer's paradise."

"I won't be here this summer, remember?" She hated voicing the words, but had no choice. "I'm leaving soon."

"You'll be back," he answered, the sentence a statement of fact. "I've been to lots of places I think you'd enjoy. Have you ever visited Michigan or California, seen the Great Lakes, Yellowstone Park, been to a Yankees or a Knicks game?"

Zoë ignored all but the last part of the question. She'd watched baseball, basketball, and football on television, but the rules of those sports completely flummoxed her. "I've only seen the teams play on TV. The rules boggle my brain."

"Trust me, watching a pro match on television is definitely not the same as seeing one in person. Every once in a while Chad and I take in a home game, and sometimes I bring my dad. The company has season tickets to a lot of the events, but we usually give the passes to the salesman of the month, or let the guys in programming use them as thanks for a job well done."

"That's generous of you."

"Chad says it's good business to parcel out the perks, and I have to agree."

They pulled into a toll booth for the New Jersey Turnpike, and Theo handed the collector a small card and money. "It won't be long now," he promised. "We should be there in about fifteen minutes."

Once off the exit ramp, they continued onto a road with fewer cars traveling at a more moderate rate of speed. Soon afterward, he turned at a sign that announced the Gentle Heart Center for Senior Care, and followed a long curving drive to a large three-story building with an expansive lawn.

"This is it." He climbed out, retrieved the plastic bag from the rear seat that he'd brought from the apartment, and walked to her side. "I always bring Dad magazines, usually stuff on sports, but lately he seems to enjoy reading about travel. He's focused on the Mediterranean, especially your home country these days. The doctor said his long-term memory is taking him back to a happier time, but talking about it upsets him. If he asks questions about your family and where they're from, just follow my lead and things should go without a hitch."

They entered the main foyer. Theo checked in at the desk while she read several bulletin boards laden with notices on upcoming events. Lists for card games, cooking classes, golf outings, book discussion groups, ballroom dancing, and a weekly movie night were among them. The home also hosted a special day each week when a group of volunteers brought animals to the center for something called pet therapy. One board overflowed with photos of aging citizens smiling as they fished from a huge boat, rode bikes, or sat in the sun, while another held sign-up sheets for more of the same.

"The wealth of activities available to the residents is one of the reasons I chose this place," Theo said behind her shoulder. "Even disabled seniors are included in the fun."

Zoë crossed her arms and turned to gaze at him. "Why would your father consider the Mediterranean a happier time? Is that where he was born?"

"No, but he spent a summer there the year after his parents passed away. It was his first time out of the country, so he did a lot of climbing and hiking. He met my mother and, according to him, they were instantly smitten." His lips thinned to a frown. "He had to leave, though I don't think it was his choice."

"And your mother stayed behind? They didn't marry?"

"They couldn't. I was born nine months later, and stayed with her until I was sent to the States."

"Then he knew about you?"

"Not until I showed up on his doorstep. But Dad took me in without a single question, saw to it I got an education, and made sure I had a purpose in life."

"And your mother?"

"I haven't seen her since I arrived here."

"That's so sad. You must miss her."

He stuffed a hand in his pocket, his expression unreadable. "I miss her, but not what she stood for, and I especially don't care for the head of her family."

"Her father?"

"Not exactly. More like a family patriarch, a man who rules with an iron fist. He made the laws and forced everyone to follow them or they were cast out, shunned . . . disgraced. My mother knew no other way of life, so she did what he wanted."

"Couldn't you write her or go back to visit her? Surely it's possible you can stay in touch?"

Theo grabbed her hand and steered her toward a bright hallway filled with more bulletin boards covered with photos. "I don't want to talk about it right now. Dad's waiting in his room."

* * *

Elise placed her pen on the desk blotter and stared at the column of numbers parading down Suited for Change's profit and loss statement; she'd been studying it for the last half hour. She'd already said good-bye to her final client of the day, then straightened the fitting rooms, righted the storage areas, and realigned the shoe boxes. She still had no idea where Zoë had found those size eleven Ferragamos for Marjorie Barris, but had to admit it wasn't unusual for the ingenious designer to unearth the perfect pair of pumps or handbag at the exact moment they were necessary.

When she started her day, she'd prayed Zoë would stop by. She needed an understanding friend who would listen to her concerns and give an opinion without being pushy or making her feel stupid. Then common sense took hold and she realized her pal was probably with Theo Maragos. Any woman lucky enough to have a guy like Theo in their clutches—and she meant that in the nicest of ways—would be a fool to ignore him on her weekend off, and Zoë was no fool.

Too bad the same couldn't be said of her.

Sighing, Elise leaned back in her chair and went over last night's "nondate" for the thousandth time. When Chad Thomas first arrived at her office, she'd been incensed. To her credit, she'd managed to act intelligent and well-adjusted for the entire evening, even though he repeatedly quizzed her on what he'd done to upset her during their so-called business meeting.

But how could she tell him she'd thought he was gay, especially after Zoë insisted she was wrong? She'd put him off by accepting his invitation to the Museum of Modern Art, because the night's exhibit featured the lesser known works of one of her favorite artists, Rodilan.

Then he'd smoothly gotten her to agree to drinks at a little bar within walking distance of MoMA. That led to a cab ride to the Village, where they'd eaten a quiet dinner in an intimate bistro with excellent food and service, something it seemed Chad naturally expected and, just as naturally, received.

He'd kept a dialogue of witty banter going throughout the evening, but even the lulls in their conversation seemed relaxed and genuine. And when they finally ran out of things to talk about and left the restaurant, he'd smoothly given the taxi driver her address from memory, as if doing so was as familiar to him as taking a breath.

The more he spoke, the more she realized he was a man who admired art, literature, fine food, and fashion, as much as he enjoyed cartoons, ball park hot dogs, and perusing the Internet. A fasci-

nating mix of couture and comic relief, he'd capti-
vated her with his witty observations and pointed
questions. There was just one itty-bitty thing that
had bothered her.

Unlike their first encounter, there'd been no ar-
gument last night over whether he'd come in for a
drink . . . and no reason to accuse him of trying to
hit on her. Instead, Chad walked her up the stairs
to her apartment, opened her door, and kissed her
hand. His farewell still echoed in her mind.

"Good night, Elise. Thanks for giving me the
chance to show you I'm not such a bad guy."

She'd stood in the hallway for a full five minutes after he left before she understood what he'd
done.

The sneaky bastard.

Fisting her hands in her hair, she called herself
a dozen kinds of stupid. What the heck was wrong
with her? First, she was annoyed that Chad had
tried to get her alone, and now she was ticked because he'd been a perfect gentleman. A sane women
would give her eye teeth for a guy that consider-
ate. If anyone was a sneak, it was her, finding a
dozen different ways to make it seem as if he were
the one with the problem.

Not that it mattered. Now that they'd firmed
up the particulars on what Marasoft was willing
to do for her company, she would probably never

see him again in anything more than a business setting

A rush of air swept through her office, and she realized someone had walked into the lobby. Darn if she hadn't forgotten to flip the Closed sign in the window and lock the front door again. Opening her desk drawer, she grabbed her can of mace. No matter how safe the city had become in recent years, a woman alone was always at risk, and more so in her line of work. Angry ex-husbands rarely entered the picture, but she'd fielded her share of phone calls from men who weren't happy she was helping their "woman" make a new life without them.

"Hello. Anyone here? Elise?"

She let out a breath when she recognized Chad's deep voice. Then her heart rate accelerated and her stomach did a flip. Hands shaking, she slipped the mace back into the drawer and straightened her hair. Chad entered the room, and she took in his leather bomber jacket, black sweater, and snug, faded jeans. He looked like an ad for Ralph Lauren, casual and elegant at the same time.

"I'm glad you're still here," he said, a grin warming his handsome face. "Do you have to work tonight, or can I talk you into being free?"

Though well aware that last minute dates were an automatic turn-down for any savvy single woman, she'd already agreed she was a fool. Besides, she wanted to see him alone again.

"I'm about to call it a day."

He held up two tickets. At least, she thought they were tickets.

"Bono."

"I though Sonny Bono was no longer with us."

Quirking a corner of his mouth, he raised a brow. "The lead singer of U2. The group's performing at a charity benefit later tonight, and I thought you might join me for dinner, then take in the show."

She opened and closed her mouth. "I read somewhere the performance was sold out."

"I know a man."

"You do?"

He stepped to the side of her desk, still grinning. "And he owed me a favor."

"He did?" Okay, foolish was one thing, but stupid, well, that was definitely a no-no. "I mean, gee, how nice for you."

"He's a stage manager at the site. Called and asked if I'd accept two front row seats. I know I should have called—"

She always dressed casually on a Saturday. Glancing down at her faded sweater, baggy denim pants, and ratty sneakers, she realized today's clothes better suited cleaning out a garage than a night on the town. Her gaze strayed to the coa-track holding her weather-beaten rain coat with the torn flannel lining. "This isn't a professional day, so I'm not exactly dressed for an evening out. Is there time to change?"

"Not necessary. You're beautiful in whatever you wear." He edged around the desk and took her hand. "Besides, if you don't accept, I'll be forced to invite my younger sister, and that's a damned embarrassing thing for a single man to do."

Elise couldn't help but smile. "Okay, but I'm buying dinner."

Theo's heart thumped a nervous tattoo as he and Zoë followed the corridor to his dad's two-room apartment. This meeting could run like the perfect program or crash like a string of bad code. It all depended on his father's mood, which was ruled by the tenor of his mind, and that changed from day to day, sometimes even minute to minute.

As far at Theo knew, Peter Maragos had never been an erratic or contrary man, at least not when they first met. Though shocked to see him stand-ing on his apartment doorstep thirteen years ago, his father instantly knew who he was and took him in without so much as a blink of his bright blue eyes.

Theo had arrived in Michigan angry, confused,

and scared to death. His dad had calmed him down, straightened him out, and eventually convinced him they should live together. Over the years, they formed a bond of trust and respect. But whenever they discussed the past or spoke the name of the woman he'd loved, his father appeared distressed, and so after a while Theo stopped mentioning her. Eventually he managed to forget her existence . . . most of the time.

From the moment they'd become a family, his father had never shown any interest in the opposite sex, and Theo came to realize that his dad was a perfect example of the theory his mother had explained so often. "When a man finds the woman of his heart, my son, he will never desire another."

He stopped at his father's door and glanced at Zoë, who looked as nervous as he felt. "You ready?"

"I guess so." She tucked a strand of hair behind her ear and gave a feeble smile. "I want him to like me."

He grinned. Until that moment she'd always acted self-assured, confident of herself, her beauty, and her appearance. Did she somehow sense how important this meeting was to him? To their future?

"You're perfect. Dad will love you—" *As much*

as I do. Certain that wasn't the right thing to say at this moment, he added, "What man could resist you?"

"I want to make a good impression," she answered. "After all, he is your father."

"Just take a deep breath and be yourself." He raised her hand and kissed her knuckles, then knocked on the door. "Dad, it's Theo. I hope you're decent, because I brought a surprise guest."

When no one answered, he turned the knob and pushed the door inward. "Dad?"

"I'm waiting for my boy," Peter Maragos answered in a hearty tone. "But since you're here, we can talk. Don't get many visitors these days."

His expression wary, Theo glanced at Zoë. "Something tells me this isn't one of his good days."

She smiled encouragement. "No matter. Let's go in."

"Don't just stand there, close the door. You're letting all the heat out," the older man complained in a loud voice. "And be quick about it."

Zoë entered the room alongside Theo, unsure of what she would find, while Theo acted as if he hadn't heard his father mistake him for a stranger.

"Hey, Dad. Sorry I haven't been here in a while. Things are jumping down at headquarters." He introduced Zoë and began an explanation of who she was and what the spread in *NYE* would mean to his career. "I'll bring you a copy of the magazine as soon as it hits the stands."

The older man, sitting in a wing-back chair situated directly across from the television, had listened with interest. Now he peered up at his son, who resembled him right down to his charming dimples, with a frown of dismay.

"It's nice to hear that you're doing so well, young man, but . . . who the hell are you?"

Theo took the comment in stride, crossed the room and handed his dad the plastic bag containing reading material. "I brought you a couple more magazines."

His father set the bag on the table, then tilted his head and focused on Zoë. After a moment his eyes brightened and he stood. "I never could resist a visit from a pretty lady." He clasped Zoë's hand. "Peter Maragos. And you are . . ."

"I'm Zoë. I'm a friend of your son," she answered, ignoring the fact that Theo had just introduced them. He continued to hold her hand while she took in his full head of wavy silver hair. Though taller and more muscular than his father, it was easy to see where Theo got his good looks. "Thanks for inviting us in."

"I don't get a lot of company these days, so it's

not a problem." He narrowed his keen blue eyes. "Do I know you? Have we met before?"

"I don't think so," she began, playing along with his banter. "I'd have remembered."

"I'll put on the kettle for tea," said Theo, walking to the small counter lining the kitchen wall. "Just give me a minute."

"Fine, fine," Peter Maragos muttered, still studying Zoë's face. "I'm sure we've met." He shook his head. "Then again, my memory isn't as good as it used to be. It's damned hard growing old."

He pulled Zoë down next to him on the sofa. "Do you know my son, Theodore? He's a handsome kid, smart as a whip too, but a little on the nerdy side. Just turned eighteen. He'll be attending my alma mater in the fall on a full scholarship."

Zoë locked gazes with Theo and he shrugged, as if to say, *Roll with it*.

"You must be very proud of him."

"That I am." He blinked, then stared at their entwined fingers. "I'll miss him the most, when I die. Even more than I'll miss his mother."

Zoë felt herself choking up. "Where is his mother? Maybe we could arrange for the two of you to meet."

He heaved a heavy sigh. "Can't ever go back, not to that cursed place." Peter set his hands on his knees. "It doesn't exist, not anymore."

The kettle whistled, and Zoë waited while Theo poured the steaming water into mugs and carried them to the small kitchen table. Rifling through a cupboard at warp speed, he found a bag of cookies and brought them to his seat.

"Tea's ready," he announced, as if he did so every day. "Dad, why don't you escort the lady to a chair."

Peter rose and took Zoë's arm, his actions relaxed. Arriving at the table, he said, "Here you go, young lady," and glanced at the cookies, then Theo. "Chocolate chip, my favorite. Where did you find them?"

"In the pantry. I brought them on my last visit," Theo reminded him.

"You did?" He studied his son's face. "You look just like your mother, you know that?"

Theo's cheeks colored a bright pink. "I look like you, Dad. Except I'm taller."

"Maybe so." Directing his gaze at Zoë, Peter bit into a cookie and chewed. "You here to visit Mindy Rooter? She told me her daughter'd be by today."

Zoë placed her hand on his. "We came to see you, Mr. Maragos. Theo's told me so much about you."

"If he's told you so much, why isn't he here?" He crossed his arms, leaned back in his chair and thrust out his lower lip, acting more like a pouting three-year-old than a grown man. "Darned kid never stops to say hello." After a moment dimples again creased his cheeks. "I swear we've met somewhere before."

"You have a beautiful apartment," Zoë said, deftly changing the subject. "This is my first trip to New Jersey."

"Mine too. Lived in Michigan my entire life, until Theo moved me here." His brows met over the bridge of his nose. "But someday I'm going back to Greece to find the woman I love, then things will be different. We'll be a family, the way it was meant to be."

Sighing, Theo gave Zoë a hesitant smile, then said to his father, "If you really want to go back, we could take a vacation together, see the sights, lay on the beach. I'd do it if you really wanted to, you know that, don't you?"

Peter jumped to his feet, his eyes sharp with panic as he pushed from the table. "You can't go there. Ever. I forbid it." Stomping to the sitting area, he muttered a string of nonsense. "Damned pagan. Son of a bitch. Ruined my life, but he won't ruin my son's. If I ever see him again, I'm gonna choke the bastard with my own hands."

"Dad. Take it easy." Theo rose and went to his

father's side. "You don't have to go back, and neither do I. We'll stay here, and everything will be okay."

His shoulders heaving, Peter turned to his son. "Promise me. Promise me you won't go there. No matter what, you won't go back to them."

"You got it, Pop." He led his father to the side chair and placed his hand on the older man's arm until his breathing returned to normal. "I'll bring your tea, and we'll turn on ESPN. I think they're carrying a basketball game right now—the Knicks and the Spurs. And there's a home game in a week. How about we ride over together, have dinner, and go to the Garden?"

"A Knicks game?" Peter's angry expression morphed to one of rapture. "Damn. I haven't been to a Knicks game in a couple of years. My son used to take me, but he hasn't been by in a while. I love that boy to pieces, but he's too busy to see me, what with him starting college and all."

"How about if I call him and invite him to come along?" Theo suggested, his voice a gentle cadence of sound. "I have great seats, so you won't miss a thing."

The love and compassion shining in Theo's eyes made Zoë's heart ache so badly it was difficult for her to sit and do nothing. She went to the kitchen, retrieved their tea, and set the mugs on coasters on the coffee table. "Here you are, Mr. Maragos. Enjoy."

"That's Pete to you, honey. Just plain Pete." He picked up his tea and took a swallow, then wrapped his hands around the cup and gazed at the liquid as if reading the contents. Raising his head, he grinned at his son. "This tastes great, Theo. Good to know you still remember how I like my tea."

Chapter 11

Theo exhaled as he took the exit for the George Washington Bridge, his quickest route back to Manhattan from New Jersey, relieved the day was almost over. Glancing to his right, he smiled at Zoë, curled up like a sleeping kitten in the passenger seat. The lights glowing overhead whipped past, casting shadows across her wide forehead, patrician nose, kissable lips, and gently rounded chin.

She'd been a real trouper today, sitting through three hours of professional basketball while dealing with his father's disjointed thoughts and rambling conversation. She'd even listened intently when his dad repeated words or changed topics at lightning speed. And when he made coherent comments, Zoë nodded encouragement, asked questions, and gave compliments as if she'd known Peter Maragos her entire life.

She'd even agreed to have dinner at his father's favorite diner. Luckily, his dad had been his most lucid while they were in public, and only needed minimal assistance with the menu and seating.

Now, past ten o'clock, Theo imagined she was more exhausted than he was, and why not? These confusing and often frustrating visits were his burden, not Zoë's, and he was certain she'd never experienced anything like them. By charming his dad, she'd won his own heart completely. He'd spent a lifetime searching for his soul mate, fearful he would never find someone he could confide in and, most important, who would accept his father, no matter the condition of his mind or his body.

Since meeting Zoë, he'd battled with his emotions, even when the cursed ring made a case in her favor. This afternoon he'd turned a corner, come to a life-altering decision, and vowed to see it through. From this point on, no matter what happened, Zoë was the only woman he would ever love.

Another grin sprang to his lips when he thought about taking her home. The faster he got to her hotel, the faster he could lay beside her in bed, hold her in his arms, and make the world disappear.

Aware he had to reveal his feelings before she left for her family reunion, Theo took another deep breath, pondering how to approach the subject. Long ago, he'd made up his mind that honesty was the best policy if he ever found the woman of his heart. Now that he had, he hoped she would believe the impossibility of his past, understand his insecurities and concerns, and accept him and his situation completely.

But what to reveal first? Should he confess that he loved her more than he'd ever thought it possible to love another human being? Or should he explain his true parentage, tell her who—what—he was? How could he admit that he'd been born in a place so removed from earth, so implausible, that he wouldn't blame her if she laughed in his face and told him he belonged in an asylum?

With no clear answer to the dilemma, he concentrated on maneuvering the sedan through the crowded streets, until he heard Zoë yawn.

"Are we home yet?" she asked, stretching her arms out in front of her.

"Almost. I'll return the car and we can take a taxi to your suite." Realizing he'd just invited himself to spend the night with her again, he gave himself a mental slap upside the head. They'd yet to establish the tenor of their relationship, and here he was automatically assuming Zoë would want him in her bed. "If that's okay with you."

She swiveled in the seat, her grin wide. "It's

more than okay. But you might want to stop at your place for a change of clothes. That way we can take our time in the morning, have a late breakfast, maybe even go for a walk if the weather's good."

Relief washed over him at her suggestion, put in a casual yet sincere manner. "Good idea. I'll drive to the loft first, then bring back the car, and we can take it from there." His cell phone rang, and he guided the car to the curb while fumbling to answer it. "Theo here."

The caller sounded agitated, so he sat back in his seat and stayed calm and in control. After his top salesman finished spouting a litany of concerns, he said, "Look, it's not a big deal . . . get Peterson or that new guy—what's his name, Frank?—to take care of it. He's supposed to be a crack troubleshooter."

The salesman's next outburst, more frantic than the last, set Theo's teeth on edge.

"I know I wrote the code," he replied, "but we hired those guys to handle the problems . . . Crap . . . Okay, okay, take it easy. I'll get to work on it ASAP."

Muttering a string of curses, he decided his next step in product development would be to set up an extended troubleshooting clinic and require every salesman and technician to participate.

"Has something happened?" Zoë asked when he disconnected the call.

He took her hand. "Apparently a customer is having difficulty with a series of modules and the men on duty haven't been able to pinpoint the glitch. Since I'm the author of the code, they believe I'm the only one who can fix it."

"Can't it wait until Monday morning?"

"I wish. But the company in question is running a recovery test at midnight, and this data is vital to its success." He pulled away from the curb, heading toward Zoë's hotel. "I built my business on customer satisfaction, so we'd stand head and shoulders above the competition. If I go back on my promise of providing exemplary service and word gets out, it could compromise the IPO."

Zoë grabbed her handbag from the floor and set it on her lap. "I understand, and it's not a problem. Take me home and get the job done. I'd rather you make things right than worry all night."

No doubt about it, the woman was a gem. "You're sure you don't mind?"

"I know how important launching the IPO is to your future. Besides, I'm being selfish. If you take care of it now, we won't be interrupted tomorrow, which means I'll have you all to myself."

When he pulled in front of the Trump Tower, he swiveled in his seat and captured her face in his hand. "What did I ever do to deserve you in my life?"

Zoë gave a strange half smile, started to speak, then heaved a sigh. Suddenly, her eyes glittered with tears. "Watching you care for your father today showed me exactly what a great guy you are. I'm lucky to have met you, and I'll never—"

"Hey hey, no fair going weepy on me. I love my dad, therefore I see to his needs, just as he's seen to mine."

"But you're so patient, so understanding with him. You act as if nothing's changed between you, when it's obvious he's not always in control of his mind or his faculties." She clutched his fingers. "I don't think I'd be that brave if my parent had such an illness."

"From the way you handled Dad today, my guess is you would." He leaned closer and brushed her lips with his. "We'll talk in the morning. Go to sleep and dream of me, because I'll be dreaming of you."

Her smile faded and she swiped at a tear. "Come over for breakfast. We can spend the day in bed."

"Is that a promise?"

"A promise." The valet opened the car door and she got out. "Until tomorrow."

"Early night, Ms. Degodessa?" the concierge asked as Zoë passed his station in the hotel lobby.

"Yes, but I've had a long day," she replied, giving the man a smile. Long and insightful, she decided as she headed for the elevator. Theo's kind words rang in her head. How *would* she treat a mother or father who became ill or infirm? Thanks to Hera and her jealousy, she and the other muses had little experience with a loving mother, and Zeus was less than an ideal father. She'd never had a role model, someone who cared for her the way Peter Maragos had cared for his child.

Until today she'd thought Theo an admirable human being, brilliant as well as fun, but his role as a loyal and loving son had won her over completely. She doubted there was another mortal like him on the planet, and there definitely was no god to compare.

Soon she would be on Mount Olympus, while Theo was here waiting for her return. Time would pass, and she was certain he'd try to reach her, but what would he do when he realized she was gone for good? There had to be some way to tell him the truth and make him understand why she couldn't stay.

"Zoë, wait!"

She turned at the sound of her name, then blinked in case her eyes were deceiving her. Was the petite blonde skittering across the lobby really Elise?

Elise gasped for breath as she placed a hand on Zoë's arm. "I'm so happy I found you. I called your suite from the cab, and when you didn't answer, I thought that maybe you were with Theo. You did have a date with him, correct?"

"We went to New Jersey to visit his—oh, never mind, it doesn't matter. Not that I'm unhappy to see you, but it's late and—" Elise's face was flushed and her eyes red. "What happened? Are you sick? Did somebody die?"

Elise dabbed at a tear, then bit her trembling lower lip. "No, nothing like that. I just needed to talk to someone, and you were the first person I thought of."

"Do you want to go to the bar for a drink or—"

"Could we go to your room, where it's private?" Her shoulders drooped as she gazed around the lobby. "I don't want to make a fool of myself in front of all these strangers."

"Sure, fine." Zoë punched the call button as she surveyed Elise's pinched expression. "Are you hungry? Do you need to eat? Are you sure nobody died?"

"Yes, I'm sure," Elise answered, her smile hesitant. "It's not a tragedy, at least not in the way you're thinking."

Tragedy? They entered the elevator and Zoë selected her floor, disturbed by Elise's vague explanation and disheartened manner. "Okay, but once we get to my room, I want to hear everything, because you've got me worried."

Elise sniffed, and Zoë decided to give her friend time to compose herself. In the suite, she hung up their coats and turned on a few lights, then went to the bar area and opened the fridge. "How about a soft drink? Bottled water? A glass of wine?"

"Water," said Elise. "And ice, if you have it."

Zoë fixed them identical drinks and brought their glasses to the table. Sitting down, she passed Elise a tumbler, then raised her own in a toast. "Here's to good friends," she said. "And trust."

Elise swallowed half the drink in one gulp. Setting the glass on a coaster, she sighed. "I'm sorry. I shouldn't have come. It's late, and you probably have a ton of things to take care of before you go to your family reunion."

Crossing her arms, Zoë leaned back and shifted to face her friend. "Oh, no, you don't. You're not leaving until I've heard what's got you so rattled. Now talk."

Her expression grim, Elise speared her fingers through her curls as she heaved another sigh. Then she adopted Zoë's pose. "I sort of had a date tonight."

"That's great . . . wait, what do you mean, 'sort of'?"

"It was a spur of the moment kind of thing, rather than a formal 'would you like to go out with me' invitation," she explained, then shrugged. "Now that I think about it, it was more like a hit and run."

"Hit and run? You're not making any sense. Start at the beginning, why don't you?"

"I was at Suited for Change, finishing up for the day, when he strutted into the office as if he owned it. He had tickets to U2, and you know how much I like Bono."

"I know, and who's 'he'?"

"That's the bad part."

"Bad? Was it your ex?"

"Not that bad." Elise sat up straight. "It was Chad."

"Chad Thomas?"

"Do you know another Chad, because I sure don't."

"Wow, things have certainly happened fast. Last I heard, you'd been rude to him, and he hated you."

"I apologized for that, and he ended up taking me to the Museum of Modern Art, then drinks and dinner at a darling restaurant in the Village."

"Wait, I thought it was U2."

"We went to MoMA and the Village last night. Tonight was U2 and Bono, after another dinner."

"Hmm, dinner and a fun time two evenings in a row. Sounds serious." She held back a grin when Elise nodded. "Was it romantic?"

"The word pales in comparison to what I felt by the end of the night. It started out nice, no pressure, just lots of small talk and banter, mostly about our families, our past . . . my divorce."

"Oh."

"Chad didn't pry, I offered. I mentioned the cheating thing, but not the gay thing, so he still doesn't know what I first suspected about him."

"And why not?"

"Why not?"

"Elise, that was a big part of why you treated him the way you did. He's probably still wondering what he did to make you think he was a serial killer."

"I didn't treat him like that last night or tonight." Her cheeks turned pink. "Not by a long shot."

"You kissed him!"

Her blush deepened to scarlet and she scowled. "Kiss him? Hah! I practically jumped his bones in the hall. I can't believe I acted so—so needy."

Zoë recalled her own attempt at seducing Theo and smiled. "Tell me every detail."

"Things moved so fast, I'm not sure if I can." She drew her brows together, thinking. "He leaned toward me as if he was going to kiss my cheek, and before I knew what I was doing, I closed the distance and started sucking on him like a shop vac. When he backed me up against the door, I couldn't control myself. I was sinking, drowning in lust, and so was he. At least it felt that way."

"Felt that way?" Zoë giggled and held her hands a foot apart. "Do you mean 'that way'?"

"I'm a tramp. I'd have done it with him there in the hall, and he knew it."

"And . . ."

"And nothing."

"Nothing?"

"After I stepped back, he stared at me as if I were a two-headed puppy. Then he blinked a couple of times, said, 'Good night, Elise,' and walked away as calm as could be."

Zoë sipped her water. It sounded like a replay of the night Theo had left her high and dry at her suite door. What the heck was up with these modern mortals? "Maybe he thought things were moving too fast. Or that you weren't ready for more."

"Not ready?" She shook her head. "He'd be an idiot to think that. I was as close to orgasm as I've ever been with my clothes on—you know what I mean . . . don't you?"

"I guess so."

She heaved a sigh. "I'm telling you he was all over me, had his hands inside my coat, under my sweater, down the back of my pants. It was . . . I've never reacted to a man's touch like that before."

"It sounds wonderful, not awful."

"Actually, it scared me senseless. Chad was moaning the whole time he had his tongue down my throat, as if he were eating the world's best tasting dessert." Elise closed her eyes. "My ex never, ever, was that hot for me. And no one else that I can remember either."

Zoë grinned. "Ooo-kay. So what's the problem?"

"The problem is, he left me standing there like a dope. An unfulfilled dope, I might add. I stood in the hall a full ten minutes, praying he'd change his mind and come back, but he didn't. I was so keyed up I couldn't imagine falling asleep, so I came here, hoping to see you."

"And you found me." Zoë was happy for Elise, provided Chad wasn't leading her on. "I told you he wasn't gay," she said smugly.

Elise *hmmphed*. "All right, I confess, your gaydar is up and running, and mine's out for repair. Now what do I do?"

"That's easy," Zoë said, raising a brow. "You wait."

"I what?"

"Wait. Like I did for—" Theo, she almost said. "If he's serious, he'll come around. Just give him time."

"Darn. I was afraid you might say that."

"Do you want to have a relationship with him?"

"I—I—" She huffed out a breath. "Maybe."

"Elise, be honest with yourself, and with Chad. If you don't want to be with him—"

"I guess I do. But I'm still scared. Relationship means commitment. I had one of those, and it was a huge disappointment. How can I be sure this is the right thing to do? What if he's just playing me in retaliation for my rudeness? That would suck."

"It would, but if you really feel the way you do, you owe it to yourself—to the both of you—to see where it goes. Date him, but keep your head on straight. At least until you're sure of his intentions."

"Is that what you're doing with Theo?" Elise asked after taking a swallow of water.

What *was* she doing with Theo? She didn't want to string him along, but Zoë knew there never could be anything between them. "I—We—We're enjoying each other. I can't let it go any further than that. I'm leaving, remember?"

"But you'll return eventually, right? Greece is just a plane flight away. Even if you can't move back here permanently for a while, he can fly out or you can fly in for a weekend."

"We haven't discussed it."

"Well, you'd better start discussing it. You're scheduled to leave in a few days. At least let him drive you to the airport, and invite him to visit you when he can."

"I don't think that will be possible," Zoë said, her heart aching more with each passing second. How could she give advice to Elise when her own life was in turmoil? "Enough about me and Theo. It's late. Do you think you can fall asleep now?"

Elise set her hands on her knees. "Yeah, sure, and thanks."

"All I did was listen."

"And made sense out of my rattled emotions." Both women stood, and Elise wrapped Zoë in a hug. "I owe you one, girlfriend. And I'm here for you too. Remember that."

Zoë walked Elise to the foyer and retrieved her coat. "I'll be in Tuesday morning. I have one last client appointment, and I won't let Rita Hepner down."

"You're a busy woman, and I appreciate all you've done for Suited for Change, and for me. Thanks again." She slipped out the door with a wave and a resigned smile.

As Zoë slid the lock home, her cell phone rang. Groaning, she hurried into the living room and searched her tote bag. When she saw the number on caller ID, she rolled her eyes. How could she have forgotten her weekly chat with Kyra and Chloe a second time?

"Hey, sorry I wasn't here earlier," she said into the phone as she plopped on the couch. "I was on a—I was out."

"Did you have a date?" asked Kyra.

"Not exactly," Zoë lied.

"Were you with a man?" Chloe prodded, cutting to the chase.

Zoë bit her lower lip. "If you must know, yes."

"That sounds promising," said Kyra. "Who was it?"

"My latest private client, the computer guy who's getting that big magazine spread in *New York Entrepreneur*."

"Have you slept with him yet?" Chloe demanded.

"That's none of your business," Zoë snapped. Then she softened her tone. "Sorry, now that our return is getting down to the wire, I'm a little on edge."

"Aren't we all," Chloe pronounced. "Personally, I can't wait for this year to be over."

"Me too," muttered Kyra. "I take it everyone's planning to return in triumph? Both of you have done everything within your power to fulfill your mission?"

"Of course," said Zoë.

"Absolutely," Chloe chimed at the same time.

"Me too," Kyra added.

But Zoë didn't think either sister sounded convincing. "And we're all safe on the 'no falling in love with a mortal' front, correct?"

"Um, sure," Kyra answered.

"Yes, me too," Chloe promised. "I'm just sitting around wishing happiness to whoever shows up at Castleberry Hall, while I bide my time."

"I'm in the middle of that singing contest. I don't have a free second for love," Kyra reminded them. "But, Zoë, you still haven't said if you slept with your client."

She bit her lower lip. Lying had never been her strong suit. "I'll tell you all about it once we're home and there's time to gossip. I'm sure everyone will want to know what we did for amusement while we were down here." She yawned. "It's almost midnight. If I don't get to sleep, I'm going to fall down."

"I'm beat too, but I need to tell you both one more thing," said Chloe. "I love you, and I can't wait to see you on Mount Olympus. We're going to kick some major butt."

"Ditto for me," added Kyra. "To the love thing and kicking butt. 'Bye for now, and I'll see you in a week."

"I love the both of you too," echoed Zoë. "See you in a week."

Frustrated, she disconnected the call and inhaled a few calming breaths. She'd just fibbed to the two women in her life who meant the most to her. She was a rotten sister. A fraud. But if she'd told them any more about Theo, she could have let slip that she'd slept with him, which might have led to a different sort of revelation.

How could she tell them about Theo Maragos when she didn't have the faintest idea of her true feelings? She'd never loved a man before, be he god or mortal, and she wasn't about to start now. Yes, she was fond of Theo. She enjoyed being with him, was definitely thrilled when they were in bed together, and was just as happy when they were sitting side by side talking.

But that certainly wasn't love.

How disconcerting that she had plenty of advice to offer Elise but not a single sensible thought for herself. She shrugged, acknowledging a smaller fib. The nap she'd taken on the car ride home had renewed her energy. Like Elise, she doubted she could fall asleep with the questions and pent-up emotions whizzing through her head.

Snuggling into the sofa cushions, she hit the TV remote, hoping to find a show that would take her mind off Elise, her sisters, and her dilemma, and flipped to her favorite channel. There, on the screen, was the mortal with whom she'd had her greatest success to date, icing a tiered wedding cake in her television kitchen.

Zoë lost herself in Martha's voice, let the woman's accomplished words soothe her as the decorating maven extolled the joys of a perfect confectionary creation.

Though Zeus disagreed, Martha was still the best in the business, even with her stock trading problems and that little stint in prison. She'd even managed to make wearing a homing device around her ankle a fashion statement.

From here on out, Zoë told herself, she was going to be like Martha after her incarceration. She'd throw back her shoulders and plow through her last week on earth without a care, taking what Theo had to offer while keeping her eyes on her goal.

She'd had a banner year. Her elegant store windows had inspired thousands of New Yorkers, and they were hard to please. Theo Maragos was a job, just like any other. He needed to be educated in both fashion and design, and she'd done that to the best of her ability. The *NYE* photo shoot was scheduled for next Friday.

Success was within her reach, and she intended to attain it, no matter what.

Chapter 12

TO: Zdegodessa@TT.com
FROM: Topgod@mounto.org
SUBJECT: ???????????

It is apparent you are ignoring my correspon-
dence. I can only assume you are engaged in some
form of mortal hanky-panky and are NOT attending to the business at hand. Missing further up-
dates will be held against you. NOW would be a
good time to explain your inability to communi-
cate. Remember, I am watching.

Sincerely,

Zeus

Your father (and still Top God)

Zoë drummed her fingers on the desk, then stuck out her tongue and shot the monitor a raspberry. She'd always been the understanding daughter, the one who gave Zeus the benefit of the doubt whenever his crankiness rose to the fore. But here he was, acting like a pompous old goat, treating her as he did every other disrespectful muse. He'd been nagging her for an entire year about her duty and job performance. Now that it was crunch time, did he think she had nothing better to do than send him a minute by minute report?

And thanks to this infernal machine, there was no escaping his bothersome questions. Zeus claimed the invention was a boon to Mount Olympus and the world. He bragged to all the gods, promising that the Internet would be their entry into the new millennium. He doted on computers; swore they were the dawn of a new era in every way. Maybe that was so, but to her, they were nothing but a damned nuisance.

Positive she'd sent him a status report only twenty-four hours ago, she narrowed her gaze and inspected the messages in her Sent folder. According to the records, she hadn't contacted him in over a week. What had happened to the note she wrote him yesterday? Was the missive lost forever or floating somewhere in cyberspace?

Tapping a finger to her chin, she recalled that just before she'd sent the e-mail, Theo interrupted her. Her heart fluttered at the memory of what the interruption had led to, and she breathed a sigh of girlish hope. If only it were possible for she and Theo to share thousands of mornings in the same erotic manner, her life would be idyllic, almost perfect . . . complete.

Their entire day had been so fulfilling, she even accepted that Theo had to work last night. He was an important man, head of a company other businesses depended upon for the running of their contrary computer systems. The diabolical machines were his livelihood, his future, his dream. Theo was a mortal with his fingers on the pulse of the IT industry, someone who knew all there was to know about databases, electronic inter-whatsis, giga-thingies, and . . . and all that other distasteful techno *stuff.*

Someday he would be a leader in the industry. A man others looked up to, admired . . . strived to imitate. A man any woman, be they goddess or mortal, would be proud to call her own.

Still, she couldn't imagine how Marasoft's promising future could aid in her quest for glory. Yes, her father was enthralled by the very business in which Theo excelled, but at the moment, Zeus was fixated on her goal. If he thought she was slacking off, wasting time daydreaming about a mortal instead of doing her duty, it wouldn't matter how many humans' lives she improved while living here. She needed proof of her ability to inspire, and a spread in *New York Entrepreneur* was the only way to state her case.

Fingers poised over the keyboard, she began to type.

TO: *Topgod@mounto.org*
FROM: *zdegoessa@tt.com*
SUBJECT: *???????????*

Father: Forgive my inattention to your notes. I'm in the middle of an important assignment, one that will attest without question to my ability to inspire in my field. I shall relate the details on my return to Mount Olympus. In the meantime, please be patient with your daughter.

                          Sincerely,
                              Zoë
                    Muse of Beauty

Satisfied she'd done her best to hold Zeus at bay, she crossed her fingers and pressed the Send key. There was little else she could do to placate the father god when he was in one of his snits. She imagined that as time neared for her, Chloe, and Kyra to return to their mountaintop home, he would grow as restless and impatient as they did. If he accepted her apology, his next e-mail would contain instructions for their return trip, and little else.

After giving the computer screen a finger-flipping farewell, Zoë pushed away from the desk, ready to prepare for her day. It was then she noticed a huge shadow hovering over her computer station, rising to cover the wall behind it and encompassing her in a veil of darkness.

Seconds passed as a chill crept up her spine. A powerful deity had entered her room, but the intruding god or goddess was unfamiliar. Even so, the imposing presence surrounded her, filled her, and wanted her to know it was there . . . watching and waiting for her reaction.

Vowing to remain calm, she straightened in her chair. Whoever the being was, it would not find her trembling in fear. Though muses were considered lesser deities, they were also daughters of Zeus, immortals with powers of their own, and though she was on earth as a punishment of sorts, she still had her dignity.

Ingrained in the citizens of Mount Olympus was a hierarchy, and each god knew the pecking order. This A-list presence could be one of Zeus's current favorites, or a Titan, one of the oldest of deities, even though they'd been overthrown by the top god eons ago. Whoever it was, they deserved respect whenever they appeared.

With her eyes open and her head erect, she turned her chair to face the room. Her gaze traveled from daintily sandaled feet, up the curve of well-muscled yet feminine legs, to a softly swirling chiton comprised of a sheer and delicate fabric.

The flowing chiton swelled over firm thighs and rounded hips, and indented to a trim waist encircled by a belt woven of purest gold. The cords parted and traced up the goddess's stomach, crossed at her ribs, and cupped the fullness of her bountiful breasts, then trailed over her shoulders to her back. From there, they disappeared, overshadowed by a pair of snow white wings made of feathers tipped in gold.

Zoë opened her mouth in awe. Aware that it would be foolish to trivialize a visit from a warrior goddess, she slid from the chair, dropped to one knee and bowed her head. "Nike," she said when she caught her breath. "It is an honor."

She felt rather than saw the figure shrink to normal size. The scent of roses filled the air, then a touch as soft and gentle as a butterfly wing brushed her shoulder. "Rise, daughter of Zeus, and have no fear, for I have come in peace."

Zoë's brain worked at lightning speed. Nike was as old as Zeus, a goddess of battle and victory. Her father was Pallas, a superior fighter; her mother Styx, the goddess of hatred; and her sisters Strength, Force, and Rivalry. Nike herself was a favored charioteer of the mighty Zeus and a fearless leader of his minions.

What was she doing in New York City? What did she want with a mere muse?

"My lady," Zoë continued. "How may I serve you?"

Nike's smile dimpled her cheeks; the warmth flowing from her ruby lips flooded the room. Her blue eyes brightened as she folded her glorious wings and crossed her arms under her breasts. "Would you believe me if I told you I was in the neighborhood and thought to drop in for tea?"

Zoë stifled a giggle. She'd never been in the powerful goddess's presence for more than a moment, but had heard of her good humor, as well as her fierce temper and righteous demeanor.

"If you say so, my lady, though I would ask what brings you to, ah . . . my neck of the woods?"

Nike appeared to think a moment before answering. "There is much talk on Mount Olympus concerning your assignment here. Since I despise gossip, I decided to investigate and form my own opinion."

"Thank you for that," Zoë responded. At least one god had made it their business to know the truth. Nike would realize the muses were doing their best and relay the situation to the others. "I'm willing to answer all your questions."

"Good. Let's sit, shall we?"

"Certainly. And allow me to offer the tea you mentioned, as well as, uh . . ." She walked to the honor bar, picked up a menu and fumbled through it. "Soda, macadamia nuts, granola bars, chocolate, or . . . or a stronger spirit." She glanced again at the imposing deity, now resting with one muscled arm stretched gracefully along the back of the sofa. "If none of those appeal, I can call room service for anything you might fancy."

"Anything?"

Zoë shrugged. "'Tis the way of mortals who are lucky enough to live in 'the Donald's' world."

"Then perhaps a mojito?"

Zoë blinked in surprise. "A what?"

"A mojito. I enjoyed the libation on a trip to Mexico last summer. It tasted quite refreshing."

Walking to the phone, Zoë dialed the bar and placed a double order for the beverage. It would be impolite not to join Nike in her libation. When finished with the request, she took her place on a chair across from the deity.

The beautiful goddess appeared comfortable

and relaxed, yet curious about her surroundings. "Please, go about your business, muse. I don't want to keep you from your tasks."

"Today is Sunday, a day of rest, my lady. Any tasks I have can wait." Zoë fiddled with the sash of her terry robe. Should she ask the deity what the citizens of Mount Olympus were saying about her, Chloe, and Kyra, or let the goddess lead the conversation? Not wanting to be rude, she asked, "Have you visited my sisters, or am I the only one you chose to observe?"

Nike's gaze reached deep, as if she were trying to see into Zoë's very heart. "Tell me, how are you faring?" she asked, not answering the question. "Will you meet the daunting challenge mighty Zeus presented?"

"I've done my best, as have, I'm certain, Chloe and Kyra," Zoë answered.

"And you've inspired many mortals to beautify their lives?"

"I believe so."

"Tell me about your time here. How did it begin? What is your latest project, the one you feel will solidify your victory?"

Zoë began with an explanation of the windows she'd decorated, noting Nike's nod of approval. "My current task is huge. Being mentioned in an earthly publication of such importance will prove without a doubt I am able to inspire that for which I was created."

"An admirable end to the father god's challenge," Nike proclaimed. "You should be proud."

When the Greeks defeated the Persians in 490 B.C., Nike was given credit for aiding them in their fight. It was said she thought of every challenge as a battle, with only victory or defeat as the outcome. No wonder she viewed Zeus's ultimatum as a challenge.

Before Zoë could answer, there was a knock at the door. She rose and allowed the waiter to push a trolley carrying glasses and a pitcher filled with a pale green liquid into the room. After signing the tab, she wheeled the trolley to the sofa, took a seat, and poured each of them a drink.

The warrior goddess accepted her mojito and raised the goblet high. "Here's to your future as a liberated muse."

Zoë had no idea why the goddess thought she should be liberated, but touched her glass to Nike's all the same. "To my future."

The liquid tasted of lime and mint, with a sweet tang that left no doubt to its potency. And potent spirits were not something Zoë tolerated well. Still, refusing to join the goddess would be disrespectful; even worse, insulting.

Nike downed her portion in one long gulp.

"Ah, what a wonderful way to meet new friends," she said, licking her full lips. "Don't you agree?"

Zoë took a second sip, then smiled. She would move up in the pecking order if a mighty goddess claimed her as a friend. "It is a refreshing drink." Setting her glass on the table, she brought the pitcher to Nike and refilled her glass. Then she sat and attempted to relax. If only she knew the actual reason for this visit.

"So," Nike continued, "tell me more about your latest project, the one that will secure your victory."

"It's been fun, as much as a challenge," Zoë said, putting the quest in perspective.

Nike's smile again showed her charming dimples. "To win a challenge is to be victorious, don't you agree?"

"I imagine so, though Zeus said he is only insisting we do that for which we were created."

The deity waved a hand. "Go on."

"I'm working for a man—a mortal with much influence in the modern world. At least, he will be an influence as his company grows. And once the magazine is out, every person in the city will be inspired by my flair and style."

"Who is this wonderful mortal?"

"His name is Theodore Maragos—"

"Then he is Greek?" Nike interrupted, her nostrils flaring.

"I believe so."

The goddess again waved her hand. "Continue."

"*New York Entrepreneur* is going to name him one of Manhattan's ten most important new businessmen."

"And this is an accomplishment mortals consider impressive?"

"According to Theo, yes."

"Theo, is it?" Nike raised a brow. "Then you have become his . . . friend?"

Heat rose to Zoë's cheeks at the deity's pronunciation of the word. Did she know of her and Theo's relationship? Why would she care? Unless she was a spy . . . but a spy for whom?

"We have a business arrangement, nothing more."

"He does well, this Theo?"

"He will, yes, once his company goes public on the NASDAQ."

"The naz-dak?" Nike parroted, drawing out the syllables. "What type of venue is that?"

"It's one of the mortal ways to measure a company's success. I predict that, someday, Theo will stand head and shoulders above other men in his field."

The goddess gave a curt nod, as if satisfied with the statement. "I have one more question, then I must leave." Tipping back her head, she drank the last of her mojito and set down the empty glass. "Do you consider Theo Maragos to be an admirable man?"

Zoë couldn't help but grin. Hadn't she just come to the conclusion that Theo was a man among men? A human who outshined the gods? "He is hardworking and intelligent. He's also kind and thoughtful. He cares deeply for his ailing father and sees to his every need while still managing to guide an entire company. He is more than admirable. He is . . . perfect."

Nike's expression flitted from pleased to puzzled in an instant.

"Did I say something to trouble you?" Zoë asked.

The deity shook her head of flowing honey-gold hair. "Nothing you need worry about, my dear." She stood, and her magnificent wings unfolded behind her. "Thank you for the drink, and the time. I am satisfied you are an honorable muse seeking only what is due her, and I shall report so to anyone on Olympus who asks. Now, I must be off."

Before Zoë could utter farewell, the goddess of victory was gone.

* * *

Theo walked the main aisle between several dozen cubicles holding computers and printers, nodding at the employees working the early shift. He'd spent the entire night untangling a problem created by one of their customer's own technicians. The smartass, who thought he knew more about Marasoft's offerings than they did, had taken it upon himself to rewrite parts of his computer code, which completely screwed things up. After Theo read him the riot act and walked the techie through the recovery process, he promised never to try anything stupid again.

Afterward, Theo decided to hang around and check out the inner workings of his company. Chad was the partner who interfaced with the programmers and sales staff, but now that the new suite of products was finished, Theo figured it was time he became better acquainted with the men and women they employed. He had a gut feeling that once the spread in *NYE* appeared, he would no longer be able to hide behind a computer terminal or use his work as an excuse to stay on the sidelines.

Not that he was a hermit or afraid of people. He simply didn't enjoy the limelight. He didn't need public adulation to prove he had great ideas or a solid product. He left the talking to Chad while he made things happen behind the scenes with his innovative designs.

The word "design" instantly brought Zoë to mind, which caused the ring on his finger to vibrate so hard it felt electrified. He grinned when he recalled her brilliant and stylish ideas, and how simply she'd brought them to fruition. He'd learned more than he thought possible on their daily trips to furniture outlets, fabric houses, and paint stores. He even felt comfortable shopping for clothes, which in the past had left him annoyed or frazzled, or both.

Thanks to Zoë, he now knew enough about color that he'd never combine gray and brown, purple and navy blue, or plaids and polka dots of any kind. But her instruction ran deeper than a lesson in fashion.

She'd taught him all he needed to know about love.

He'd become so used to the heat and tingling on his hand, he sometimes missed the buzz when it was gone, almost as much as he missed having Zoë by his side. All he had to do now was tell her how much she meant to him and ask her to share his life.

Share his life? He gulped at the idea. Growing up, he never thought he'd find a woman who would understand the oddity of his birth and his unbelievable heritage . . . or his miserable excuse for a grandfather. Knowing the man was not truly a blood relation kept him sane, but it didn't help when he recalled the way the dictator had torn his family apart.

While trying to decide if he should call Zoë or wait a while, he wandered into the break room and discovered a fresh pot of coffee and a box of pastry. After helping himself to the coffee, he selected a cheese Danish, set it on a napkin, and brought both to his desk. Chad had left a few suggestions about the IPO, and this was a good time to look at them and give his opinion. As soon as he finished, he'd phone Zoë and invite her to lunch, after which they could spend the rest of the day in her bed. Maybe by then he'd figure a way to explain his past and convince her to join him in the future.

A knock at the door caught his attention and he raised his head.

"You're in the office? On a Sunday morning at . . ." Chad glanced at his watch. ". . . eight o'clock? Let me guess, the end of the world is coming and I missed the announcement."

Theo grinned. "Be prepared, because I'll be here more often once the IPO is announced."

The COO walked in and took a seat. "I'd hoped as much. Rumor has it your presence boosts moral.

I heard a pair of programmers talking on the way here. They were impressed that the 'big boss' actually took the time to come in and personally handle a problem."

"To tell the truth, I wouldn't have, if one of the troubleshooters had been able to fix it."

Chad frowned. "Maybe we should can the guy."

"Fire him?" Theo shook his head. "We need all the bodies we have. Besides, I already gave him a lesson in customer service. I plan to set up a couple of training sessions on how to manage the same glitch if it reoccurs."

"Think you'll have time to do that?"

"Time? Sure, I will. Why?"

"Oh, I don't know. Maybe because a certain interior designer will be eating up your days off?"

Heat flooded Theo's chest. Great, just what a man needed—the ability to blush like a girl. "Zoë's going to a family reunion, remember?"

"I remember. My money says she'll be back."

Theo drummed his pencil on the blotter. They had yet to discuss her trip, but he was certain once Zoë knew how he felt, she'd return to him. "I'm going to see to it."

Chad's eyebrows rose to his hairline. "Really? And how are you going to do that?"

"Simple. I'm going to propose." Now that the

words were out, he couldn't take them back. "Think you're ready to be a best man?"

"Whoa." Chad leaned forward in the chair. "That's a little radical. Are you sure?"

"As sure as I can be," Theo said, unable to tell his best friend that his special ring had already given its blessing. "She's the perfect woman for me."

"I'll admit, you two look good together, and she seems to like you, but . . . love? What if it's only infatuation, or raging hormones or—"

"It might have started out that way, but my feelings for Zoë grow stronger each day. I know I love her," Theo stated.

"Yeah, but how do you *know*?" Chad asked, his expression pained. "Marriage is a big step, and divorce can be devastating. What tells you it will last?"

Theo grinned and put a hand on his chest. "This tells me. My heart rate triples when I think about her, and when she comes near, it's off the chart. When I hold her in my arms, I can't breathe, and the sex is—" He shook his head. "It doesn't matter what the sex is. By then I'm a goner. I want to dive into her and stay with her until the planet turns to dust."

Chad rested his elbows on his knees and clasped his hands, then quirked his lips. "That's almost poetic. And kind of geeky at the same time. But hey, that's just the kind of guy you are."

"Joke if you want, but I know my future is with Zoë. Take it from me, you'll understand when you meet the right girl." When Chad didn't come back with a snappy retort, Theo asked, "What's wrong? Don't think you'll ever meet your Ms. Right?"

The COO stood, shoved his hands in his pockets and walked to the windows.

Theo frowned. "Hey, what did I say?" A moment passed. "Chad? You okay?"

"Yes . . . no . . ." He whirled on his feet. "Hell, I don't know."

"Sounds serious," said Theo, preparing to listen. "Care to tell me about it?"

His partner paced for a full thirty seconds, then returned to his chair. "It's Elise."

"The woman from Suited for Change? Zoë's Elise?"

Chad dragged his fingers through his hair until it stood on end. "The very one."

Stifling a grin, Theo inhaled a breath. Gauging his COO's reaction, he could tell it was serious. "I know you hit a rough patch when you first met, but what's happened since? Did you go out? Have dinner? Holy hell. Don't tell me you already slept together."

"I wish," he said with a snort. "In fact, I'm fairly certain if we'd spent time in the sack, I wouldn't be so frustrated right now."

"Okay, I'm confused," Theo began. "You want to have sex with her but you haven't, correct?"

"Correct."

"And you've been on how many dates? One . . . two . . ."

Chad shrugged. "Two, not counting that first dinner."

"So number three's the charm. Once it passes, you'll move on." *Just like you always do.* "You'll get her out of your system and say good-bye."

"Fat lot you know."

"Excuse me?"

"You heard me. You don't have the faintest idea what I want, or how I'm feeling. Hell, even I don't know."

"You're not having a breakdown, are you? Maybe you should seek professional help. I'm pretty sure seeing a shrink is covered under our health insurance policy."

Chad heaved a sigh. "I don't need a shrink, you moron. At least, I don't think so."

"Well, you need something. It's early, but maybe a good stiff drink?"

"I've tried that, and it didn't help."

Theo exhaled, flummoxed by his best friend's problem. "Look, just spit it out. What the hell's up with you and Elise Sutton?"

The COO gazed at him and shrugged.

Theo shook his head. With his disheveled hair, hound dog expression, and deflated body language, Chad appeared pathetic, almost a beaten man. "You sure you don't need a doctor?"

"I doubt a medical man will help."

"Then what?"

"I have the same symptoms you just described, and it bites."

Before Theo could comment, his cell phone rang.

"Mr. Maragos?" said the voice on the other end of the line. "This is the Gentle Heart. It's about your father."

Chapter 13

Zoë paced the lobby of her hotel, troubled at the turn her morning—nay, her entire day—had taken. First, a surprise meeting with Nike, one of the most powerful and righteous of deities, and the not-quiet-believable reason for her visit; then a frantic phone call from Theo.

The fact that his dear, sweet father was missing from the Gentle Heart was a shock, but she had enough good sense to insist that she be allowed to ride with him to New Jersey. Theo shouldn't have to handle such a dire emergency alone.

He had argued, of course, that he didn't want to impose by dragging her along on the trip, but she'd battled back, telling him if he didn't bring her, she'd find her way to the senior care center by herself. This crisis was huge, and he needed a friend by his side.

After hanging up, she dressed in a beige cashmere sweater, navy wool slacks, and a pair of low-heeled navy boots, threw her coat over her shoulders and raced to the lobby. Theo wasn't scheduled to arrive for at least fifteen minutes, but she wanted to be ready for him. Now, gazing at the darkening sky, she thought about the morning paper's dire prediction of a snowstorm. Peter Maragos had disappeared from his apartment and couldn't be found. What would happen to him if he were lost in a blizzard?

After a few rounds of pacing, she spotted Theo pulling his rental car to the front of her hotel. Charging from the lobby, she opened the passenger door and slid inside. Theo gave her a sad smile as he reached over and took her hand.

"Are you sure you want to do this?" he asked.

"Absolutely," she said. "Let's get going."

Zoë didn't have a clue as to the fastest route to New Jersey, but trusted that Theo did. She gripped an overhead handle as he clenched his jaw, weaved around a string of double-parked vehicles, and headed into traffic.

Once they were on the George Washington Bridge, he pulled his cell phone from his pocket and passed it to her. "Do me a favor. Hit the Recall button and talk to whoever answers at the Gentle Heart. See if there's any news."

She did as he asked and spoke to someone at the front desk, but all they said was, "Sorry. Mr. Maragos is still missing. We've phoned the police. There isn't any more we can tell you."

Zoë relayed the message as she disconnected the call. "I'm so sorry. What are your plans, once we get there?"

"I guess I need to work with the authorities. Maybe you can sit in his apartment in case he returns? It's possible he's somewhere in the building and they missed him, which means he might wander back on his own."

Snow began to fall when they got on the New Jersey Turnpike. By the time they reached the Gentle Heart grounds, the flurries were so heavy she couldn't see a foot in front of her. Theo slid into a parking space labeled DOCTORS ONLY, directly next to the entrance, and shot from the car. She followed him through the main doors and to the desk, where two police officers stood waiting.

"Mjr. Maragos, we have an APB out on your father," said the taller patrolman. "Do you know of any place he might have gone?"

"No," Theo answered immediately. "He's always lived in Michigan. I brought him here because my company is based in Manhattan and we'd be close." He turned to the attendant. "This is supposed to be a guarded facility with guaranteed supervision of its residents. How the hell could my dad slip away without someone noticing?"

"We do a room check every two hours, Mr. Maragos. The attendant on duty reported your father was asleep in his bed at six A.M. and again when he looked in at eight. Pete likes to eat in his room on Sunday morning. That's the reason no one missed him at breakfast. It was the ten A.M. attendant who reported him missing."

"Then it's possible he disappeared just past eight?"

"Yes, sir. It's possible."

Theo swiped a hand over his face and rubbed his eyes. Zoë knew he'd been in his office overnight, because he was still dressed in the clothes he'd worn last evening. She could only imagine how exhausted he was, and how worried.

"I take it you've checked the grounds?" he asked.

"We did a thorough survey of the building and gave the exterior a quick perusal, then waited for the police." The woman shifted her gaze to the patrolman. "We thought they might bring a few more bodies to help with the search."

The police officer frowned. "We're in the middle of a snowstorm, which translates into traffic tie-ups and accidents. Most of the department is on the road seeing to spinouts, fender benders, and collisions. For now, we're all the department can spare."

"Fine," Theo muttered. He turned up the collar on his jacket and pulled on his gloves, then handed Zoë his keys. "I'm going out to look for him. Let yourself into his apartment and wait there in case he finds his way home."

He huddled with the patrolmen. When he headed for the door, she touched his arm and he turned. "I'll keep my fingers crossed. Please be careful." He opened his mouth as if to speak, then nodded and forged out the front door with the officers on his heels.

"Do you know the way to Mr. Maragos's room, miss?" the desk attendant asked.

"I can find it," she answered, turning down the hall.

Inside the apartment, she slipped off her coat and glanced around the room, hoping to spot something that could tell her where Peter might have gone. The magazines Theo brought yesterday still sat in a pile on the coffee table; a travel publication open to an article on the Aegean lay on the older man's chair.

She picked up the magazine, closed it, and set it next to the others. Plopping into the chair, she heaved a sigh. Poor Peter. What had happened that made him leave his home? Where would he go? She couldn't imagine being unable to remember the people she'd known and the places she'd visited in her life. Theo had explained the devastating effects of Alzheimer's, but it was difficult to envision the thoughts that took place when a mortal was afflicted with such an illness.

On a whim, she decided to search the drawers and closets, even if it was considered impolite. She walked to his bedroom door and peeked inside. Except for an unmade bed, the room was neat and tidy, no clothing on the floor, the dresser bare of all but a comb and a few toiletries. She stepped into the room to get a better perspective and checked around the bed, scanning carefully.

Gazing at the carpet, she lowered herself to her knees, then picked up the large white feather tipped in gold lying next to Peter's worn slippers. Rising, she let the feather rest in her palm as she studied it. Feathers on earth were commonly used in pillows, she reminded herself. She tested the two on the mattress and found them stuffed with foam. Staring again at the feather, she touched its golden tip.

For a moment she thought about where she'd

last seen one so similar. Then she shook her head. This piece of fluff couldn't mean what she thought it did. Peter Maragos was a mortal, a nice man who'd once visited Greece and was now trapped in the world his lonely mind had created, nothing more.

Clutching the feather, she returned to the living area, where she stopped short. "Mr. Maragos?"

Sitting in his chair, Peter raised his head and smiled at her as if she showed up in his apartment every day. "Well, hello. You're my son's friend, aren't you? What brings you back here so soon?"

Zoë tucked the feather into her pocket and walked to his chair. "Yes. I'm Zoë." Reining in her curiosity, she remained calm in order not to frighten him. "Where have you been, if you don't mind my asking?"

"That's right. You're Zoë." His smile grew. "Did you come alone, or did Theo accompany you?"

"Theo's here," she said, noting he hadn't answered her question. "Just give me a minute to locate him." She hurried to the wall phone in the kitchen, dialed the front desk and gave them the news. Then she took a seat, hoping Peter would shed some light on his disappearance.

Instead, he turned on the television. "Hope you don't mind," he said. "But I don't want to miss this basketball game."

* * *

Later that evening, Theo sat across from Zoë at the dining table in her suite while snow still swirled outside, creating a wonderland of white. They'd ordered room service, and were just finishing the meal while discussing his father's early morning escapade.

They'd gone over the details a dozen times and still couldn't figure out where he'd been. Not outside, that was certain, because Peter had returned dry, warm, and perfectly content when he'd reappeared. Unfortunately, they'd had no luck getting his dad to focus and shed light on the mystery.

Overcome with exhaustion, Theo wanted nothing more that to spend the night wrapped in Zoë's arms, but told himself it wasn't practical. He'd worn these clothes far too long and hadn't shaved in almost forty-eight hours. It was a miracle she could stand being in the same room with him.

"I guess I'd better be going," he said as she began to clear their dishes, stacking them on the serving trolley.

"What?" She gazed at him as if he'd confessed to a crime.

"I'm rank, Zoë. I smell like a . . . a Dumpster in August, and I'm sure I look like I belong in one. I need to shower and shave, get clean clothes—"

"You can do that here," she told him. "There are

shops downstairs that carry men's wear, or I can call housekeeping and have them launder what you have on."

"It's a Sunday night. I don't think—"

"Nonsense. I do it all the time." She dialed the phone before he could continue. "This is Zoë Degodessa. I need a few things washed and pressed, and delivered to my suite first thing tomorrow morning . . . I'll leave the garments in a laundry bag outside the door. Thanks." She hung up and flashed a smile. "That's one advantage of living in a penthouse suite in the most expensive hotel in Manhattan. Housekeeping guarantees your items will be back by eight A.M."

Theo ran a hand over his stubble. "Yeah, but what about a shave? My hair?" He grimaced. "A shower?"

Zoë had already walked to a closet and retrieved a white plastic bag. Sitting at the table, she marked off the list. "Let's see, one white dress shirt, one pair of gray slacks, a pair of socks, an undershirt, boxers . . . you are wearing the silk boxers we bought, correct?"

He felt another blush coming on. "Yes, I'm wearing the silk boxers."

"And you like them?"

Leaning back, he crossed his arms. "You're enjoying this, aren't you?"

"Enjoying what?" she asked, her face a mask of innocence.

"Taking charge, asking about my underwear—embarrassing me?"

"I helped you choose those boxers, Theo, and I've already seen you in the buff. There's no need for you to be embarrassed. Now, strip and stuff everything in the sack."

"Strip? Here?"

"Yes, here, unless you'd prefer doing it in the hall?"

Okay, so he was being a prude, but he was new at this man-woman intimacy game. "How about the bathroom? Then I'll hop in the shower."

"Fine." She pushed from the table. "But hurry up. The man who answered said someone would be right up."

Bag in hand, he headed for the bathroom and did as she'd ordered. When he peered from behind the door, she was waiting. Muttering a thanks, he passed her the bag, ducked back inside and walked to the shower. If nothing else, he'd be clean. But he'd have to wear one of those girly terry robes in order to remain decent.

Moments later, water running, he hopped into the steaming spray. Shortly after that, the bathroom door opened and, before he knew it, Zoë was in the stall with him, in all her naked glory.

"I thought you might need someone to wash your back," she said in a voice tinged with amusement. Then she slipped under the downpour, drenching her hair and body. Ignoring what had to be his shocked expression, she grabbed the washcloth and started soaping up.

Theo's penis jumped to attention. Zoë took the foaming cloth and began a slow massage of his neck, his chest, his stomach. By the time she reached his hips, he had a hard-on to rival an iron spike and was ready to take her there on the stall floor.

Instead, he fisted his hands. What did Zoë expect him to say? To do?

"You seem tense," she stated in a matter-of-fact tone. "Never showered with a woman before?"

"Um . . . no," he admitted. But that didn't mean it hadn't been one of his lifelong fantasies. "Not really."

"Then this must be your lucky day." She ran the cloth over his engorged shaft and under his balls, squeezing gently as she tended to him.

Bracing his legs, Theo closed his eyes, unable to ignore the heat racing through his system. When he glanced down, she was on her knees, her luscious lips inches from his pulsing cock while she soaped his legs, his thighs, his butt. The erotic picture made his body sizzle. She was an angel, a siren, a tempting cross between the two, and she'd been created just for him.

"Hang on a second," he muttered, dragging her to a stand.

"What's wrong?" she asked, again with a tremor of amusement.

"Nothing's wrong, exactly, it's just that . . . jeez, Zoë, you're driving me crazy." When she giggled, he pulled her to his chest. "You're doing it on purpose, aren't you?"

She batted her lashes. "Whatever gave you that idea?"

Well, hell. Two could play at this game; once he learned the rules, that is. He slipped a leg between her thighs and guided her to the wall. Then he ran his hands to her back and hoisted her onto his knee. Raising a brow, he said, "Oh, I get it. You want to be in charge."

"Not in charge," she corrected. "But I do want you inside me. I was afraid you'd never take the initiative on your own, so I—"

He caught her breast and brought a budded nipple to his lips, sucking the tip deep inside. Zoë's words melted away as she moaned in approval. Moving against his thigh, she rocked in tandem with the rhythm of his tongue.

Theo cupped her other breast, circling with his finger, drawing the nipple out and flicking it to hardness. Then he trailed his lips upward, sipping droplets of water as he feasted on her neck, her shoulder, her earlobe . . . her mouth.

Probing deep, he tasted her, drinking in her sighs of desire. His fingers reached between her legs, delved into her secret core, touched her sweet spot and teased it to attention, encouraging her to enjoy the sensations and find her release.

Zoë's moans turned to cries of passion. Riding his hand, she clenched her inner walls around his seeking fingers as she called out his name. He encouraged her journey, reveling in his ability to make her shatter. Moments passed as she quivered from head to toe, then slumped against him and rested her face in his chest.

"That's not fair," she admonished. "I was supposed to do that to you."

He tilted her chin and kissed her. "You still can," he murmured. "But cut a guy a break. I'm already worn-out, a trembling pathetic mass of manhood, a glob of putty in your capable female hands."

Smiling, Zoë slipped her arms around his neck, wrapped her legs about his waist, and eased down until she settled on his shaft and he slid inside of her. Theo held his ground, managing her weight, and she sighed. He had the strength and physique of a god, this mortal, and he was exactly what she needed.

"You are so strong. Are you sure you don't lift weights?"

He nibbled on her neck. "I'm sure."

"Amazing," she commented. "And how lucky for me."

Rising up, she tightened over his throbbing shaft and began a motion as old as time. He spun in a half circle, rested his back against the tiles and levered his body to carry her fully. Zoë tasted his lower lip, then teased his tongue with hers, hoping to show him how much she cared, how much she wanted him to remember her when she was gone.

Theo arched into her, clutched her bottom and surged upward, shouting his release. Zoë followed, panting as she crested and fell with the waves of passion rolling through her. Gasping for air, her heart slowed, and he guided her to her feet.

The thought of leaving Theo forever burst inside her brain. She couldn't imagine living without his kisses, his smiles . . . his love.

Nike's surprise visit came to mind. Perhaps the powerful goddess would stand beside her when she asked Zeus for a boon, a bonus for achieving her goal. More than likely, her father's answer would hinge on the layout in *New York Entrepreneur*. If the photo shoot and accompanying article were a success, the top god would have to reward her for going above and beyond his demands, but it wouldn't hurt to have a great warrior by her side pleading her case for a return to earth.

Until then, she would continue to spend her nights in Theo's strong, capable arms, giving him pleasure he would remember long after she was gone.

Theo woke to complete quiet and calm, and gazed around the darkened room. He couldn't recall when he'd had such a restful night, or when he'd last slept as if he didn't have a care in the world. And considering what had gone on with his father, that was amazing.

To find that his dad had simply returned to his apartment as if nothing was wrong still boggled his mind. Without a clue as to where Peter had been or what he'd done, it was damned difficult coming up with a way to prevent it from happening again. At least he'd gotten the nursing home to promise they'd perform more frequent checks and be more diligent in their surveillance.

Still mulling over his dad's escape, he smiled when Zoë moved against him. Rolling to his side, he drew her to his chest and she gave a throaty moan. The ring he wore tingled, warming his finger, and he realized the token had ceased emitting crazed jolts whenever they were together. Instead, it only zapped him when he concentrated on his future and pondered the best time to tell Zoë how much he loved her.

Okay, so the damned thing was trying to convey a message. It was time he revealed his feelings, now, when she was half asleep and sated from their night of passion, so she'd commit to a future.

He blew softly in her ear. "You awake?"

"How can I sleep when I know you're watching me?"

"I enjoy watching you. You're beautiful."

"Nice to hear you think so, but that doesn't mean you have to keep an eye on me."

"I just can't believe you're in my arms. I worry that someday I'll wake up and you'll be gone, simply disappear as if you've never been here."

She tensed in his arms. "Theo, I will be gone soon. I'm going home, remember?"

"But you'll return, at least I hope you will after I tell you something."

Reaching behind her, Zoë grabbed his penis and stroked. "Tell me later."

Cupping her breast, he nuzzled her neck. "It's important. I have to tell you now, or I'll wimp out, lose my courage, stutter like an idiot, and make a fool of myself."

He trailed a hand over her stomach and down to her thighs, slipping his fingers in her warm wet heat. Zoë sighed her pleasure, squirming against him. Then she shifted in his embrace, guided him to his back and climbed astride. Settling over his hips, she eased onto his cock and gave a dreamy grin. "This is so much better than talking. Don't you agree?"

Theo clutched her hips as she continued her assault. There could never—would never—be another woman for him, in his bed or out of it. Before he was carried away in a sexual frenzy, he had to tell her.

"You're the one I want, Zoë," he managed to groan out loud. "The only woman I intend to do this with for the rest of my life. I love you."

Her sensuous rocking stopped, and he opened his eyes. She gazed at him with an expression so odd it almost froze the beating of his heart.

"What's wrong? Are you all right?"

"I'm fine," she answered, sighing.

He rose up and caught her as she rested on his thighs. He'd hoped for a flood of words from her, telling him she felt the same, but instead Zoë appeared petrified. "I mean it. Tell me what's wrong and I'll do whatever I can to make it right. I swear I will."

She shook her head, then leaned into him.

Had his heartfelt confession saddened her or shocked her? "Surely, you realized we'd get to this point when we began going out? You must have known from our first night together that I was falling in love with you."

She shrugged, but didn't speak.

"Is it so terrible that I care for you? Are we . . . am I moving too fast? Do you need more time before I say the words again?"

Stiffening in his arms, she whispered, "You can't love me, Theo. You hardly know me."

He tilted her chin and stared at her. "I know all I need to. You're funny, smart, and clever. You make me feel ten feet tall, as if I could leap skyscrapers in a single bound or fight a dozen suitors for your hand. And the unbelievable thing is, you get along with my father. I never thought I'd find a woman who could handle his problem, never mind sit and talk to him as if he were a healthy normal man."

"Peter is a dear. He's easy to like."

When she swiped a tear from her eye, Theo winced. "You're crying?" He drew her to his chest and wrapped her in his arms. "Please, don't cry, Zoë. I'm no good with tears. I don't want to hurt you. I never want to hurt you. Just tell me how to make it right and I'll do it."

Though she remained silent, her body trembled.

He was such a fool, jumping to conclusions, assuming she felt the same thing for him that he felt for her just because they'd slept together. *Just because the cursed ring told him so.* Modern women were pragmatic, took a more casual view of sex, were more cautious when it came to love.

"How about we spend the day together? I won't mention the L word again until you let me know you're ready. I'm a patient man. I can wait a day or so."

She chuckled, and he breathed a sigh of relief.

"See. I'm a dope, but at least I'm a funny dope. We'll do whatever you want today . . . walk in the snow, bundle up and take a carriage ride around Central Park. I'll even let you drag me to a clothing store and buy me more underwear."

She turned her head and peered at him from between a fall of cascading hair. "You're not a dope. You're a handsome, sexy, and very nice man. And I know exactly what I want to do today."

He cupped her cheek and swiped the last of her tears with his thumbs. "Great. You name it and we'll do it."

She pushed at his shoulders, guiding him to the mattress. Then she smiled, a slow sensual grin, climbed onto his hips and wiggled against his penis. "This is what I want."

He heaved a breath of relief. "Well, what do you know. It's what I want too. I told you we were compatible."

Bending forward, she kissed him slow and deep, then ran her mouth to his nipple and bit down gently. Theo gasped, rising up into her, and she again began to rock. He clasped her hips, guiding her rhythm, slowing her pace, until he was ready to burst inside of her.

Zoë deserved the very best of him, his patience, his respect, every iota of his care. Shifting their bodies, he maneuvered her to her back, rose above her and wrapped her legs around his waist. Then he plunged into her core, driving to the hilt, taking her the way a man took the woman he loved. If she didn't want the words, at least he could give her the actions.

She clutched his shoulders, met his pounding thrusts, and allowed him to lead her to fulfillment. Quaking beneath him, she hung on as if she would never let him go.

Theo waited until she drifted in the aftermath of her orgasm before he began to soar to his own release. This morning, this moment, was for Zoë.

And today was the first day of the rest of their lives.

Chapter 14

Zoë heaved a sigh as she took a seat in the Suited for Change break room. Last night's snowstorm had turned Manhattan into a wonderland of white, but it also mucked up travel for anyone taking part in the morning rush hour. She'd reminded Theo that the painters and furniture delivery were scheduled for today and kissed him good-bye at 7:00 A.M. Since learning of the traffic tie-ups and cancelled appointments rampant throughout the city, she kept her fingers crossed that he made it to the apartment on time to let everyone in.

Elise entered the room, and Zoë studied her face. The last time they'd talked, Elise had been confused about both her feelings for Chad and her ability to keep things in perspective. This morning she was back to her smiling self, as if without a worry in the world. What had happened to change things?

"Mary Beth is thrilled with her new look, Zoë. I think it gave her the confidence she needs to ace that job interview this afternoon. It's good they didn't cancel because of the snow."

Mary Beth Borden, a forty-five-year-old mother of three, was on her own for the first time in her life. Her tyrannical and abusive husband had died after a massive coronary just six months ago, and in that time she'd become a changed woman. He'd left insurance money, but not enough to give her and her children the life she now realized they deserved, and she'd come to Suited for Change hoping for a fresh start for her family.

"Mary Beth was a snap to transform. I'm happy for her," Zoë stated, wondering if now was the right moment to bring up their last conversation. Then she thought, Why not? She'd be going home in a few days. Knowing her friend had found someone to count on would make it easier to say good-bye.

"May I ask you a question?"

Elise set her coffee cup on the table. "Let me guess. You want to know about Chad."

"Am I being too personal?"

Elise shrugged her slim shoulders. "Heck no. If not for you, I wouldn't have met him. Unfortunately, there's nothing I can tell you."

"Nothing?"

"Nope. I left your hotel the other night and didn't hear from him once over the weekend. No call, no surprise visit, zilch, nada, zip."

"I'm sorry."

"I'm not, so why should you be? It's not like we had a commitment or anything."

"I know, but I also got the impression you were taken with him. I was hoping he'd be your entry into a new round of male companionship or maybe . . . something more."

Elise grinned. "Something more as in hot steamy sex?"

"Well, yes, now that you put it that way."

"Ah, so you're one of *those* women."

"*Those* women? What does that mean?"

"You know, a woman who's so blissfully happy having hot steamy sex with her own guy, she wants the same for her friends. But I doubt that will happen between Chad and me."

Zoë frowned. "Why are you giving up on the idea so soon? He may have had something else scheduled he couldn't change, or he's planning on calling you today."

"I'm not giving up, just accepting reality. If Chad Thomas wanted hot steamy sex, even lukewarm sex, he would have hit on me by now. And don't try to tell me he didn't because of my negative signals, because I gave him plenty of opportunities."

"Oh," Zoë asked, raising a brow. "What exactly did you do?"

The director's cheeks turned pink. "I already gave you the lowdown on my lust."

"Well, fill me in again," said Zoë, her expression purposely innocent. "My memory is failing me."

"You want to hear about the drooling or the panting?"

"Oh, come on. You weren't that bad."

"Bad enough. I sucked on his mouth like a darned vacuum cleaner and wound myself around him like a . . . a sex-starved cat. Now that I've had a chance to think it over, it's a wonder he didn't run down the hall instead of merely walking away."

"Maybe he did try to phone and there's something wrong with your house line or—"

"Nope. In a weak moment, I checked. Of course, with this storm and all, I imagine there are parts of the city with no service, but it was up and running fine last night."

Zoë heaved a sigh. "Okay then, at least it shows you can get fired up over a guy. That's something positive."

"I suppose so." Elise brought her cup to the sink, then turned. "What did you and Theo do yesterday?"

"How do you know I spent the day with Theo?"

The director folded her arms, taking on the stance of a school principal. "It's written all over your face, my friend. You positively glowed when I mentioned hot steamy sex, and you always light up when I mention Theo's name. If I was a betting woman, I'd take odds you're in love with him, or very close to it. And it's obvious how he feels about you."

"I like him very much," Zoë confessed. "But I'm leaving town—"

"An airplane flies both ways, so buy a round-trip ticket. I already told you we'd welcome you back here with open arms."

"Thanks, but I'm not sure—"

"Your customers would do the same. Once that magazine article appears, you'll be able to contract for whatever type of work you want in the world of fashion and design."

If only Zeus believed that to be true, thought Zoë.

"And I'm sure Theo's already asked when you'll be returning. Right?"

"Yes, he's asked." *And I've told him I won't be.* "He knows I'm not looking for anything . . . permanent."

"Why not, if you don't mind my asking?"

Elise was her closest friend in the mortal world.

They'd shared so much more than the superfluous gossip she and her cousins on Mount Olympus usually discussed. The director had become her confidante, more like Chloe or Kyra than an acquaintance.

"I have a duty to my family, and I have to put that duty before my own needs."

"A supportive family would want you to be happy, even if it meant you had to be away from them for months at a time. And what with all the airlines, that wouldn't happen. As I've said already, you could live anywhere in the world and reach them with a simple plane ride."

"You don't know my family."

"You're right, I don't." Elise ran a hand through her golden curls. "I'm sorry if I've pushed my way into your personal life, but I care about you. I want you back here too."

"I understand, and it's—" Zoë's gaze strayed to the wall clock. "Oh, no. I'm late."

"Late?"

"I was supposed to be at Theo's loft by now. The furniture's being delivered this afternoon, and I'm the one directing the show." She rose to her feet and shrugged into her coat. "Thanks to this snowstorm, it's going to take me forever to get there."

"I'd call the delivery company before I race to TriBeCa. Everything in the city has slowed to a crawl since yesterday. They may not even make it today."

Not good, thought Zoë. Not good at all. "I certainly hope the painters were on time this morning. I'd hate for them to collide with the deliverymen."

"Painters? This morning?" Elise returned to her chair. "Have you called Theo to check?"

"Why would I? He was supposed to get home before they arrived. He would have phoned *me* if they didn't show."

"I hate to be the one to break this to you, but it's been my experience that most men aren't as flustered by decorating delays as women. Are you positive Theo would be concerned enough to let you know?"

"It was the last thing I said to him before he left my suite."

"Uh-huh."

"You don't think he remembered?"

"I'm sure he did, but he's lived in this city long enough to know how crippling a snowstorm can be. I'm sure he's taking a delay—if there is one—in stride."

"I'm telling you there cannot be a delay. That will give us one day less to get the apartment ready for the *New York Entrepreneur* photographer." She found her cell phone and dialed the furniture store. "If they don't make it today, I'll . . . Hello? Grandby Furniture? This is Zoë Degodessa and I'm calling about a delivery . . . Yes, I'll hold."

Gazing at Elise, she rolled her eyes. "I hate it when they put me on hold."

"Me too. I swear it's a ruse some companies use to keep you from finding out what's really going on."

It was another five minutes before the line went dead.

"It's not the end of the world, Zoë," said Theo, watching her pace his living room.

"Why didn't you call me?"

"I told you, due to the storm, my apartment line is out of commission, and when I phoned Suited for Change on my cell, all I got was a busy signal."

"What about my cell phone?" she challenged.

Theo hunched his shoulders. "Honestly? I got involved in a computer glitch and lost track of the time. I didn't think it was that big a deal."

"So you have no idea what happened to the painters?"

"I just figured the storm held them up."

She waved her hands at the walls, covered in Sheetrock and prepared for the painters. "This is a disaster."

"No, it's not. The shoot is scheduled for Friday. We have three more days."

"If the furniture looks awkward or doesn't co-ordinate with the wall color, the pictures will be a failure."

"Zoë, come on. You were careful to measure everything, and we had samples of the wall colors with us when we made our final choice of the fabrics." He set his hands on her shoulders and began to rub. "Trust me. It's going to look great."

Zoë gazed at the ceiling, then her feet, and stiffened under his kneading fingers. "The rugs! Why aren't the rugs down?"

"The rugs? Uh . . . when were they supposed to be here?"

"The end of last week. Didn't I ask you about them?"

He wrinkled his forehead. "I don't remember."

Tears welled in her eyes. "This cannot be happening to me."

"What do you mean, to you? It's my photo shoot."

"But it's my reputation on the line." She realized how angry she must sound and shook her head. "Sorry, it's just that I don't take scheduling problems very well."

"While I've learned to roll with the punches,"

he said with a smile. "Let me try the painters. Maybe their phone is up and running now."

She walked to the windows and stared at the blue sky, then focused on the street below. The snow had already begun to melt. The roads had been plowed, and people were digging out their cars or shoveling walkways in front of buildings. The pristine view of early morning was turning into a slushy mess that was still going to hold up traffic and make deliveries difficult. Theo spoke to someone, and she realized the phone was back in working order.

"I know the storm put you behind, but I'm in a bind. The painting was supposed to be finished today." He held his palm over the receiver. "They say they'll try to make it first thing tomorrow morning. It's the best they can do."

She stomped toward him and held out her hand, and he passed her the phone. "Hello. This is the interior designer. I'm the one who hired your company. To whom am I speaking? . . . I see. No, I don't understand. But we have a contract. If it's not honored by end of day tomorrow, future dealings with your firm will be severed. Thank you."

"Wow," said Theo, shaking his head. "Remind me never to tick you off."

She inhaled a breath. Why was she acting like a harridan instead of calmly handling the problem?

"Maybe you should try the delivery service again. They wouldn't dare hang up on a man."

He dialed Granby's number, spoke to someone, and was put on hold. After several minutes a woman took his call, after which he hung up and gave the report. "She promised the truck would be here today, probably after six P.M."

"Great . . . fine . . . it'll be a miracle if the shoot actually goes as scheduled."

"It will happen. We just have to take a more creative approach. We'll push all the furniture to the middle of the room and have the painters cover it with drop cloths when they arrive tomorrow. What's next?"

"The rugs," she replied, frowning. "Can you see what happened to them?"

"No problem." He made another call, spoke to someone, and told her, "They're putting me on hold." After pacing for several minutes, he said, "Okay . . . I see . . . No, it's not acceptable. If they aren't here in twenty-four hours, we don't want them." He gave the Marasoft number and turned to her. "I'm sorry to have to tell you this, but it looks as if the rugs are lost."

Zoë inhaled another fortifying breath, and sucked back a second round of tears. Was this Hera's nasty way of making her appear a fool?

"We can't have a photo shoot without rugs."

She walked to the kitchen, hitched a hip on one of the bar stools lining the island and rested her head in her hands. "This is terrible. What are we going to do?"

Theo reached her side and began another calming massage. "You're still wound tight as a drum. Try to loosen up." She moaned when he touched a knot of muscles. Once she relaxed, he kissed the nape of her neck. "Hey, I have an idea."

"What?" she muttered, leaning into his still circling fingers.

"First tell me, are you free for the rest of the day?"

She shrugged. "Seeing as my day was supposed to be spent here, supervising the painters and deliverymen, yes."

"And you're game for whatever I want to do?"

"I could be . . . I guess."

"Great. Just give me a couple of minutes." He pulled out his cell and headed for his office. "I'll be back."

She raised a brow. "Why am I getting worried?"

"Beats me," he answered, grinning as he walked backward. "Just chill, and trust me, okay?"

Chad disconnected Theo's call and shook his head. Damn but his buddy had it bad, especially if he was willing to go to a place he'd sworn up and down he wouldn't be caught dead in . . . ever. Love sure made a man do crazy things.

And he ought to know, he thought, grinning like a fool, because he'd been concocting his own special event for Elise all weekend. The storm had almost ruined the gesture, but he'd rearranged a few things in order to stay on track. He only hoped she would approve of his plan.

He checked the pile of goods he'd collected for his surprise a third time, then took a gander in the mirror. The rugged look wasn't his usual style, but today was an exception. His shearling jacket made sense, as did his jeans, red turtleneck, and plaid wool shirt. Combined with his leather hiking boots, he resembled a citified Marlboro Man, without the cigarette or Stetson, of course. He'd even used the lousy weather to cancel an appointment with his stylist, because the longer length of his hair seemed just right for his man-of-the-outdoors persona.

Since he'd already escorted Elise to her favorite museum, a couple of great restaurants, and a sold-out concert given by her favorite artist, he felt positive today's jaunt would put a lock on his all-out effort to impress her. After this clever gesture, she'd have to admit he was a nice guy . . . and someone she could see in her future.

Their last good-night kiss had been hot—very

hot—but he still had the feeling she was keeping him at a distance, as if she wasn't sure they were compatible. But being compatible was just a small part of what he desired from Elise Sutton. She'd consumed his thoughts since the night they met, popping into his mind at odd moments to knock on the door to his sanity, until he realized he wanted more from her than he'd asked of any other woman.

Shifting gears, he hoisted everything in his arms and headed out the door, ignoring his wavering confidence. It wouldn't be the first time in his life he went to great lengths to impress a woman, but he'd never allowed failure to enter the picture. This afternoon with Elise was different . . . special. More important than all the other times with other women combined.

Downstairs, he caught a taxi to Central Park South and carted his gear to the only hansom in line. He'd been told when he made the arrangements that if it snowed as predicted, many of the carriages and their drivers would be holed up, safe and warm for the day. If he wanted a guaranteed ride, he'd have to pay double the fee in advance to assure a driver would take the job. Only the most stalwart made an appearance in bad weather, and only if they knew it was worth the effort.

"Harry." Chad nodded at the driver, who was wrapped in so many layers of clothing his laughing brown eyes were all that showed. "Thanks for doing this."

"Believe me, since you've paid double, it's not a problem," Harry responded. "I just hope the lady realizes what a special thing this is."

Chad levered his supplies into the hansom, then pulled himself up and got settled. "I'm counting on it. You have the address, right?"

"Got it," Harry said, glancing over his shoulder. "Just keep your fingers crossed we don't get stopped by a cop. We're not exactly staying 'in the zone,' but this kind of weather usually allows for some rule breaking, so I imagine it'll be okay."

"I told you I'd cover any fines."

"Damn straight you will," the older man responded. Clucking his tongue, he snapped the reins and steered the carriage into the street.

They headed toward the fashion district, home to the Suited for Change office, staying off the beaten path as much as possible. When Harry had the balls to wave at a pair of cops directing traffic at a clogged intersection, Chad decided to triple the guy's tip.

"Okay, there's the building," he shouted thirty minutes later. He pulled the blanket off his legs and slid out of the buggy. "Say a prayer for me, pal, and pull up a little. I don't want her to see you first thing. With luck, I'll be back with my fair lady in a couple of minutes."

Chad heaved a sigh of relief when he saw lights burning in the front office. He hadn't called Elise because he didn't want to alert her to his surprise. Instead, he'd counted on her devotion to Suited for Change and guessed she would be hard at work. If he'd been wrong, he would have asked Harry to beat tracks to her apartment in Gramercy Park.

He gave himself a mental high-five when the door opened. Slipping inside, he walked quietly to the rear office and eased his head around the corner. Elise sat at her desk studying a file. From what he could see of her clothing, she was dressed perfectly for the frigid temperature and his planned outing, in a forest green sweater over a beige turtleneck.

"Knock, knock," he said softly, not wanting to startle her.

She raised her head. "Chad?"

He grinned. "I was hoping you'd be at work today."

Her cheeks turned bright pink. "I'm always here. I have a responsibility—"

"Yeah, me too." He stepped into the room. "But this lousy weather gives us workaholics a reprieve."

"Workaholic? You?"

He managed a wounded smile. "Yes, me." When she opened and closed her mouth, he said, "What, you think I don't work for a living like the rest of the world?"

"No—I mean yes, I know you work, but I didn't think you did it with total . . . dedication."

He came around her side of the desk and hitched his hip on top. "Even though I don't have controlling interest, Marasoft is my company too. Just ask Theo."

"I don't need to ask Theo. I believe you."

"I hear what you're saying but your tone screams of doubt." He frowned. "I'm not a dilettante."

"I never said you were." She crossed her arms. "But you do come from money."

"So what?"

"I don't."

"And your point would be . . . ?"

She shrugged, then sat up straight and ran a hand through her riot of golden curls. "No point. If you're here about the employment agreement, I was just going over the contract." She held the folder out to him. "I believe you'll find every—"

He grabbed the file, set it on the blotter, and pulled her to her feet. Before she spoke, he leaned forward and kissed her.

At first she flattened her palms on his chest and tried to push him away, but when his arms slid to her back and he drew her closer, she softened against him. He let her set the pace, and she melted into his chest, opening her mouth as if she wanted to dive inside of him.

Gratified by her reaction, Chad deepened the kiss and pulled her between his legs so she could feel his arousal. Her hands slipped underneath his heavy coat and around to his back. Her moan told him she wanted him, and damn if he wasn't ready to take her right there on her desk.

Then she broke the intimate contact and set her forehead on his shoulder. "I can't . . . we can't . . ."

"Oh, but I say we can," he teased.

She shook her head. "I'm not ready for this—for a man like you."

"You mean a man who has money?"

"Not exactly, no."

"Are you upset because I didn't call you this weekend?"

"Upset? Of course not."

Ah. So she had wanted him to call. "I spent the weekend clearing my calendar for today, and then, when the storm warnings began, I had to pull a few strings. But I'm starting to believe it was worth it."

She raised her head and gazed at him, one brow

raised in question. "Clear your calendar? Pull a few strings?"

"You're curious. Good."

Stepping back, she heaved a breath. "What are you talking about?"

He took note of her wool slacks and heeled black boots. "I hope your outerwear is warm."

She nodded toward the coatrack, and he saw her full-length coat. "How about a hat and gloves?"

"I have both, but I still don't understand—"

"Okay. No more talk. Are you done here?"

"I don't have any more appointments, if that's what you mean."

"That's what I mean." He removed her coat from the rack and helped her slip it on, then he sat the fuzzy dark green knit cap hanging from a hook on her head.

"Hey, you're messing my hair," she muttered as she rearranged the hat and tucked her curls under the band so the cap framed her face. "I still don't see—"

"You will. Gloves?"

Elise pulled a pair of leather gloves from the coat pocket and slid them on. "Now what?"

"Do whatever you need to do to close this place for the day."

She rolled her eyes. "Okay, but this had better be good."

He followed her from room to room, watching while she turned off lights and made sure things were tight.

"All set?"

"I guess so."

He took her hand and tucked it in the crook of his elbow. When they reached the front door, he turned her around. "Don't look, just lock up."

After she did as he asked, he put his fingers over her eyes and guided her toward the hansom. "My lady," he said, dropping his hands, "your carriage awaits."

When she didn't respond, he swallowed his frustration. Maybe he should have asked if she was allergic to horses or, God forbid, had her ex done this with her often enough to bring back bad memories?

Stepping in front of her, he tipped up her chin. "Elise, are you all right?"

She gazed at him through glittering tears. Then she began to cry.

Chapter 15

Zoë closed her eyes and moaned her appreciation. She was back on Mount Olympus sitting atop the highest peak while she watched fluffy clouds of white float past on a soft fragrant breeze. Relaxed, warm, almost asleep, her veins hummed with contentment while beautiful music surrounded her and her muscles melted into a single mass of pleasure.

The sound of footsteps faded, and her peaceful cocoon dimmed to a pale golden glow. Then a door closed and seconds ticked by as she considered Theo's thoughtful gift: an afternoon at a spa. The pedicure and manicure had been wonderful, but the best part of the experience was sitting next to Theo while he received the same intimate attention that she did.

She knew he'd swallowed a lot of manly pride by allowing himself to be pumiced, pampered, and pummeled, but he'd done it just for her. His generous gesture of arranging this afternoon made her all the more miserable about leaving him. She couldn't imagine never seeing him again, whether it be sharing ideas and jokes or sleeping by his side.

"Are you awake?" Theo's voice came from a few feet away. It sounded as if he read her thoughts and sensed her confusion. Laying on separate tables in the same room, they'd just finished getting a full body massage and were waiting for an attendant to lead them to their next appointment.

"I'm floating," she answered. "How about you?"

"It wasn't too bad, once I got used to being touched and fussed over by strangers . . . and buck-assed naked in front of a guy who probably wrestles for the WWF in his spare time."

She giggled. "A masseuse is asexual. Man or woman, they don't notice a thing about you personally. Their job is to knead your muscles into a pulpy mound of pliant flesh, until you're so relaxed you don't care where you are or who's touching you. And strong hands and arms enables them to do fabulous things to your body."

"Maybe I should call you Ms. Expert, because

it's obvious you've experienced this kind of thing before."

"I have, but this establishment is one of the best I've tried. How did you find it?"

"Chad. He comes here every couple of months for the full treatment. He's been trying to convince me to tag along for years, but I always said no—screamed no, if you want the truth. Now that I see what I've been missing, I could kick myself."

"He's certainly full of surprises." *And he'd better not hurt my friend.* "Can I ask you something?"

"Anything."

"Was Chad always so . . . so . . . uh . . ."

"Pompous?"

"No."

"Smug?"

"Of course not."

"Too bad, because if I told him you thought he was either, he'd have a fit. So what is it about him you want to know?"

"I'm not sure how to phrase it. Has he always been so self-confident where women are concerned?"

"Self-confident? I guess so. I didn't know him until college, but I've met his family. He grew up with sisters who treated him like a prince. I think he always expected other women would, and they complied."

"How did he come to know so much about fashion and things most men avoid?"

"I've asked him the same thing a couple hundred times, and he just says it's in his genes. He thinks I'm an insecure male who worries too much about appearances instead of doing what feels good. When we first met, I was positive he was gay, so I understand what you're saying."

"I know he's not gay, but he's certainly into the finer things in life. Things some men wouldn't dare do, never mind think about doing. I doubt they'd even feel comfortable taking part in a conversation on all the things he knows about culture and clothing. Art too."

"Amazing, isn't it? But it only took one night out on the town with him while we were in college to realize he was part of a new breed."

"New breed?"

"Men in tune with their feminine side, who care about their personal appearance, what they wear, that sort of thing."

"And they take women to bed . . . and only women." She had to ask in order to protect Elise from another heartache.

Theo laughed. "I don't know about the others, but Chad loves women, maybe more than he should. If he was an ordinary guy—"

"Like you?"

"Hah! I'm far from ordinary, and as a bona fide geek, proud of it. Chad is actually a hound dog, but a sensitive hound dog." He groaned. "I'm not explaining this correctly at all. He's not sensitive . . . I mean, he is, but not in a bad way—"

"I think I get it," Zoë interrupted, chuckling. "And it doesn't matter, as long as he doesn't make Elise unhappy. She hasn't had the best of luck with men."

"Uh . . . I don't think that's going to happen."

"Oh? How do you know?" When he didn't answer, she shifted to an upright position on the padded table, clutched the large cotton towel that covered her and set her feet on the floor. Wrapping the towel around her middle, she took five steps to a still silent Theo, and bending forward, whispered, "I'm waiting."

He jumped and turned to look at her. "Jeez, next time warn me before you sneak up on me, please."

"Then answer my question."

"I just know, okay."

"Hmm, something tells me you're not being entirely truthful."

His continued silent treatment forced her to take charge. She tickled his ribs and he skittered off the opposite side of the table, grabbing his own towel. Standing, he held the cloth like a shield.

"No fair. At least, it's not fair unless I can tickle you too."

She raised her nose in the air. "Go ahead, see if I care. I'm not ticklish."

"Oh, yeah? Maybe I'd better test that theory out." He circled his table and walked toward her.

With one hand raised in protest, Zoë took a step back. "I'm not, honest."

He advanced slowly, waggling his eyebrows and grinning. "Hmm, why do I think you're not being entirely truthful?" he asked, repeating her teasing question.

She reached the wall, but he kept moving toward her, one step at a time, while his expression turned from playful to powerful. In fact, he reminded her of a warrior of old marching into battle. A vision of Nike came to mind and she pushed it aside. This wasn't Mount Olympus and Theo certainly wasn't a Greek god.

Backing her into a corner, he grabbed her waist, pulled her to his chest, and brought his lips to hers an inch at a time.

Ready for his kiss, Zoë closed her eyes, then trembled when his fingers brushed her sides. "Hey, that's not nice," she shouted, trying to wiggle free. "Stop," she gasped, refusing to give in to her laughter.

"I thought you weren't ticklish," he said, still plying her with skimming touches from his seeking fingers.

She bent forward and pushed him away, giggling. "You're evil, and not very nice."

He moved closer, and his hands began a different kind of action. "I'm not evil, I'm obsessed."

She met his heated gaze. "Obsessed?"

"With you. Being with you, talking to you, laying next to you in bed . . . making love with you. It's all I think about." He nuzzled the tender spot under her ear. "I love you, Zoë."

She sighed, arching against him. "You don't know me well enough to love me."

He kissed her neck, trailed his lips to her chin, her mouth, and shared her breath. "I don't need to know anything more than I do. My heart's told me enough."

Before Zoë could argue further, there was a knock on the door. "Excuse me, folks, but I'm here to escort you to your private hot tub," a woman said. "It's your final treatment of the day. I'll be waiting in the hall."

"Hang on a second," Theo called out. Backing away from Zoë, he wrapped the towel tighter around his waist. "What's this hot tub thing supposed to be again?"

She grinned. "I believe the description in the

brochure said it was 'a warm and soothing soak in a combination of essential oils and herbal essences designed to privately pamper the most discriminating of couples.'" She tightened her own towel as her smile broadened. "I think that means we'll be alone in a hot tub that will smell divine and feel even better."

He gave another eyebrow wag, then took her hand and led her to the door. "Don't tell Chad I said so, but I think I could get used to this."

"Never fear, macho man," she whispered. "Your secret is safe with me."

That evening, Zoë gazed at the drop cloth draped over a mound of what she hoped was furniture piled in the center of Theo's living room. "It was nice of Sally to come over and let the deliverymen in," she said, setting her purse on the kitchen island.

"Chad gave her the day off because of the storm, but the streets were clear so she didn't mind coming over. Besides, I think she was dying to see what you'd done to this place."

"Has Sally visited here in the past?" Zoë asked, trying to keep her curiosity in check.

He walked to her side and enfolded her in his arms. "Is that jealousy I see in those beautiful amber eyes?"

Okay, maybe she was a little envious of any woman who'd been intimate with Theo before her, but he didn't have to know that. "It's unrealistic for me to believe you've been celibate your entire life, while waiting around for me," she offered, hoping to sound blasé.

His face turned red, and Zoë grinned. The man was too cute for words. "Your assistant is very attractive, and you're a single man, so it's perfectly natural that you might have dated."

"Sally is, first and foremost, an employee, so she's off limits as a date. Besides, she has a boyfriend, and he's training to be a professional kick boxer, which means I don't want to tangle with him for any reason."

"But she has been here before."

"Once or twice, when I was up to my eyeballs in program development, she delivered documents that needed my signature. That's all."

"Okay, I believe you had no ulterior designs on the lovely Sally, but remind me to thank her personally if I see her. She did us a big favor." She moved to walk around him. "Why don't you pick up a change of clothes while I earn my outrageous fee by inspecting our finds?"

"What? Why?" he asked, stepping in front of her.

"To be sure Granby's delivered what I ordered

in the correct fabrics and colors. If there's another mix-up, we'll never recover before the photo shoot." She moved left and he followed, then she danced to the right, and he did the same. "Theo, what is wrong with you?"

"With me? Nothing. But we don't have time for that now. Sally had the list and she's smart enough to match stuff up. If there'd been a problem, she would have called. Plus, it's dark in here, and without lamps, which are under the tarp, we won't be able to see much."

Zoë gazed longingly at the pile of shrouded furniture. "What about the bedroom? Maybe we should check in there and make sure everything is right?"

"No!"

She shook her head. "Are you certain your brain didn't turn to mush during that massage?"

"I'm fine, just . . . just anxious to . . . to spend the night at your hotel. We'll have plenty of time to check things out after the painters leave tomorrow. If there's a mistake, we can't do a thing about it tonight anyway."

She took note of his pleading look and shrugged. "Okay, but do me a favor. While you're packing your bag, make sure there really is a mound of furniture in the bedroom. It wouldn't do if we only received half the delivery."

"Sure, fine. But promise you won't do any peeking while I'm in the other room."

Had the man lost his mind? "No peeking? Theo, what's going on?"

"Nothing. I just want us to look at everything together. We've come this far, I want to see what you see, when you see it." He crossed the living room walking backward. "So don't raise that drop cloth, okay?"

Zoë rolled her eyes. "All right, I promise, but I think you're being silly. This is my job, my final project before . . . before I take that trip to see my family. I have to be certain everything's on track so the *NYE* article turns out like we want it."

"I understand, but it can wait a day." He disappeared into the bedroom, still talking. "Besides, if we did find a problem, it would only keep you from getting a good night's sleep. You don't want that, do you?"

"All right, you've made your point," she said, fisting her fingers into her palms. She itched to flip up just one corner of the tarp and check out the goods, but she never broke a promise. Instead, she paced the kitchen, wondering why he was acting so strange.

Theo quickly stuffed a change of clothes into a gym bag. Today had been great, an afternoon of togetherness he was positive had shown Zoë how much she meant to him. He'd told himself to take things step by step and woo her slowly, but her reminder that she'd be leaving to visit her relatives in a matter of days had practically slapped him upside the head.

He needed to prepare for his grand gesture, not jump in without thinking. If she saw some of the changes he'd made in the order before he had a chance to explain, well, it just might ruin everything. And if he lost Zoë—

No, he refused to even consider that might happen. Minute by minute, day by day, he'd forged a path to her heart. He had to remain strong and carry things through. His ring finger tingled, again reminding him of how right it was to have her in his life. Maybe someday, if he renewed his relationship with his mother, he'd thank her for giving him the token, and tell her how well it had worked. But for now, he had to center on his quest for Zoë.

"Ready," he said, sauntering to her side. "I'm starving. Shall we stop for a late dinner or use room service at your hotel?"

"The hotel is fine. The kitchen knows what I like, and room service is often faster than waiting in a crowded restaurant." Together, they entered the elevator, and she smiled at him. "Did you pack your pajamas?"

"Very funny," he responded, waggling his eyebrows again.

"You look adorable when you do that."

"Great. Now I'll have to remember to stop doing it."

"Stop? Why?"

Theo hailed a taxi while they stood on the sidewalk. "Because I don't want to be 'adorable.' It's sissy."

Sighing, Zoë gazed at the star-filled sky. "It's not another 'girly' term, if that's what you're suggesting. Sometimes, a woman is drawn to a man when he's adorable."

A cab pulled up and he opened the door, then climbed in behind her and gave the driver their destination. "Not this man. It's taken me a while to whittle the negatives from my geek quotient. From here on out, it's nothing but macho, all the way. In fact, I think I'll have a beer with dinner tonight."

"Drinking beer with your evening meal makes you macho?"

"And one for breakfast. I might even pour a little on my morning oatmeal. It might grow hair on my chest."

"You already have a nice dusting of hair on your body," she said, snuggling closer. "I like your chest just the way it is."

"You do?" he asked, his voice wavering. "I mean, of course you do. It's a great chest. Very manly."

"And muscular. Are you sure you haven't pumped iron or lifted weights in the past?" She ran her hand over his abs and slipped her fingers beneath his belt. "Or maybe practiced a different, more interesting form of exercise?"

"I'm sure," he muttered. Grabbing her wrist, he nodded toward the driver. "Uh, we're not alone, Zoë."

"I know," she teased. "But so what?"

"I'm not used to doing personal things in public."

"Are you telling me I have to control myself until we enter my hotel suite?"

"Yeah, I guess."

"And after that?"

"After that, you can do whatever you want," he promised her. "I'll be yours to command."

She rested her head on his shoulder. "You mean I can command you to do anything I want, and you will?"

"Um . . . sure . . . within reason."

"No fair, putting a fence around my creativity." She walked two fingers down his chest, again stopping at his belt. "Given enough incentive, I can be a very creative woman."

Warmth flooded Theo's neck and face, a sure sign that he was blushing—another *un*-manly trait. He also had a hard-on that was almost painful in its intensity. If Zoë's hand traveled any lower, which it might if she was bent on teasing him, his condition would only encourage her game of torture.

Turning on the seat, he cupped Zoë's jaw and gazed into her amber eyes. Then he lowered his mouth to hers. Why the hell should he care what a cab driver thought, when loving Zoë was all that mattered?

He kissed her, inhaling her essence, drawing it into him as if he never wanted to let her go. And he didn't. Not now, not ever.

She moaned in appreciation, twined her arms around his neck and climbed into his lap, straddling him. Lost in a slow burn of desire, he barely realized the cab had stopped.

"Good thing we're at your hotel," said the disapproving driver. "Because you two definitely need a room."

Elise's insides quivered as she and Chad took the stairs to her apartment. The past few hours played over in her mind and she heaved a breath. She couldn't remember the last time she'd felt this relaxed or had this much fun. She'd been giggling all afternoon. *Giggling!* It was so unlike her, she was embarrassed just thinking about it.

Chad placed a hand on her back, guiding her as they climbed the steps, his touch gentle but commanding, and it took all her self-control not to turn around and kiss him as she'd longed to do several times that afternoon. The moment she'd seen the carriage, she knew he'd gone to great lengths to surprise her, and it had been a very long while since a man—since anyone—made that type of gesture.

Once he'd helped her into the carriage, he covered her with a mound of blankets and told the driver to head into traffic. Then he'd pulled a thermos from a wicker hamper and poured them each a steaming cup of tomato bisque. The hansom stopped at Rockefeller Center, and they spent the next two hours ice skating, something she remembered telling him she'd always wanted to do but had never gotten around to in her years of living in the city. He'd held her hand, picked her up when she fell, and traced perfect circles around her as she wobbled like a newborn colt.

After that, he'd taken her to a private table at a fancy restaurant and had a wonderful meal that he told her he'd ordered in advance, complete with a shrimp tart appetizer, lobster and pasta main course, and a decadent chocolate dessert.

For her final treat, the hansom took a long lazy ride around Central Park, and while she and Chad snuggled under the blankets, he'd gazed at the stars, pointing out the different constellations and telling her how and why each had received their name.

She still found it difficult to believe that during their final ride, as he entertained her with romantic tales of the stars, all she'd wanted to do was cuddle into his lap and kiss him until her toes curled and she lost herself in his arms.

Now at her door, she spotted a huge basket wrapped in colored plastic sitting on the hall floor.

"What in the world is that?"

Chad took the key from her hand, undid the lock, and picked up the basket. "Wild guess, it's a gift for you. You can figure it out once we're inside."

He followed her in and set the basket on her kitchen table, then helped her out of her coat. Elise couldn't wait. She tore into the plastic while he undid his scarf, removed his gloves, and shrugged from his jacket. Once the wrapping was gone, she found a bottle of champagne, two crystal flutes, and a red satin heart-shaped box nestled in the tissue paper.

She placed the champagne and glasses on the

table, took out the box and dug through the nest of tissue. "I don't get it. There's no card." She raised her gaze and found him grinning. "This is from you?"

He shrugged. "Me? How could that be from me? I was occupied all afternoon."

She opened the box and selected a cocoa-covered truffle. Biting into the creamy goodness, she moaned. "This is so good." She held out the box and he chose one. "You aren't going to get a second helping unless you tell me who this is from."

"You're a big girl. You figure it out," he countered.

She rolled her eyes and dug farther. "There has to be a card or something." Finally, at the bottom of the basket, she saw an envelope. "What do you think this is?"

"An envelope?"

"I can see it's an envelope, smarty pants. What do you think it's for?"

"Probably a bill for the contents. Maybe you ordered it and it slipped your mind?"

She frowned. "Trust me, I'd remember if I ordered this champagne. Tattingers is one of the most expensive on the market." When he didn't answer, she looked up and caught his grin. Then reality dawned on her. This mystery basket was more than she could handle. The entire day had been too much, the most lovely day she could re-member having in the past several years. Tears welled behind her eyes and leaked down her cheeks, and she brushed them away.

"Aw, sweetheart, I didn't mean to make you un-happy."

"I'm not unhappy." She sniffed as he pulled her to his chest. "This is so—so—it's—I—"

"If you're at a loss for words, I'm a happy guy. I never thought I could do anything to impress you that much." He clasped her upper arms. "Why don't you open the envelope?"

She gave a watery laugh. "I can't imagine what else you could do to surprise me. Today was per-fect."

"Would you stop crying if I told you what's in the envelope isn't for today? That it's not going to happen for a few more weeks?"

Concert tickets, Elise thought, or tickets to a Broadway play. She slit the flap and pulled out a pair of airline tickets. "You're taking me on a trip?"

"If you agree to go." His teasing expression turned serious. "There are no strings, Elise. Trav-eling with me is your decision, and I'll under-stand if you say no."

She read the destination. "Cancun? In Mexico?"

"Unless they moved it, yeah, it's in Mexico. I think they call it the Mexican Riviera."

She inhaled a breath. "But why?"

"Why? Why what?"

"Why all the wining and dining? The shows, the museum, the surprises?" Her gaze centered on his eyes, which she believed were the windows to a person's soul. "Why me?"

Chad narrowed his gaze. "I thought I was being fairly obvious. I want to spend time with you . . . alone, where we can explore our feelings and see if we're compatible."

She shook her head. "I can't leave my job."

"Sure you can. The reservation isn't for two more weeks. That'll give you plenty of time to clear up whatever is hanging. You can hand the rest off to an assistant." He frowned. "You do have an assistant, don't you?"

She counted the days in her head and came up with a trip over Valentine's Day. She'd spent the last four of those sappy holidays alone, watching rented DVDs and drinking hot chocolate laced with brandy. "Part-time, though I suppose she could work full-time for a week."

"There's something else you should know," he said, back to grinning. "I've booked a suite—*one* suite."

"One . . . oh."

"I want to be alone with you, spend time with you where we can get to know each other, talk about things. Be a couple." Leaning forward, he brushed her lips with his own, sweetly at first, then with more intensity.

Drawn into the kiss, Elise opened her mouth, and the chocolate on his tongue melted like the truffle she'd just eaten.

He pulled away slowly and they locked gazes. Chad brushed a strand of hair off her forehead. "I want us to be lovers."

Her heart stuttered at the words. Then she realized he had to know the truth about her past. "Before I agree, I have to tell you something."

His hand slid down her back to cup her bottom, and he pressed against her so closely there was no doubt of his arousal. "Anything."

"You know I'm divorced—"

"Stupid men abound in this world. It's your ex's loss, Elise."

"It ended badly, but it wasn't his fault . . . exactly. At least, it wasn't anything he could control." She focused on his shirt buttons. "He was gay."

Scowling, Chad opened and closed his mouth. "Your ex was gay—and you married him anyway?"

She *tsked*. "I didn't think he was gay when we got married, but he dropped the bomb a couple of years later. The incident made me wary of all men, but especially those who came across as—as—"

He smiled. "Articulate? Well-dressed? Confident?"

"Then you're not insulted by my concern?"

"I might have been a dozen years ago, but I've grown used to people and their preconceived notions of the way a man is supposed to act. I'm secure enough to know I'm one hundred percent straight. Just ask a few of the women I've dated."

"A few out of how many?" she asked, grinning.

"Uh, scratch that idea. Right now, I'd say yours is the only opinion that counts."

She edged closer, hoping against hope she wouldn't be hurt again. "And how, exactly, do you intend to prove it?"

Bending down, he swooped her up in his arms and walked out of the kitchen. "I guess there's only one way to do that, sweetheart. So hang on and prepare to be amazed."

Chapter 16

Zoë and Theo ate a quick breakfast at the Trump Tower and hurried to his loft to wait for their scheduled deliveries. Now, in his apartment, she walked the kitchen, fighting the urge to phone the day's workers. As Theo had already warned her, it wouldn't be smart to lose her temper and alienate both the painting company and the carpet store. Better to have someone calm and assertive, namely him, make the necessary calls to be certain their appointments went as planned.

While she paced, she kept her eyes on the mound hidden under a tarp in the middle of his living room. Theo's mysterious request, asking her to stay away from the furniture, had rankled. He'd acted odd, ridiculous even, when he made her promise not to peek. It was only sofas, chairs, tables, and lamps. Nothing that would end the world or create a tsunami in the middle of Manhattan. What was the big deal?

With Theo in his office, she made her way around the tarp and peeked past the door frame. She saw him hunched over his computer monitor staring at a display she privately referred to as "gobblydegook."

She knew he'd used the computer to escape from an unhappy past, get through his difficult college years, and start his adult life. With Chad as a partner, Theo had found his niche in the world, in a business that was his passion and his dream. When she left, she knew that technology would be his comfort, his business a diversion, and in time he would forget about her. Chad would see to it that he made new friends, met the right woman and found a future with her.

Biting back a tear, she pasted a smile on her face. "What are you doing?"

Theo jumped and spun around in his chair. "Holy crap, Zoë. You scared the piss out of me."

She walked to his desk. "It serves you right for keeping me waiting. What did the painters and carpet store have to say?"

"Oh, them." He leaned back and made room for her on his lap. "The painters should be here in . . ." He glanced at his watch. ". . . ten, fifteen minutes, and the carpet company found a set of identical rugs in their warehouse in New Jersey. They promised to have them delivered by mid-afternoon."

"That's a relief." She snuggled into his chest. "Speaking of New Jersey, have you talked to your father lately?"

He frowned. "No, but I probably should check in with him. Since I haven't received a call, I have to assume he didn't do another disappearing act."

"I'm sure he'd enjoy hearing from you in any case." She wrapped an arm around his neck and pointed to the monitor. "What is all that gibberish on the screen?"

He rolled the chair closer. "That 'gibberish' is going to take our company in a new direction, and if all goes well, make us a couple of trillion dollars in the process."

"Trillion? Sorry, that's too many zeros for me." She curved her body against his. Why did mortals always have money on the brain, when there was so much more to life? "Is amassing a fortune really that important to you?"

He kissed her forehead, then sighed. "Money is a necessary evil. Without it, I couldn't afford to give my dad the top notch care he's receiving in the nursing home."

"So you've done all this for your father?"

He shrugged. "Partly."

"Only partly? Then share the rest with me. I'm a good listener, honest."

"I know you're a good listener, but the other reason is harder to put into words. Sometimes I want to pretend it doesn't matter, but I know it does."

"That what doesn't matter?"

"That the amount of money I make is not the way to prove to a certain someone that I'm worthy. That I mean something to the world."

She jerked her head back and stared at him. "Who dares think you aren't a worthy mor—person?"

"It doesn't matter, and even if it did, I doubt there's a thing you could do about it. I don't think anyone can."

"At least tell me his name." *Because if I ever meet him, I'm going to set him straight in a very serious way.* "Just so I'll understand why he has you so upset."

"It's a . . . man. Someone you'll never meet, but he has a hold over my mother that can't be broken. For any reason."

His description reminded Zoë of the iron grip her all-powerful father had on the citizens of Mount Olympus. It was strange to hear there were mortals of the same ilk: unbending, unforgiving, and never happy unless they were in control. She'd been the one muse who gave Zeus some latitude when he made ridiculous demands or demeaned his subjects, but over this past year she'd begun to wonder if the others were right, that Zeus was a tyrant who didn't deserve their respect.

"Since he doesn't sound like anyone I'd care to meet, good," she said with a pout. "I have no patience for anyone who is purposely cruel to others."

"I don't think he does it on purpose, exactly. My mother used to tell me that he can't help the way he is. It's in his DNA or something."

"It sounds as if you're making excuses for him," she scolded. The buzzer rang and she stood. "The painters. They're here."

"Sounds like," said Theo, following her from the room.

Zoë pressed the entry buzzer, then spun in a circle of joyful expectation. "I can't wait for them to finish. Then we can move the furniture and lay the rugs. Once they're down, we'll arrange things perfectly. Tomorrow, when the paint's dry, we'll hang the art work and meet with the drapers." *The drapers!* She'd been spending so much personal time with Theo, she'd forgotten all about them.

"Theo, please. Let the workmen in." She pulled her cell phone from her tote bag. "I have to call Finnety and Sons and set up a time for them to install the window treatments."

He opened the door and stood aside to let the men enter, then waited while Zoë spoke with the drapery people. He knew that the worst thing he could do was get in her way. Once she went on a tear, there was no stopping her. In fact, it was probably better if she involved herself in another project for the next couple of hours. If she decided to micromanage the painters, they'd get annoyed and things would fall apart for sure.

Gently, he grasped her upper arms and headed her in the opposite direction of the flow of traffic. Where could he send her? Who was important enough to Zoë that she would take the time to visit them? When Elise and Suited for Change came to mind, he stepped to her side. "Good news?" he asked when she snapped her phone closed.

"Great news. Mr. Finnety had a cancellation for tomorrow, mid-morning. His installers are going to arrive between nine-thirty and ten with the merchandise."

"Sounds good."

She peered over his shoulder. "Hold on a second. I'm going to make sure the workmen brought the proper paint. We wanted a matte finish, if memory serves me."

She marched to the cans of paint and started sorting through them, while Theo stood and recalled that they'd chosen two accent shades and one basic color, a brick red, to pull everything together. He cringed when Zoë's cheeks turned pink.

"This can't be right. It looks too dark."

When the painters made their second entrance, carrying ladders, drop cloths, and the rest of their paraphernalia, she latched onto the first man through the door and began her diatribe. "Can you do me a favor? Don't do a thing until you put a swatch of the burnt sienna on the wall. I want to get a good look at it before you continue."

The workman, who wore a T-shirt that read YOU WANTED IT WHEN?, rolled his eyes. "It's gonna hafta be the right color, lady, because we're booked solid for the next seven days. If we don't finish today, the job won't get done until the end of next week or later."

Zoë's eyes grew wide, but before she spoke, Theo grabbed her around the waist, lifted her off her feet and walked her into the kitchen. "It's the shade we chose," he said setting her down. "I remember because we thought it might be too dark, until we decided that, with all the light in the room, it would be perfect."

The men, of course, snickered as they went about opening paint cans and setting up drop cloths and ladders.

"Are you sure?" she asked. Brows raised, she peered over his shoulder.

"I'm positive." He cranked his brain into overdrive. "I have an idea. Why don't you let me take care of things here while you treat Elise to lunch?"

"Hm? What?" she muttered, still scoping out the painting crew.

He raised her chin with a finger, forcing her to pay attention. "Take Elise to lunch, Zoë. You only have a day or two before your family reunion, which means you probably won't see her for a while."

Meeting his gaze, she narrowed her eyes. "You're sending me to Suited for Change?"

"Well, yeah." He grinned. "You've been under a lot of stress lately, and I know Elise would like to see you."

"Oh? How do you know that? And don't try to tell me she called and left a message, because neither my phone nor yours has rung, and I'm certain I don't have any more appointments at the office."

"No, she hasn't called, but I think you should stop in and say hello. I can't spill the beans, but I bet she has something to tell you." He picked up her coat, slipped it over her arms, and pulled it onto her shoulders. Then he passed her the tote bag. "I can handle things here."

Zoë marched into the director's office at Suited for Change, hung her coat on a wall hook, and slammed her hat on another. Then she stomped to the chair across from her friend's desk and sat with a plop.

Elise arched a brow. "Well, hello. I didn't expect to see you today."

"I didn't expect to be here." Zoë bit back a curse. "Theo threw me out of his loft."

"You're kidding."

"Not physically, though I think that might have been his next move. But he made it very clear I wasn't needed for the afternoon. He claimed I'd only get in the way and pester the painters." She folded her arms and huffed out a sigh. "Can you believe it? Me, being a pest?"

"Wherever did he get that idea?" Elise asked, her lips inching upward.

"It isn't funny," Zoë responded. "I don't pester, but I do try to keep things moving. I want the work done a certain way, and I make a point of seeing to it my vision becomes a reality."

"You want to know what I think?"

"Probably not, but since I have nowhere else to go . . ."

Elise gave a full-fledged grin. "Think a minute and see this from Theo's point of view. With him, everything is black or white. There's no decorative eye needed to write a computer program, and he's not under any deadline except the ones he makes for himself. You, on the other hand, are an artist with a vision. His loft is a very important project, and it's coming to an end. The pressure is mounting, so you're doing everything you can to make certain this final job is a success, and possibly throwing your weight around in the process."

"Well, thank you, Dr. Sutton. I only have one question. Tell me the name of the university you attended to get your degree."

"Don't get defensive. You know I love you, and so does Theo. He must have a good reason for sending you here."

She shrugged. "Theo only thinks he loves me."

Elise's expression turned thoughtful. "Do you truly believe that?"

Ignoring her blossoming sadness, Zoë forged ahead. "Look who's asking that question. You've told me often enough how unstable most couples are. Has something happened to change your mind?"

Elise picked up a pencil from her blotter and

drummed it on the desk. "I can't lie to you. Something did happen this weekend. Something I . . . I didn't expect."

"Really?" Zoë gazed into her friend's eyes and caught the concern resting there, along with another, more intense emotion. "Oh, my gosh. You slept with Chad."

Elise stared in surprise. Then she scowled. "Am I that transparent?"

"Not really. But I know you, and I can tell that whatever took place had to do with your heart. Since Chad's the only man with an interest in that part of your life . . ."

"Great."

"It is great, if it's what you want."

"I do want it." Elise gave her a rueful grin. "There's no longer a doubt in my mind about his sexual preference, by the way."

Zoë hadn't doubted Theo or her own intuition, but hearing Elise say it was a relief. "So why do you look so miserable?"

"I'm not miserable, I'm . . . confused. It happened so fast, I'm still reeling." She proceeded to tell Zoë, in detail, about the carriage ride, ending with, "It was the most wonderful twenty-four hours of my life."

"Sounds very romantic, almost like a fairy tale."

"The entire experience made me feel like Cinderella going to the ball and meeting Prince Charming. I just worry that, like all fairy tales, it will come to an end."

"Don't think that way. Knowing what you went through in your first marriage, you deserve a terrific guy and a happily-ever-after."

Elise worried her lower lip. "There's just one small problem. He bought tickets to Cancun. For Valentine's week."

"And that's a problem because . . ."

Elise heaved a sigh. "How can I be certain Chad isn't playing a game? When will I know if this relationship is right? That I'm the only woman he'll ever want?"

"How about asking yourself this," Zoë offered. "Is he the only man *you* will ever want?"

Elise leaned back in her chair, still struggling with her thoughts. "I guess so."

"Guessing isn't good enough. You need to be absolutely positive. You've already been hurt enough for two lifetimes. Your next experience with love should be the last, a perfect relationship in every way, and exactly what you want."

"I want what you and Theo have."

Zoë crossed her arms and gazed at the ceiling. "Theo and I do not share a forever kind of love."

"Nonsense. All I have to do is take one look at

the two of you together to see the truth. When Theo's near you, his feelings are written all over his face, and so are yours."

"I wish you'd stop harping," Zoë said. "Once I leave, he'll forget about me and move on, just as I will." Until that moment, she had no idea the words would be so painful.

"That's silly. Once you finish your family visit and return to New York, your lives will move in the right direction. Seems simple enough to me."

"There are other things at work here, Elise. Situations I can't explain."

"They can't be that bad. Surely your family will understand when you tell them what a great guy Theo is and how you feel about him."

Zoë's heart ached and tears welled in her eyes. "I can't explain it. It just won't work."

"Oh, honey, don't cry." Elise walked around her desk and dropped to her knees in front of Zoë. "Nothing is that bad."

"You don't know the half of it," she answered with a sob. "It's hopeless."

"Can you tell me about it?" Elise grabbed a tissue from her box on the desk and passed it over. "There's not much happening here today, and I'm a good listener."

Zoë blew her nose, then wadded the tissue in a tight ball. "If there was anyone I could tell, it would be you. But I can't. How about we just leave it at that?"

"All right. I'm not going to pressure you. But I'm here if you need me."

"Thanks, I appreciate it." Zoë cleared her throat. "And I know the perfect way to cheer up both of us. We'll spend the afternoon doing what women do best, if you're game."

"Uh-oh. I'm not sure I like the sound of that."

"Oh, but you will. And it consists of a single word: shopping."

"But I don't need—"

"Clothes? Nonsense. No woman ever has enough clothes."

"I must have resort wear in my closet."

"Uh-huh, sure. But shorts and T-shirts aren't enough. You'll need a half-dozen sundresses, a bathing suit, sandals, some sexy lingerie." Zoë set her hands on her hips. "I know you don't have any sexy lingerie."

"Because I never had a reason to own any."

"Ah, but now you do. Chad is a man of taste and sophistication. You'll need something understated but so sexy it will knock him off his feet. I'm thinking silk tap pants and a demibra so sheer nothing will be left to the imagination. A set in black, for sure, and one in red . . . and a couple of thong undies, maybe in pink or cream. Men love that prim-yet-oh-so-naughty look."

Elise's cheeks brightened. "God lord, you're making me blush. Are you sure—"

"I'm positive." Zoë stood and retrieved her coat. "Come on, a thousand calorie lunch and an afternoon at Bergdorf's will do us both a world of good."

Theo stood back and admired his handiwork. Though the living room walls were bare of paintings, the apartment still appeared put together and elegant. He'd done his best to recall Zoë's diagram and put each piece of furniture where she said she wanted it. If he'd screwed up the plan, they'd rearrange things later.

He and Chad had spent the last hour setting up and installing the ventless fireplace and decorative mantel Zoë had adored but he'd vetoed. He told her it was too costly, and she took the words to heart, but he was positive she wanted something just like it when she got a place of her own, and now he was giving it to her.

"I hope you know what you're doing," said Chad for the tenth time, resting his hands on his hips. "Are you sure Zoë is going to approve of the changes?"

"Why not? There aren't that many." He took in the matching chairs flanking the fireplace, proud of the fact that he'd called the store and exchanged one of the chairs for a smaller "ladies" version in fabric identical to his own. Soon, he and Zoë would be sitting across from each other, sipping hot chocolate in front of a cozy fire, while she flipped through a decorating magazine and he read the latest *Computer World*. "She made plenty of comments about what she'd do if this was her place. I'm only giving her what she said she'd like."

"I don't know . . ." Chad turned in a circle. "She seems like a pretty thorough woman who knows exactly what she wants for the projects she works on. And this isn't her place—"

"Yet. But it will be."

"If she agrees to live with you, pal."

"You mean, if she agrees to marry me, which she will."

"You don't know that for certain. This little surprise could be enough to push her over the edge and send her running from you forever."

"Don't be such a pessimist. Think positively. That's what I'm doing." Sitting in "his" chair, Theo studied the sofa Zoë had gazed at longingly in the showroom. He'd told her it was too "girly," so she moved to another, more masculine piece while he revised the order in secret. It was only furniture, after all, and he'd kept everything top-of-the-line, as Zoë had insisted. But he'd added the pieces he was positive she would like in her own place, just to show her how much he wanted her in his life. How much he wanted to live with her forever.

"Admirable, but she did this design for your magazine spread. Not a lover's retreat."

"What's wrong? Isn't the stuff I chose upscale enough?"

"As far as I'm concerned, everything appears fine, but I'm not the one you have to worry about. Think of if from Zoë's perspective." Chad sighed and headed for the door. "I have to meet Elise for dinner. She's cooking at her place tonight. It's phase one of our plan."

"Sounds too organized for me," said Theo, following him.

"It's what Elise wants, and I'm not going to blow it. Which might be something you start thinking about."

"Don't worry about me. And thanks for the hand at putting it all together. I can take it from here. By the way, you made the right decision about Elise. Zoë and I are going to take a vacation too, only it'll double as our honeymoon."

Theo closed the door and returned to the living area, viewing the space as if for the first time.

Since there was nothing more he could do until the pictures were hung and the drapes installed, he went to his office and scanned the large U-shaped computer station. Attractive yet practical filing cabinets and tall bookcases lined the walls, giving the room a professional flare. He took a seat in his old swivel chair, the lone piece they hadn't replaced, and exhaled a breath. The only room yet to be tackled was the spare guest room, and that could wait. It was time to put the finishing touches on the final but most important area of the loft.

Walking to the master bedroom, he tried to envision it as if he were a woman. His father's massive armoire flanked a far wall, while fresh flowers sat in the center of the new triple-mirrored dresser. He'd left the drawers empty for Zoë's things, and had even found a service that agreed to pack and remove his old clothes so there was room for her hanging apparel in the closet. If she needed more space, he'd move his stuff to the guest room closet. Anything to make her comfortable here.

The nightstands and lamps Zoë had ordered sat on either side of the king-size bed, and blended perfectly with the room's most imposing piece. The one object she'd told him she would die to have in her own home: a beautiful vine-and-flower-carved headboard and matching footboard.

Now that it was here, Theo was happy he'd

taken the initiative and placed the change order. The bed suited the room, complimented the other furniture, and pulled everything together, giving the space a seamless appeal, just as Chad had said.

With the photo shoot a mere forty-eight hours away, he was certain his loft would be the most exceptional of those featured in *New York Entrepreneur*. And he'd be certain to mention Zoë's name enough times that whoever read the article would know she was the designer, even if he had to sound like Chad to get the point across.

He walked to the kitchen and called in an order for dinner. Zoë had already phoned and told him she'd be there in an hour. He had just enough time to shower, shave, and dress for their special night.

Chapter 17

TO: Zdegodessa@TT.com
FROM: Topgod@mounto.org
SUBJECT: Your return to Olympus

In preparation for your journey home, it is impera-
tive I remind you of the rules. Plan for retrieval
anywhere from 6:00 P.M. until midnight, earth time,
Friday. Attire: chiton and sandals only. No earthly
items will be allowed on Olympus, including clothing,
jewelry, and documentation of your successes or
failures. Avoid transporting the following contami-
nants: chewing gum, breath mints, cosmetics.

> I look forward to your arrival,
> Zeus
> Your father (and still Top God)

Zoë read the e-mail a third time. She'd said good-bye to Elise when they left Bergdorf's and decided to stop at her suite to pick up messages and a change of clothes. Since she hadn't corresponded with her father in a while, she felt certain there would be a message detailing her return to Olympus, and she was right.

Slouching in her seat, she rested her chin in her hand and stared at the screen. She longed to ask questions, test the waters to ascertain his mood, get an idea of what he might accept or reject if she made a special request. First and foremost, could she return to earth to visit Theo?

There was no doubt in her mind she would be victorious in her quest, but annoying Zeus was foolish. Concocting a plan that would enable her to share a life with Theo had been on her mind for several days . . . and nights. He'd told her he loved her and wanted to be with her forever. The confession had awakened a yearning deep inside of her, a longing to spend whatever time she could with him, and if possible, make his wish come true.

There were ways to get what one wanted from the powerful top god, but only if one approached him carefully. Irritating her father before he declared her triumphant would be foolish. Pleading the favor after she'd won the challenge was best. And she intended to do just that.

Zoë saved the e-mail and walked to her closet, where she surveyed the items she'd acquired while on earth. Zeus had provided her with an outrageously expensive wardrobe upon her arrival, but there were things she'd purchased for herself that she hadn't been able to resist. Her favorites were the stylish Prada pumps, several hundred dollars a pair; the Dolce & Gabanna evening gown she'd worn to the opening of a high-end design showroom; and the diamond earrings she bought after decorating the Harry Winston window for Christmas. Though she would miss them, she didn't need them on Mount Olympus.

But the women at Suited for Change might.

Coming to a decision, she picked up the phone and dialed housekeeping. She had to make the arrangements now, otherwise she would forget to place the call or lose her courage altogether, and her lovely things would be given to whoever cleaned out the hotel's vacant rooms.

"I'd like six good-sized boxes please, and someone to help me pack them," she said when a woman answered. "Two o'clock tomorrow afternoon will be fine. Thank you."

She retrieved her overnight bag, set it on the bed, and packed for her stay at Theo's. She'd purchased some lovely lingerie that afternoon, all of it LaPerla, and every piece made to titillate a man.

If the next few hours were all she had with Theo, she would make the night a memory to warm him until he found someone new.

When through, she went to the lobby, where the doorman hailed a cab. Thirty minutes later the taxi dropped her at Theo's building. She met a deliveryman at the door, holding a sack from a restaurant she recognized.

"Is that for loft 3A?" she asked. "Theo Maragos's apartment?"

"Yes, ma'am." The man smiled. "You on your way up?"

"I am. How about if I save you a trip and take care of it?" Theo had treated her to meals for weeks. It was her turn to do the same for him. "I'll bring it there myself."

She paid the deliveryman and added a tip. Hoisting the carryall on her shoulder, she grabbed the food bag and rode the elevator to Theo's floor. Inside his apartment, she snapped on the light, set her bag and the food on the island, and took note of the spotless kitchen, its beautiful granite counters, dark wood cabinets, and top-of-the-line appliances. It was a cooking space any woman would be thrilled to own, herself included.

After hanging her coat in the closet, she peeked in the powder room. Decorated in a bright and airy motif, with pale blue wallpaper, snow white fixtures, and beige and navy striped towels, it was welcoming and cozy, yet very stylish, and the idea of an important magazine like *New York Entrepreneur* taking pictures of a the bathroom made her smile.

Preparing for her first look at the living area, she inhaled a breath and cleared her mind, intent on walking into the room as if she were an observer, a design professional there to scope out a project and report on its success or failure.

She stood in the entryway and flicked the switch for the overhead light and matching wall sconces she and Theo had found in a store famous for restoring antique fixtures. When the room blazed into view, a chill of excitement danced up her spine. The wall color was perfect, as were the accent shades. The rich tones gave the room an elegant yet comfortable feel, as if touting the upscale design while embracing a friend.

But when she focused on the sofa, she did a double take. Though the piece blended well with the setting and looked charming nestled between a pair of antique tables, she recalled ordering a Chesterfield covered in a rustic and very masculine fabric. Had she somehow made a mistake? Her gaze shot across the room, to the formal seating arrangement she'd planned to use to break up the comfort zone supplied by the sofa.

Instead of the bookcases she'd requested, the wall held a fireplace complete with the carved, dark green marble mantel she'd admired on their last shopping expedition. But she also recalled Theo deciding against it. And where had that chair come from? She definitely had not ordered the smaller version of Theo's oversized armchair and ottoman.

She checked her watch and her heart sank. It was too late to get hold of the furniture store and demand they pick up the incorrect items. And how long would it take to get the proper replacement pieces? Her stomach heaved as she plopped onto the smaller chair and stared at the faux logs burning a bright and very lifelike electric fire.

She'd worked so hard to get the atmosphere of the apartment just right, to showcase Theo as a man to be envied. And now, through some clerical error, it was ruined.

Seconds ticked by. She heard the shower and figured Theo was getting ready for her arrival. Why had his assistant accepted the incorrect pieces? Why hadn't he called her about the error?

She heard Theo whistle a happy tune, then a drawer slid open and slammed closed. Preparing her speech, she stood and walked to the doorway, but stopped in shock when she viewed the spacious room. The bed—her bed—in all its fabulous glory, called to her like a siren's song.

The hand-carved headboard and its delicate design of intricately twining vines, flowers, and leaves provided a beautiful counterpoint to the richness of the dark wood. Massive in size, the matching footboard only added to the grandeur of the king-size mattress.

Theo turned when she gasped, watched as she stared at the bed, and grinned at her reaction. "Do you like it?" he asked, mentally crossing his fingers. "I did it for you."

Glittering with tears, Zoë's eyes met his. "Oh, Theo. What have you done?"

His hands stilled on his shirt button, and his heart thudded in his chest. Were those tears of anger or joy trickling down her pale cheeks?

"Please tell me you approve of the changes." He crossed the room. "The store assured me it could all go back, but it will take a couple of days to arrange the pickup and delivery of switching out the pieces."

"When did you . . . how did you do this?" She swiped at a tear. "And why?"

Moving closer, he cleared his throat. "I just said why. I did it for you . . . for us. I know the apartment isn't as fancy as the Trump Tower, but we can find a new place anywhere you want after the photo shoot. Just say that you'll move in with me so we can be together."

"But I'm leaving." Her lips trembled with the words. "I don't know if . . . when I'll be back."

He took her hand. "It doesn't matter when, because I'll be here waiting."

Lying on the massive bed, Theo held Zoë close to his heart. They'd eaten dinner in silence, though he'd tried time and again to make pleasant conversation. But his jokes had fallen flat and his compliments on the new apartment fared no better. Zoë hadn't said she hated his changes, but she didn't say she approved either. Her lack of opinion made the food he'd swallowed sit in his stomach like a lump of bread dough.

Moonlight filtered in from the window above the bed, casting a pale golden glow on their bodies. He'd stripped down to his boxers, while Zoë still wore her street clothes, but he was comforted by the fact that she intended to spend the night. If they made love, he was certain things would be better, but he didn't want to appear insensitive to her feelings, so he restrained himself to holding her close and letting things evolve.

Unfortunately, even more frustrating than her

silence was the fact that he couldn't figure out why she was disappointed.

Everything he'd done had been for Zoë. It was all he could think of to show her how much he loved her, how he longed for them to be together Had that been so wrong?

The sound of her sigh set his heart to aching. He'd never meant to confuse her or make her sad. He'd never wanted to hurt her. "Let me guess. You're hoping to wake up and find that all of this was a nightmare," he said, striving for levity.

"It hasn't been a nightmare."

"Then you want to whack me on the head for going behind your back and making changes."

"I'd never lay a hand on you in anger, and I'm not upset that you did something without my permission either."

"Funny, but that's not the impression I got. I would have sworn you wanted to boil me in oil."

She placed her palm on his chest. "It was a foolish thing to do, Theo. For so many reasons."

"Trust me. I know that now."

"On a positive note, the new pieces are passable. I was hoping to project edgy and professional to enhance your business acumen and high-tech vision. The cozy yet stylish look you've created is fine, but unfortunately it's not the image I thought *NYE* would expect from one of its ten rising stars of industry."

"If it's any consolation, I like what I changed."

"And that's most important. Just keep your fingers crossed that the new things photograph well."

"Do you think the pictures will be a disaster?"

"Of course not. Especially if I go out first thing in the morning and get a few accessories to add to the tables and mantel."

If the magazine shoot wasn't bothering her, that left only one sticking point: his presumption that they would live together.

"It won't be the end of the world if you don't move in with me, Zoë." At least, not her world. "You don't have to lie to me."

"Lie to you?"

"You know, let me down easy, give me the brush-off, tell me I'm a nice guy but I'm not your type." He tucked a strand of hair behind her ear. "And please don't use the most disheartening line of all—it isn't you, it's me—because that would really suck."

She nestled into his side. "I've always been honest with you. I would never give you a line. I've said all along I might not be able to return to Manhattan, and you shouldn't get your hopes up."

"Then you do love me?" The moment he blurted the question, he longed to take it back. "Sorry, forget I asked."

Zoë's body tensed, and he had a good idea what was coming. She took a deep breath, and he cringed inside, waiting for the negative words.

"I can't love you. It wouldn't be right."

Since the statement was a hell of a lot better than *All we can be is friends,* he continued making his point. "Wouldn't be right for who? Because I certainly know it's right for me."

"I'm not who you think I am, Theo."

"You mean you're not a talented interior designer with a fabulous body, gorgeous face, and a wonderful sense of humor? Darn, you really have been fooling me."

She poked his chest with her forefinger. "Cute. Very cute." After heaving another sigh, she said, "I have other commitments."

He could only come up with one thing that would make her so reticent. "Are you in love with another guy?" He hated the way his voice quivered, but damn, he wasn't going to lose her without a fight "Tell me who it is, so we can have a little talk."

"It's not another man," she said, her tone a hair lighter than it had been a moment ago. "You're exactly who I want too, but life—my life—is complicated. I might not be able to work it out. Remember, I'm leaving very soon."

He rolled into her, saw the tears in her eyes, and

knew he'd taken the discussion as far as he dared. "Then I have another idea." He waggled his eyebrows, hoping to make her smile. "Care to hear it?"

She softened in his arms. "Does it involve this lovely bed?"

He kissed her forehead, trailed his lips down her cheek, and gently bit her jaw. "Yeah, but not for sleeping."

"Hmm. What else do people do in a bed? Watch television, maybe?"

He inched his hand under her sweater and palmed a breast, teasing the nipple to attention. "I hate to break it to you, but this room doesn't have a TV."

"Then how about a midnight snack?" she asked, gasping when he squeezed her swollen flesh.

Nuzzling her neck with his mouth, Theo slipped his fingers down her stomach, under the waistband of her slacks, and onto her silken panties. "I'm hungry, but not for food."

Squirming, Zoë arched against him and moaned. After undoing her zipper, she wriggled out of her slacks, and he pulled the sweater over her head. She raised her hips, and he tugged her panties off, then got rid of her bra.

"My turn," Zoë whispered, thumbing off his boxers. When his impressive erection sprang to life, she smiled. Bathed in moonlight, his rigid penis resembled the sword of a warrior god come to free her from her past.

"Never doubt that I want you, Theo," she said, emboldened by desire. Raising up on her knees, she straddled him and settled on his shaft. "We may not have more than a night or two left, but if you let me, I'll make them memorable."

With his fingers on her hips, he guided her down, hissing as she gloved him inside of her. Then he held her in place and arched up, sheathing himself to the hilt. His handsome face glowed golden in the moonlight, while his expression turned taut and determined. Then he pumped his hips, showing her what he wanted.

"I'll take that as a yes," she murmured, bending to bring a nipple to his lips.

Using his teeth, he tugged on her breast to heighten her pleasure, and a wave of sweet abandon swirled to her heart. In perfect unison, they rode the crest, taking each other higher, until Zoë collapsed to his chest and trembled with the force of her orgasm.

Theo stilled and heaved a breath. "I can't let you go, Zoë. If you don't come back to me, I swear I'll find you and make this work. Whatever it is that has you worried is my worry too, and my battle. I can't—I won't—let you fight it alone. We'll be together for a lifetime, no matter what it takes."

His vow was a balm to her desolate heart, a caress that touched her deep inside, giving her the courage to dream of their future. She melted against him, wanting his words to come true more than anything she'd ever wanted before.

Somehow, some way, she would make it happen.

The next morning, Zoë went over the installation with the drapery expert, left Theo working on his computer, and taxied to the Trump Tower, where she packed her possessions and instructed the bellman to send the cartons to Suited for Change the following Monday. Elise would recognize her clothes and shoes, but Zoë knew she'd be gone before the director could refuse her gift.

She gave her suite a final glance, noted the laptop on the desk, and shrugged. Perhaps Zeus would collect it, perhaps not, but it wasn't her concern. She'd return here tomorrow for her escort home. She had but one night left with Theo, and she planned to make the most of it.

She found a few smaller items to enhance the new look of his apartment at a shop in Decorator's Row, carried the shopping bag to the curb and caught another taxi. Then she stopped at Balducci's, picked up dinner, and brought everything to his home. Inside the apartment, she set her belongings on the island, flicked on the lights, and walked into the living room.

A chill coursed down her spine when she viewed the final feather in her cap. The remodeling of Theo's loft was definitely her finest creation. The drapes hung exactly as she imagined they would, and the wall colors complimented the furniture, even the pieces Theo had chosen. Her accessories would set a tone that was formal yet inviting, and the yellow chrysanthemums, white lilies, and blush roses she'd bought from a street vendor blended perfectly with the furnishings. It was as lovely as she'd dreamed it might be.

And she would give it all up, if only she could remain here on earth with Theo, for as long as they both lived.

Tiptoeing to his office, she smiled in spite of the approaching deadline. Theo stared at the monitor in the exact position she'd last seen him, studying a screen of gobbledygook. If any mortal could overcome Zeus, this mortal, with his determination and passion, was that man.

Unfortunately, he had no physical weapon to wield against the top god, and no magic to counter Zeus's power. No mortal did.

"I heard you come in," Theo said without turning around. "I have a few things to finish here, and I'm free."

"Did you get a chance to inspect the drapes?"

"Uh . . . sure. The curtains look great."

"Curtains?" Zoë grinned as she marched to his desk. "I'll have you know those 'curtains' cost a thousand dollars a panel. Have a little respect, if you please."

He stared up at her, his mouth open. "A thousand bucks per panel? You must be joking."

"'Fraid not. And with six windows and two panels per window, that comes to a pricy—"

"Never mind, I can do the math," he muttered. "This entire remodeling business gives me a headache. I don't know how you handle it all."

"It's my job. Luckily, you won't have to decorate again for a long while. Just send the drapes to the cleaners once a year, preferably before the holidays so they'll be ready when you entertain."

"Entertain?" He raised a brow. "Who the heck will I entertain?"

"Clients, business contacts, Chad and Elise— whoever you invite over." He was such a guy. "Find a caterer and tell them what you want to serve, and they'll send people to take care of it and do the cleaning too. Simple."

"Find a caterer? You make it sound so easy." He pushed away from the desk and, still sitting, encircled her with his arms. "Unless you're willing to do it for me?"

She bent and rested her cheek on his head. "I'm sure Chad knows a dozen companies that do a competent job."

"I don't want Chad or a dozen companies." Drawing back, he looked at her. "I want you."

"But I'm—"

"Leaving. I know." He turned the chair to his desk and picked up a pen. "I forgot to ask. What airline are you flying and what time's the flight?"

"Airline?"

"You know, American, United, or does Greece have its own national airline? Sometimes you can get a better deal on those flights."

Zoë swallowed, thinking. "Um . . . it's one of the first two, but I don't remember which."

"And the time?"

"Uh . . . tomorrow night. I have to leave the city by—by six to get to Kennedy on time."

"That means the photo shoot has to finish by seven."

"Six? But why?"

"Because I'm taking you to the airport. I want to help with your luggage and make sure you get to Security without a hitch. Then I'll come home, pour myself a stiff drink, and spend the night thinking of you."

"A drink?" The plans he'd just announced had her so flustered all she could say was, "But you never drink more than a glass or two of wine."

"Not usually." He slid the chair out again and pulled her near. "But I've grown so used to sleeping alongside you, I'll need something to knock me out." Standing, he wrapped her in his arms. "I'm really going to miss you."

Zoë stared at his shirt buttons. "I'll miss you too."

"How about a phone number?"

"A phone number?" Duh, could she sound any dumber?

"For your father's house. So I can call and make sure you arrived safely."

"I don't have the number," she lied.

"You don't have the number to your father's home?"

"He moved recently, so one of my cousins will be picking me up at that end."

"Then give me their number." He grinned. "You do realize that, eventually, I will meet your family."

"Sure, okay . . . I'll get you the number, but first we have to—to hang a few more pictures, and I want to show you what I bought for the living room." She backed out of his office, still talking. "And you'd better tidy this place, in case they want a photo of your work space."

Wearing a puzzled expression, he gazed about

the room. "Why in the heck would they want that?"

"Because you're the IT industry's next rising star. The readers will expect to see where a genius works. Come out when you're done and give me an opinion on things."

Theo picked up a couple of folders, then set them back down. If the photographer wanted pictures of this room, he'd take them as is, period. Right now he wanted to be with Zoë. Standing in the hallway, he watched while she set a clock on the mantel.

"That's nice, but I hope it didn't cost a thousand bucks."

"Not even close. But it's cloisonné and imported from France. The minute I saw it, I knew it would be a perfect accent for the fireplace."

Theo dropped into his chair and focused on Zoë fussing with the flowers. Closing his eyes, he imagined her sitting across from him on a cold winter night with the fireplace aglow. Maybe they'd get a dog when she returned from her family reunion, and the animal would lay between them as they read or worked on a project. If they were lucky, there might even be a baby or two playing on the floor, building block towers or shifting furniture in a doll house.

He didn't regret his childhood. His mother had

taken pains to protect him and see to his happiness until he was old enough to live with his father. And his father had shared with him all that he had from the moment they met. But they'd never lived together as a family, and that's what he wanted with Zoë.

"Everything looks great," he said when she fulfilled a part of his fantasy and took a seat across from him on her chair.

"I'm glad you like it."

"What time is the photography crew supposed to arrive tomorrow?"

"*NYE* said they'd be here by ten, and I don't think there's much more we have to do. Are you ready for dinner?"

"Italian?"

"Of course," she said, grinning. "It'll just take a second to reheat. We can eat at the island."

Theo stood, admiring the view as Zoë made her way to the kitchen. As soon as they finished dinner, he'd help her clean up, then convince her it was time for bed. Since tonight was all they'd have for a while, he was going to make it as perfect as possible. He'd done all he could to show her how much he cared. He had to believe his love would win out.

Chapter 18

Theo and Chad stood in a corner of the living room, watching the flurry of a half-dozen stylists, assistants, and other bodies that had hustled into the apartment at ten that morning. The way everyone flapped around reminded Theo more of a sale at a discount department store than a professional endeavor.

"She's quite the director, isn't she?" Chad commented when Zoë resituated a table the stylist had just moved into place. "Zoë's even got the lead photographer eating out of her hand, though he doesn't seem to realize it."

Theo had to agree. "She's comfortable being in charge, but I don't like the way that guy with the pencil behind his ear is staring at her ass. Maybe I should have a talk with him and suggest he stick his clipboard—"

Chad laid a hand on his arm. "Do me a favor— break his nose when the job is over. I'd hate for your petty jealousy to ruin our best opportunity at making the company famous. Besides, you can't blame the guy for ogling Zoë's figure. It's world-class."

Theo raised an eyebrow. "You have your own woman to ogle. Stop staring at mine."

"It never hurts to stare, pal. It's the touching that gets you in trouble. And I do ogle my own woman. Elise is dynamite to look at, and she has world-class body parts too. Only Zoë happens to be more, uh, more."

"And she's all mine. I just wish she'd let me make an honest woman out of her."

"Do people still use that ridiculous adage?" Chad asked, his eyes wide in false horror.

"Probably not, but it's how I feel." Theo fisted his hands and stuffed them in his pockets. "She's leaving tonight, you know."

"Yeah, Elise mentioned it a couple dozen times, in between griping about how much Suited for Change is going to miss Zoë and her expertise. Says she prays every night that Zoë will come back and make her home here instead of with her family."

"It's good to hear that Elise and I got the same story."

"Why? You think Zoë would lie to you?"

Theo stepped aside when one of the assistants came over to move a lighting stand. "Not lie, exactly, but I don't think she's telling me the whole truth. I just wish I knew why."

"Maybe she'll tell you on the drive to the airport."

"I hope so. All I know is I'm going to worry until I hear she's landed safely, and be miserable until she returns."

"Elise and I will keep you company if you get restless. Maybe you can take some time off and fly over there when we return from Cancun, introduce yourself to Zoë's family, and try to score some Brownie points. It couldn't hurt."

"I'd do it in a heartbeat, but I'm afraid she'd get upset," said Theo. "She sort of goes nuts whenever I bring up meeting her relatives, especially her father." Zoë headed their way, and he smiled. "Are they through in here?"

"Just about." She folded her arms and nodded to Chad. "How is Elise? I'm sorry I haven't had a chance to meet her for a formal good-bye."

"She's missing you already. Said you should call from the airport. If the people from the Suited for Change headquarters hadn't picked today to

pay her a surprise visit, she'd be here to cheer
you on."

"I'm sure she would be," Zoë agreed.

"You coming, Zoë?" The lead photographer
walked to her side and draped an arm over her
shoulder. "I'd like your professional eye for the
next couple of shots." He focused on Theo. "Guess
I don't need to tell you how fabulous this place
looks. Anyone who sees the layout will be impressed. Zoë's going to be a big name in the design world after the article appears in print."

"She deserves every bit of praise," Theo said.
"Can you tell me how much longer this will take?"

"A couple more hours. The bedroom is next,
then your office, then the kitchen." An assistant
called and the photographer waved his hand.
"Gotta go. Zoë, you coming?"

"In a minute." She stepped closer to Theo. "You
seem a little tense. Maybe you and Chad should
go to lunch?"

"Not on your life. Besides, Chad was just
leaving."

"I was?"

"You were," he answered, wrapping an arm
possessively around Zoë. "Elise is waiting, remember?"

"Right, but I'm not going until I kiss my favorite
interior designer farewell." Chad leaned close and

brushed her cheek with his lips. "Hurry back, Zoë, or this guy is going to be hell to live with."

"Tell Elise I'll be in touch—if it's possible."

"Will do."

He sauntered from the room, and she turned to Theo. "Things are moving along. As soon as we're finished, I'll get my bags from the hotel."

"I still don't understand why you didn't bring them over yesterday."

"I told you, they'd only clutter the place, and we needed room for the equipment."

"Then I'll come with you now."

"No! I mean, you can't leave until the *NYE* people are through. I'll call when I'm downstairs, and we can take the same cab to Kennedy. It'll save time."

"No cab. I'm getting a rental, because I plan to drive to Dad's nursing home tomorrow. Maybe a couple of hours with him will help lessen my misery."

"I'm sure your father will be pleased to see you. Now, how about watching the rest of the shoot with me?"

Hours later, Zoë breathed a sigh of relief as the camera crew and person responsible for the article walked out the apartment door. They'd taken down her name and praised her on the design of

Theo's loft throughout the day, promising she'd get at least two mentions in the story and credit for the layout.

"Your phone's going to ring off the hook once that article hits the stands," Theo told her. "Be prepared for a flood of business when you come back."

Zoë laid her hand on his cheek, felt the warmth of his skin, and read the concern in his eyes. She'd held back tears all day, and wasn't about to cry now. There'd be time enough for that on Mount Olympus.

"You're sweet." Leaning into his chest, she kissed him a final time, molding her lips to his, determined to memorize their shape and taste. "I'll be back, Theo," she said, softening the lie with a half-truth. "I just don't know exactly when that might be."

"Sounds like you're saying good-bye forever," he scolded. "Wait until we get to Kennedy before you make such dire predictions. It almost sounds as if you don't want to see me again."

"I do, very much," she confessed. "It's just that—"

"You have to leave. Don't remind me." He smiled. "Bring your luggage back here and I'll have the rental waiting. That way, we can spend more time together before your flight."

Zoë pressed her forehead against his chest to stem the flow of tears. She had to be strong and put up a brave front. She had barely enough time to arrive at her suite, change into her chiton and sandals, and wait for her escort. When Theo realized she wasn't coming back, she would already be gone.

"I'll see you soon," she said, crossing mental fingers. Then she gave him a final passionate kiss of farewell. She planned to remember this moment for eternity, much as she hoped he would, if he ever thought of her again.

"Wow," said Theo when she drew away.

She cupped his cheek a final time. "Take care of yourself."

She walked to the hall and rode the elevator to the street, where she caught a taxi to the Trump Tower. Entering her hotel, she waved fondly at the bellman and desk clerks. They'd taken good care of her this past year, but they'd probably forget that she existed in a few days, just as Theo would. Unfortunately, an eternity would pass before she forgot about him.

In her room, she undressed and slipped into her chiton and sandals. Then she sat on the sofa and closed her eyes, hoping her escort would give her some information on her sisters. When last they'd spoken, both Kyra and Chloe sounded odd, almost as if they weren't looking forward to their return.

Had they too met mortals and fallen in love?

Before she could dwell on the possibility, thunder rumbled, shaking the hotel walls. Wind whistled through the room, rustling the drapes and fluttering the papers on the desk. She sat at attention as a mist rose before her and Zeus's winged messenger appeared.

"Hello," he announced. "Long time, no see."

Zoë smiled. "Hermes, you look well. How are things at home?"

The messenger shrugged. "Unfortunately, disasters abound. The computers are totally fubar, and the system is down more than it's up, so the big gas bag is on a tear." Hermes nodded toward the desk. "I've even been instructed to leave your laptop, which is fine with me. It'll be one less piece of equipment I have to worry about."

"Maybe Zeus should send you to earth for some classes," Zoë offered. "Microsoft certification is a plus in any job. I have a friend who's an expert."

"It's a thought, but there's no time to talk about that now." He glanced around the room. "It looks like you're ready."

"Fill me in first. What happened to Kyra and Chloe? Has Zeus called for them? Did they win the challenge?"

Hermes frowned. "Sorry, but his mightiness swore me to secrecy on that score." He held out his hand. "Off we go."

Zoë stood and grasped his fingers. A gust of wind swirled around them. Hermes lifted her up and, together, they rose toward the glittering night sky.

Theo paced the apartment in a rush of frustration. He'd picked up the rental car and parked it downstairs. When Zoë didn't arrive as expected, he checked the apartment, thinking she'd let herself in to wait. When he realized she hadn't, he called Trump Tower and was told she'd checked out several hours ago. Then he called Kennedy, where every airline he reached informed him they were not allowed to reveal the names on their passenger lists, for any reason. He even asked the airport personnel to have her paged, but they refused.

With no other idea in mind, he drove the rental to her hotel, tossed the keys to the doorman, and raced to the elevator. He still had the key card Zoë had given him on one of the evenings he stayed overnight, and he intended to use it.

Inside the suite, he took a quick inventory. The empty closets, bare bathroom, and naked shelves confirmed his worst fear. Zoë was gone, and she hadn't trusted him enough to bestow a final fare-well.

He ran his fingers through his hair and stomped to the living room, where he spotted her laptop sitting open on the desk. These days, most people made plane reservations online. Though Zoë wasn't computer savvy, maybe she'd done it too.

He sat at the desk and tapped a few keys, re-lieved to learn she had no password protection or secret code needed to access her files. In fact, there was hardly any information on the system at all, except for a few e-mail communications with someone called Topgod at—

Theo peered at the screen and read the signa-ture line again, and a chill snaked up his spine. Scrolling back to the first round of messages, he read them from day one—January of last year.

No, it couldn't be. He refused to believe Zoë, the woman he loved, was a citizen of Mount Olym-pus. She would have told him if she were, and he would have understood. Why hadn't she trusted him?

Just like I trusted her.

He shook his head at the idiocy of his words. He hadn't trusted her enough to tell her about his past, so how could he blame her for not taking him into her confidence? He read the e-mails again, noting that his name was never mentioned, which meant she hadn't been sent to earth to torment him, though he wouldn't have been surprised if Zeus had done that very thing.

In fact, it sounded as if the old goat had issued some sort of challenge to Zoë and her sisters. A challenge that frightened her.

He was well aware of the power Zeus held over his people, so her reticence at returning finally made sense. He only vaguely recalled the muses and other deities living on Olympus, because they resided at the main temple while he, his mother, and her handmaidens had been banished to the far fringes until he'd grown to manhood. When that time came, the jerk-in-a-box had sent him to live with his father and allowed his mother back into the fold. He'd heard rumors of Zeus ordering other gods to earth, some as a reward and some as a punishment, but he had never met one . . . until now.

Standing, he circled the room, noting the ring was burning his finger. His mother had given him a lesson on its use and made him promise to return if ever he needed her. But he'd given his father a promise too. He'd sworn he would never go to Olympus again. For any reason.

If he went, he'd be a traitor to his dad, the one man who'd given up everything to see that his son had a home and a good education. An honorable guy who'd done all in his power to keep his boy safe.

Remember, son, when you find the right woman, do whatever it takes to keep her at your side. Make a life with her and never look back, no matter the consequences.

Now, his dad's warning tore at his conscience, exactly like his heartfelt advice. Theo loved his parents. Both had done their best to raise him and make him happy. Which one should he be faithful to now?

The ring throbbed, burned his finger, and sent a jolt up his arm straight to his heart. The shock gave him the courage to make a decision. He knew, without a doubt, this was the proper moment to be his own man and follow the advice that would serve him best. Both his parents would expect nothing less.

Stiffening his spine, he turned the ring three times and faced the lightning bolt toward his palm. Squeezing his hand into a fist, he raised it toward the heavens. "Mother, bring me home," he whispered. "Bring me home now!"

Zoë studied her reflection in the mirror hanging on the wall of her room. She'd fixed her hair and changed into her best chiton, but waiting to be called for her final reckoning had churned her stomach, and it seemed that the constant pacing wore holes in her sandals.

She'd been alone for hours. Why was she being tortured in this horrible manner? Why hadn't Zeus called her to his throne?

When a bolt of lightning split the sky, she exhaled a ragged breath. Thunder roared, its deep boom calling out her name, and she held her head high. Marching into the marble hall, she passed the rooms reserved for the graces and her sister muses, raced through the hanging gardens, zipped past the bathing pools, and headed straight to the first of one hundred steps that led to her father's boardroom and private chambers.

Her fellow gods lined the stairs, some reclining alone, some standing in groups, whispering as they viewed her ascent. Raising her eyes, she spotted Zeus, hands folded across his chest, standing on the highest platform, glaring down at her as only the top god could.

Reaching the last stair, Zoë made a graceful bow. "Father, I am here as you demanded."

When he didn't speak, she lifted her head. His bushy brows arched as he narrowed his gaze. "I sent you to earth and gave you a chance to redeem yourself, and this is how you repay me? Why did you betray me, daughter?"

Zoë cringed inside when she heard his disapproving tone. Had her accomplishments on earth been that terrible? "Betray you? I'm sorry, Father, but I don't understand."•

"I gave you but one command—well, two, actually. First, you were to inspire mortals in fashion and design—"

"Which I did," Zoë insisted. "My windows were greatly admired, and the women I dressed for success found new jobs and bettered their way of life."

"I never said you failed in your design tasks. In fact, you did exactly what I asked. That's not the part I'm talking about," he spat out. "It's the falling in love order you disobeyed."

"You know about Theo?" She opened her mouth, then snapped it closed, regretting that she'd mentioned Theo's name. If her father was angry enough to punish her, he might do the same to the man she loved. "I'm sorry, but he is wonderful. I'm proud to say I loved—that I love him still."

"The fact that you fell in love with a mortal isn't as infuriating as who that mortal is," he sneered. "And do not say his name again in my presence."

"I can't even say Theo's name? But why?"

Zeus threaded his bony fingers through his hair and pulled. "Arghhh! The boy is a changeling. A mutant. An abomination to our race."

"My Theo?" she asked again, still confused.

"Don't play the innocent with me, daughter. He must have told you of his past and explained the foolishness of his parents."

Confounded by his statement, Zoë crossed her arms and tapped her foot. "I have no idea to what you're referring. Stop speaking in riddles and get to the point."

"You mean he never told you?"

She heaved a sigh of impatience. "Told me what?"

Before Zeus could answer, a gasp rose from the crowd.

"Zeus!" a voice called, shouting the top god's name from below.

Zoë turned and watched as Theo made his way up the marble staircase. Dressed in a chiton that showed his mighty physique to perfection, his eyes focused on her father as he climbed the steps and took his place beside her.

"What are you doing on Mount Olympus?" she whispered.

Smiling as if he'd met her there a thousand times before, Theo took her hand in his. "I told you I'd make certain we were together, sweetheart, and I meant it."

"Silence!" Zeus shouted.

All heads swung from the couple to the top god. Zoë's gaze darted from her father to Theo. "I don't understand."

Still grinning, Theo focused on Zeus. "I've come for the woman I love, old man, and I dare you to stop me."

"Uh-oh," said a member of the audience, causing others to mutter the same.

Zeus glared at his curious subjects, then back at Theo. "Pah! She is a pure and true daughter of Mount Olympus. You don't deserve her."

"Oh, but I do," Theo proclaimed. "She is the woman I love, will love for eternity. We belong together."

"Ridiculous. You've done nothing to earn her love," Zeus raged. "She is my daughter. Only I will decide her fate."

"And if I told you I had something you needed? Something I'd be willing to trade to prove my worth?"

"You have something I need? Impossible!" Zeus cried, his hands fisted at his sides.

Before Theo could argue, a shout echoed from the boardroom behind the top god. "Oh great one, I implore you." Hermes flew through the archway, his winged sandals fluttering. "Listen to the boy, my odious liege, or we are doomed."

Zeus focused on his clearly flustered messenger. "I told you not to disturb me unless you had good news."

"Sorry, O Malevolent Master, but—"

"Then remove yourself from my presence." The top god waggled his fingers, as if shooing a bee. "Now, where was I?"

"Theo?" Zoë said, more confused than before.

"Stop saying his name!" Zeus ordered. After giving a full-body shiver, he again placed his hands on his hips. "Woe to whoever tries to stop me in this. I banished the son of Nike once, and I shall do it again."

"You? The son of the great goddess Nike?" Zoë asked. Suddenly, so many things fell into place. Nike's surprise visit to the Trump Tower; the questions Nike asked about Theo; the gold-tipped feather she had found in Peter Maragos's room.

The air grew still as they spoke. Then the daylight faded and the crowd gasped. A shadow loomed over the open hall, covered the gods and inched up the staircase. Zeus and the others gazed skyward and Nike appeared, a giantess framed against the brilliant sun.

"Mother," Theo said, breaking into a smile.

Nike floated to the ground and walked up the steps, her shimmering wings folding as she shrank to a more human size. "My son," she said when she arrived on the landing. "Knowing you recalled the power of the ring is a great relief to this worried mother." Taking her place alongside Theo, she peeked around him and nodded politely at Zoë. "How nice to see you too, my clever girl."

Zeus harrumphed his displeasure. "Leave us, Nike. This has naught to do with you."

"Naught to do with me?" The warrior goddess's laughter floated like thistledown on the wind. "I beg to differ, you old goat. 'Tis my son's future at stake here."

The audience murmured, shocked by her effrontery.

"I knew I should have punished you more rigorously for falling in love with that pathetic mortal," Zeus said.

Hermes fluttered near. "Before you go any further, I must speak with you, my detestable dictator."

"Not now, you idiot," muttered the top god, his voice a growl.

Theo stepped forward, and Nike laid a hand on his arm. "That pathetic mortal is my father, so show some respect."

"The boy is right," Nike pronounced.

Zeus glowered at his warrior goddess. "Perhaps I should have banished you as well as the boy."

"Then do banish me now. I'm sure you'll find another god powerful enough to smite your enemies and drive your chariot to victory." Nike grinned, as if she just remembered she had the upper hand. "Wait, I'll find one for you."

Facing the audience, she made eye contact with the men, and each dropped their gaze. Then she focused on the women. "Come now, ladies, which of you is prepared to take my place as the despot's warrior at arms?" She nodded toward two goddesses huddled on a lower stair. "Will it be you, Athena, or you, Circe?"

The women cowered in fear, and Nike continued the hunt. "Perhaps you, Leto?"

Leto shrieked. Her eyes rolled up into her head and she fell to the ground in a faint, and not a body moved to help her.

Nike returned her gaze to Zeus. "How sad that once I am 'banished,' " she singsonged the word, "there will be no one to protect you."

"I don't need protection." The top god raised a finger. "I've led Olympus into the modern world, where battles are fought and won in the boardroom, on the Internet, through technology and—"

"But, sire, that's what I keep trying to tell you," the still-blathering Hermes interrupted. "All is lost. The system cannot be saved."

Zeus furrowed his brow as he gazed at his IT

expert. "I ordered you to leave me until you had good news, you fool. Can't you see I'm busy?"

The messenger floated nearer, cupped his hand and raised it to Zeus's ear. Whispering ensued, most of it muffled but frantic. Zeus reared back and snarled, then cast a dark glance at Theo.

Hermes nodded and more discussion transpired until, finally, Zeus said, "I've just received some interesting and rather unhappy news." He cleared his throat. "I know you have some measure of influence in the computer industry. This buffoon insists you are a man among men in the field of Internet Technology."

Theo squared his shoulders. "I run my own business, and as of the spring edition of *New York Entrepreneur*, I'm one of the top ten rising stars of the systems world," he bragged.

"Yes, yes, so all the geeks and hackers say." Zeus gave Hermes a disgruntled stare. "We're in a bind, and this fool can't seem to solve the problem. Something about bugs and worms and a contaminated network, whatever that means."

"Sounds serious," Theo said, an evil grin lighting his face. "Maybe bad enough to shut you down for good."

"Stop your crowing, boy, and answer the question. Can you or can't you fix the problem?"

Hermes fluttered closer and again whispered in the top god's ear.

"You can't be serious," Zeus said, staring at him.

"Oh, but I am, your flatulence," muttered the messenger. "Dead serious."

Zeus thrust out his lower lip in a pout and closed his eyes, then opened them and trained his gaze on Theo. "And once you repair the system, are you willing to be put on retainer, so that my IT department can call on you if there are future problems?"

Theo glanced at Zoë. "That depends on what you're offering in return."

Scanning the crowd of tittering deities, the top god growled. Then, as if realizing he was beaten, he shook his leonine head. "Do you truly love Zoë, the Muse of Beauty? Do you promise to honor her and care for her until your dying day?"

Zoë held her breath. This entire debacle had played havoc with her nerves. She was still trying to accept that Theo was really there and was Nike's son. It explained so much about his past and his father's ramblings. But she also recalled the negative words Theo had used to describe Mount Olympus and its hedonistic citizens; words that were degrading and unflattering, and included her.

She held her breath, wishing with all her heart

that he would put her out of her misery and give the right answer.

Theo pulled her near. "What do you say, Zoë? Will you live with me on earth and stay with me until your dying day?" He lifted her hand and grazed her knuckles with his mouth. "Do you love me as much as I love you?"

Though tears trickled down her cheeks, Zoë's lips quivered with joy. "I love you more, but I have questions, lots of questions. Are you prepared to answer them?"

Theo cupped her jaw. "I'll explain everything, as soon as we're back on earth."

She frowned. "But are you certain you can fix a problem that isn't running entirely on earthly technology?"

He grinned. "Didn't I tell you that someday the gobbledygook would come in handy?"

She rolled her eyes. "Silly me, doubting a man with the brains of Einstein and the body of a warrior god."

"Just promise to always be my goddess, and I'll forgive you," he said, his expression filled with hope, his blue eyes twinkling.

"Deal. Now go do whatever you must to bring us home."

Theo kissed her, passionately, slowly, deliberately, not only to show the top god who was in charge, but to show Zoë, once and for all, that she was the woman of his heart. Then he put Zoë's hand in Nike's. "I leave my future wife in your capable hands, Mother, until I finish here and bring her to my . . . to our home."

Standing tall, he faced the father god. "I will do what you ask and take you at your word. When I'm through, you will allow the Muse of Beauty and I to live with no further interference from you." He took a step forward. "But if you go back on your word, I'll see to it your system is breached and your network is so unsalvageable no one will be able to sift through the rubble to perform a rescue. Is that understood?"

Zeus muttered a curse and nodded in agreement. Hermes darted to his ear and hissed more words of advice. Finally, the top god waggled his fingers, ordering the messenger god to take over.

Raising a brow, Hermes said to Theo, "This is a tough one. It may take a while."

"Then we'd better get started," Theo answered. "Time's a'wasting."

Epilogue

Six months later

Kyra and Chloe lay side by side on identical lounge chairs on an exclusive private beach off the coast of Bali. The sun sparkled on the turquoise water and bounced off the white sand, while the air smelled of tropical flowers and the salty sea. It was rumored that Angelina and Brad, and their brood of children, had left the day before the goddesses arrived, and the sumptuous vacation spot was expecting Tom, Katie, and Suri in the next two weeks.

"I can't believe the front desk has something one of us had to pick up personally," said Kyra. "What do you suppose it might be, and what is taking her so long?"

"It's probably nothing. But knowing Zoë," said

Chloe, "she's stopped to lecture the help on the proper way to tie their sarongs."

The sisters sighed as one.

"I wouldn't put it past her," Kyra agreed. "She's so determined to make her design firm a success that she can't seem to stop fussing. I think she'll be the only one ready to leave here at the end of the week."

"Much as I like it here, I want to go home too," Chloe pronounced. "I miss Belle and Ruby."

"Then I guess it's all right to confess I miss Vegas. I can't wait to start summer promotions for the hotel." Kyra laid a hand on her rounded belly. "And start shopping for baby clothes."

Chloe reached out and clasped her sister's hand. "I can't wait to be called Auntie Chloe. It sounds so right."

"It's going to be a busy first Christmas on earth," Kyra said, squeezing her sister's fingers. "But Vegas weather is pleasant in December, and our house is huge. There'll be room for everyone, including your beloved Miss Belle and Ruby."

"Chloe! Kyra!"

The goddesses turned at the sound of their names and spotted Zoë in the distance, waving a package in her hands. She walked faster when she saw that she'd caught their attention, and soon dropped onto the third chaise on the beach.

"Mail?" asked Chloe. "Who sends mail on a honeymoon?"

"Miss Belle, from the look of the postmark," said Zoë, passing her sister a large manila envelope. "It's addressed to the three of us, but I'll let you have the honor of opening it. It must be important."

Chloe tore at the flap and pulled out the folded sheet of newspaper from inside. "What in the world . . ." She raised her sunglasses to the top of her head and peered at the paper, then smiled and held up a sticky note stuck to the page. "Belle said she couldn't wait for us to read the notice." She narrowed her gaze. "Listen to this. It's from the society page of the *Chicago Tribune,* and the headline reads, 'Triple Wedding at Castleberry Hall.'"

"Well, don't stop there," said Kyra. "Let's hear it all."

Chloe took a sip of her mai-tai and cleared her throat. " 'Castleberry Hall, the preeminent wedding venue in this city, is pleased to announce its first triple wedding ceremony and reception. Ms. Kyra Degodessa and Mr. Jacob Lennox, Ms. Chloe Degodessa and Dr. Matthew Castleberry, and Ms. Zoë Degodessa and Mr. Theodore Maragos, were joined in matrimony on Saturday, June first, in identical ceremonies.

'Guests included Isabelle Castleberry, grandmother of Matthew, Dr. David Jones and Dr. Lloyd

Kellam of Chicago, prominent business tycoon
Socrates Themopolis of Las Vegas, and the COO
of Marasoft, Inc., Chad Thomas and his wife, Elise
Sutton Thomas, director of Suited for Change,
both of Manhattan.

'Mr. and Mrs. Lennox will reside in Las Vegas
to jointly manage the multi-million-dollar Acrop-
olis Casino and Hotel, while Mr. and Mrs. Maragos will make their home in Manhattan, where
Mr. Maragos is CEO of Marasoft, Inc., a rising giant in the computer industry, and Mrs. Maragos
leads her newly formed company, Musings in Design. Dr. and Mrs. Castleberry live in Chicago,
where Dr. Castleberry practices medicine and
Mrs. Castleberry will continue in her position as
manager of Castleberry Hall.' "

"Wow! Don't we sound important?" Zoë said
with a giggle. "They even gave the name of my
firm."

"And our hotel," Kyra added proudly, as if she
and Jake were the owners. "I guess we're a success."

Chloe folded the paper and slid it back in the
envelope. At the sound of a whoop and her
shouted name, she shaded her eyes and stared out
into the ocean. "I don't know about the two of
you, but there's only one measure of success in

my life, and right now, if he isn't careful, he's going to kill himself on that jet ski."

She stood and stomped to the water's edge, Zoë and Kyra on her heels. "Just look at the three of them. They're acting like children. When I get that man alone, I'm going to . . . to . . ."

"I know, and I plan to do the same," said Kyra. "After I get through making love to him, he'll be too tired to ride a jet ski or do much of anything else. That ought to keep him safe until we fly home."

"Sounds like a good idea to me," Zoë agreed. She waved to Theo, probably the most sensible of the husbands. "It's time for lunch!" she yelled. "Come in and join us!"

Waving, Theo headed for shore, followed by Jake and Matt. When the trio reached the sand, they hopped off, grinning as they steered the jet skis toward their brides.

"The water's warm, the perfect temperature for a ride," Matt said to Chloe, pulling her near. "I'll take you for a spin after we eat."

"That sounds like fun," said Kyra as Jake wrapped her in his arms.

The handsome security expert furrowed his brow. "Not this trip, wife. You're carrying our child, and I'm not taking any chances with either of your lives."

"By my calcualtions, the probability of an accident is one in 117,000," Theo noted. "Pretty good odds, if you ask me."

"One of the benefits of being married to a nerd," said Zoë, "is always knowing the odds."

"Hey, odds are my expertise," said Jake. "And no matter how good, I wouldn't play them for all the sand in the ocean where my wife and baby are concerned. I'll never do anything to screw up my life with the woman I love."

Chloe punched Matt in the shoulder. "That's so poetic. How come you never say things like that?"

"Because I'm the one who'll always be around to kiss it and make it better, sweetheart. Who needs words when you're married to a man of action?" asked the doctor.

"With brains, beauty, and luck on our side," said Zoë, "I'd say we have everything we need, ladies. And we owe it all to you know who."

"You know who?" said Jake. "I wish one of you would tell us this guru's name. Someday, I want to meet him and thank him in person for sending me the woman of my dreams."

Theo grinned. "I already did, and believe me, you don't want to know who he is."

"I still don't understand why you're the only one who met the guy," said Matt, raising a brow in Theo's direction. Before he could say more, thunder rumbled in the distance, and he peered at the crystaline blue sky. "Sounds like there's a storm brewing, but not here. It wouldn't dare rain on our honeymoon."

The sisters winked at one another as they strolled alongside their husbands. "There's no doubt in my mind. Each of us will have a perfect life, filled with happiness," said Chloe. "And we'll make it happen on our terms. Free from anyone's rules or warnings."

"Perfect and full of good luck," echoed Kyra.

"And forever love," pronounced Zoë. "I feel it in my bones, but more importantly, I know it in my heart."

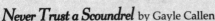

AVON

978-0-06-052513-2

978-0-06-087137-6

978-0-06-084798-2

978-0-06-124110-9

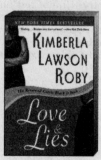

978-0-06-089251-7

978-0-06-137321-3